Brimstone and Mystery

"THEN," little Jack Pennywort went on, working sweeping gestures into the retelling of the amazing story, "as I followed along, there was a pale sort of flickering just up around his shoulders. Just before I saw the yellow gleam . . . and then I tripped over a stone, and fell down in the road.

"As I looked again, the flames came right up out of him—all around! They rose with a *roar*, they did—rose up and danced like Satan himself, all around the old man right where he stood, waving his arms up in the air before he disappeared! Black smoke, first, black as night . . . and when the wind took it off, all I saw was a white mist rise up, and a spot of blue fire, *damme* if I didn't! There was heat enough to water my eyes, and the Devil's stink of hellfire and brimstone!"

"Sulphur, most likely," Longfellow commented from one side of the crowd.

"And after that he was gone," Jack continued, raising his voice to be heard by all, "*disappeared*, from what I could see!"

A Wicked Way to Burn

Margaret Miles

BANTAM BOOKS

New York   Toronto   London
Sydney   Auckland

A WICKED WAY TO BURN

A Bantam Book/February 1998

All rights reserved.

Copyright © 1998 by Margaret Miles.

Cover art copyright © 1998 by Daniel Craig.

No part of this book may be reproduced or transmitted in any
form or by any means, electronic or mechanical, including
photocopying, recording, or by any information storage and
retrieval system, without permission in writing from the publisher.

For information address: Bantam Books

ISBN 0-553-57862-6

Published simultaneously in the United States and Canada

Bantam Books are published by Bantam Books, a division of Bantam
Doubleday Dell Publishing Group, Inc. Its trademark, consisting of the
words "Bantam Books" and the portrayal of a rooster, is Registered in U.S.
Patent and Trademark Office and in other countries. Marca Registrada.
Bantam Books, 1540 Broadway, New York, New York 10036.

PRINTED IN THE UNITED STATES OF AMERICA

OPM   10   9   8   7   6   5   4   3   2   1

For Richard, with love.

Search me, O God, and know my heart:
Try me, and know my thoughts:
And see if there be any wicked way in me,
and lead me in the way everlasting.

PSALMS 139: 23–24

A Wicked Way to Burn

Chapter 1

Monday

"DAMN THEM ALL!" cackled the merchant, not for the first time. Then his smile broadened as he glimpsed, through autumn leaves, the upper arm of Narragansett Bay.

Duncan Middleton had ridden out from Boston early, taking the post road whose windings had carried him inland for many wearisome hours. Far from streets full of people and fine carriages, he had lately seen only villages, tedious stretches of woodland, and empty stubble fields left to the crows that cawed from the treetops, well above the rustling, slithering, hopping life that foraged below.

Carefully, he uncurled gnarled fingers and reached beneath the scarlet cloak that covered his bent and withered form. It should be said that his curious shape was due to a gouty disposition of the joints: the merchant was barely fifty. But he had already acquired the face of an old man who cultivated a wintry soul. Certain acquaintances had been heard to comment, in private, that both face and twisted skeleton served to warn men of the merchant's undernourished and corrupt spirit . . . as Jehovah had probably intended when he made him that way.

But now, on this mild October evening, the wizened rider felt almost kindly as he gently stroked something held against his chest. Satisfied, he breathed deeply of the brisk salt air. Was it a love of the sea that made Middleton's small, sunken eyes lift and sparkle briefly? Unhappily, no—the merchant's pleased expression was born of his belief that what he smelled on the air was profit. He already had a hoard of money—enough to buy courtesies from others whose manners and breeding were far better than his own. But, as he often said, more money never hurt . . . and everyone knew that a shipping fortune was never entirely safe. With a few fierce storms, or an unseen reef or two, one could be ruined. And who would shed a tear?

Well, at the next milestone, he would see. The next milestone . . . one of those set up by order of the Great Man, Middleton sneered to his mount in lieu of anyone else to complain to. He'd always said the stones were a waste of money, erected only to mark Franklin's own advancement on Fortune's road. But on this evening, in a rare burst of good humor, the merchant decided to excuse "Poor Richard." At the next milestone, Middleton intended to do a quiet bit of business himself.

The thin, tired nag that carried him stumbled over the deeply rutted soil, occasionally lifting its head to the whine of gulls above. Ill-fed and rarely rested, the horse had again grown used to shivering under the cut of its owner's whip. Now, although it had no way of knowing, its troubles were nearly over.

Middleton continued to strain his eyes across the glinting waters ahead. He entertained mixed feelings about what he saw. Like many others who took their living from the ocean, he rarely allowed his own body to brave her rolling green waves. In fact, the death of his last brother by shipwreck three years before had hardened his suspicion of the sea, however much that event had pleased him. Oh, young Lionel had been a worthless relation—shunned by a family who disapproved of his gambling and lusting after things he was unable to pay for—forced to become a sailor. When he eventually sank to his final reward, Lionel followed the lead of the merchant's pious brother Chester, a truly tedious soul, and was followed in turn by a spinster sister, Veracity, who had been "as chaste" (and as cold) "as unsunn'd snow."

Middleton didn't miss any of his siblings at all. With the pack of them gone, none were left to try to steal from his corpse, with the help of their lawyers, what he'd managed to pull together into a considerable fortune even by Boston standards. His own death would simply be the end of the line. And the ornate tombstone he planned would be a fitting memorial to the last and best fruit of a dead branch of the family tree. Where the rest of the money would go would be Duncan Middleton's final surprise for the good people of Boston.

Curiously, there were still several gentlemen living in that city, entirely unrelated to him, who believed they might receive a piece of his fortune when Middleton went to meet his Maker. These birds of prey (who nested in law firms and merchandise warehouses) had lately given him far more entertainment, as he watched and baited them, than Lionel, Chester, and Veracity together had ever managed to do. The crooked man looked forward to keeping the vultures guessing. He would continue to enjoy seeing them squabble among themselves, making flattering, unctuous bids for his favor. Just let them try to gain from his death—it was years away, at any rate. Recently, he even thought some of them had secretly followed him about Boston . . . probably trying to glean details of his holdings, or to find something in his activities that might be held over his head.

Damn them all!

The purpose of this particular trip might have surprised even those who thought they knew the worst about the merchant's ways. Middleton had started out after receiving an answer to a letter of his own on the previous evening. The missive had made his lips curl with its promises.

"*I foresee no trouble in transporting the commodities you require, and selling same, regardless of their eventual use. . . .*"

The merchant had wisely burned that letter to keep it from Mrs. Bledsoe's notice. The old biddy only knew that he would be gone for at least two days. She would be free to gossip and pry where she might, as she went about her housekeeping duties. Still, she would never guess what he was up to, nor see the end of the lucrative plan he was about to set in motion.

Abruptly, the traveler's thoughts of home were interrupted by the hurrying approach of another horse and rider. After a few moments, they overtook him and passed by, probably making for shelter before night fell. Duncan Middleton averted his face, giving the passing stranger only the back of his wig and an edge of his tricornered hat, until the other had gone.

If all went well, he thought as he rode on, it would be a simple matter, this buying up of cheap turpentine and black powder (but quietly, through an agent) before mixing them with a bit of rum from his stores. Once the doctored item had been recasked, it would be sent inland by someone who had nothing to do with the coast trade.

The deadly new product would be difficult to trace back to him. On the frontier, it would be as welcome as any other intoxicant, and would be bought up by enough willing customers to make him a quick and satisfying profit. If a few delicate guts were poisoned by the drinking of it—why, they might have known better, and couldn't they follow their noses to save their lives? Most who bought would be heathens and savages anyway, and good riddance.

His knobby hand continued to fondle the bag of Dutch gold kept snug and warm beneath the red wool cloak. If all went well, he could soon laugh at the backs of the blasted customs men who peered out to sea. Not that he generally disliked these men; most of them were quite sympathetic, and took pity on a hard-pressed merchant—took bribes, really, for overlooking the outrageous duty of sixpence a gallon on non-British molasses brought up from the Caribbean.

(The commodity was, after all, one of the mainstays of colonial shipping. Everyone knew that much of the coast lived by sending fish, lumber, and livestock to the British, French, and Dutch sugar islands, in exchange for their dark syrup. Brought back to Massachusetts, it then went into dozens of distilleries, and came back out as rum that could be easily moved, and sold for a large profit at home or abroad. Some went as far as Africa, where it was traded for slaves, who were shipped to the sugar islands, where they were sold for more molasses, which would again be brought back to the colonial distilleries. It was a system that worked and would continue to work, because everyone concerned could share in the profits. Well, nearly everyone.)

Lately, however, rumors from London suggested that special interests might soon prevail, and that far stiffer controls could be expected within the coming year, now that Grenville had hold of a depleted royal purse . . . as well as the young George's ear. The coffeehouses had been full of it for weeks.

Thirty years before, old George's infernal Molasses Act had threatened to stop the Triangular Trade with its tariff on the foreign syrup that now satisfied more than two-thirds of the distilleries' demand—had even with the war going on! Thankfully, war or no, the Act's provisions had never been much enforced. But what if that were to change?

There was even an absurd new idea of requiring customs officials to actually *live* in the colonies—instead of staying safely at home in England, leaving their responsibilities to colonial men who were paid nearly nothing.

It was almost unnecessary to pay such men anything at all. Everyone knew where to find their pockets, and had long stuffed them with a little something extra, to feed their families. If the Crown started paying them a decent wage, their eyesight might improve dramatically. Next, they'd be expecting shipping manifests to actually agree with goods carried! Then, where would everyone be?

Long an avowed Tory, Duncan Middleton had lately become interested in Whiggish ideas of liberty, and British abuse of the colonies—which he often read about in the newspapers—although he also felt it was a shame they gave encouragement to the rabble. Still, noisy mobs might keep the long arms of the king and his advisors busy, and away from things that didn't concern them, like warehouses, and cargo holds.

Suddenly the sea wind hit him fully, and he had a clear view of a nearly spherical moon rising through the trees. Pulling wool closer for warmth, Middleton gave a harsh laugh.

In Rhode Island, away from the old Commonwealth, Britain saw far less, and a man of business could do far more. Of course a great many of Providence's men of business were pirates plain and simple—if few went to the trouble of stealing on the high seas. Not unlike himself, smiled the sly old merchant. Let Sam Adams and the rest in Boston earn His Majesty's displeasure: the Crown would soon make it hot enough for the City on the Hill. Meanwhile, *he* would build a second home to the southwestern, while he fleeced the frontier.

And so, thoughts of death and taxes, pain and profits winged peacefully about the merchant's head on this quiet evening, complimenting each other pleasantly. The fading light had left the sky a soft rose, and the sea sent up moonlit reflections of lilac and silver.

That must be the final milestone up ahead, and there was a figure waiting just off the road, standing in the shadow of a leaning pine. Next to it stood two oxen and a loaded wagon, as promised. Soon, Middleton thought, he would go on alone to Providence. He looked forward to a very large bowl of crab bisque, and a dozen or two of oysters, for he was keenly hungry. But business first.

Once more, capriciously, he whipped the shuddering animal beneath him, and hurried on his way.

It might be mentioned that the gold the merchant carried was of an interesting and unusual stamp. Several pieces of it would soon leave a glittering trail as they lay about the countryside like autumn crocuses. And watching them from the shadows would be an old reaper. He, too, would appreciate their bright, ageless bloom, while he held a scythe to the ready in his grasping, bony hands.

Chapter 2

⎯⌐ *Tuesday*

THE SUMMER OF 1763 had sent a good harvest to the village of Bracebridge, just west of Boston. Now, with Nature's work nearly done, the countryside caught its breath. A well-earned calm, buzzing like a gentle spell, settled over all.

All, that is, except the kitchens, for truly, woman's work is never done. This was the season of preserving and laying away for the long New England winter. And in more than one house, the steamy air was full of apples—small, striped apples bubbling into applesauce and apple butter in black pots suspended above steady fires, while sliced apples dried slowly on threads among the rafters.

Inside one such kitchen at the edge of the village, close by cupboard shelves lined with crockery, pewter, and china, a young woman stood in a warm ray of amber light. She sighed as she passed a sticky wrist over a wisp of hair that had fallen from its pins. It was the color of clear, sweet cider, glinting richly with red and gold. To-day, Charlotte Willett would not have been pleased with the comparison. She longed to be out walking, waiting for a cool twilight. Thoroughly tired of bending, carry-ing, peeling, and coring, she tossed down a paring knife with a defiant glance at her stout companion.

"Any more outside?" Hannah Sloan inquired with-out looking up. She paused to catch at a billowing linen sleeve.

"Three more bushels. And that's the end. Thank heaven."

Hannah kept peeling and slicing on the boards that stood between them, her broad back to the fire. The mo-notonous routine of several days had taken its toll. Words were currently few and far between.

Charlotte leaned back to squint through one of the open windows, adjusting the light muslin bodice that stuck to her skin. Above the house, the barn, and the farmyard between, a huge white oak dropped acorns and leaves around chickens scratching and muttering below.

In the same shade, an old dog lay stretched and doz-ing, his brown, curling fur dappled with sun and flecked with gray. Once a herder of sheep, Orpheus was now re-duced to lifting an eyelid occasionally when a hen came to close. But he *would* stay within earshot, his mistress thought fondly.

Charlotte turned again to watch Hannah reach deep into a basket. On most days, the older woman walked up from her home by the river bridge to work with Mrs. Willett for several hours, leaving her own household to the care of daughters who were in no hurry to see their mother return. Now, her face below her mobcap was col-ored like an Indian's—red from the fire on one side, blue from the cooler reflections of a late October sky on the other.

"Hannah, will you still go at four?"

"I'll stay until we're done."

Another hour—maybe two!

Abruptly, knowing there would be eyebrows raised behind her, Charlotte spun around in the heat, and lunged through the open door to freedom.

THE SUGARED STEAM of the kettles was no match for the whispering breeze outside.

As Charlotte, led by Orpheus, rounded a corner of the house, she was humming an appropriate hymn to the world's blessings, her plain skirts swinging gently over the cropped grass. Before long, she took stock of all she saw, each thing hers to care for.

The little cherry's summer leaves were curled and faded, nearly ready to fall. She and Aaron had planted it together. Six years ago they had set the tree in, the same week Reverend Rowe had joined them together. Now, almost three years had gone by since another Sunday— when ropes in loving hands had lowered Aaron into nearby ground. That unbearable winter, Reverend Rowe had counseled Mrs. Willett to listen to the Lord and her elders, and to avoid examining her own inclinations, at least until she married again. The memory of this advice caused Charlotte to lower her round chin thoughtfully and kick a little at the grass.

The first time Aaron had come up from Philadelphia, he had only planned to visit the Quaker community near Boston. A young gentleman of some means, he'd also hoped to take home one of his own for a bride. Instead, he had been taken with Charlotte Howard, and finally chose to stay in Bracebridge. Her family were not Friends. Still, she shared her husband's trust in an inner light, in the truths revealed by Nature, and in the virtues of simplicity. They both knew that they were fortunate, and blessed, in each other. But even as they started their life together, they also knew that what comes to a young couple can as easily go.

Well, life *had* moved on, even without Aaron Willett, although it had taken a while for her to accept the idea. Now, it looked as if the country entered a great new era. There was a new king, tall, boyish George III, who promised to take good care of his subjects while he tended his own fields. (Farmer George, they had begun to call him.) The Great War that had unsettled much of the world, fought in North America against the French and their Indian allies, was over. And the peace treaty signed in Paris the past February had given Great Britain uncontested right to Canada, as well as most of the country east of the Mississippi. People were flooding back to abandoned settlements, and pushing the frontier farther west.

For her part, Charlotte Willett had for three years been the sole manager of a farm that had once held a whole family. Still held them, she thought with a familiar stab, in the high, fenced plot that overlooked the river, above the hillside orchard. Not so long ago, her parents had been carried there to join three infants who'd never grown to childhood. Then, suddenly, her sister Eleanor had been taken on the eve of her own marriage. And Aaron had died of the same choking fever within a few weeks, leaving the sharpest ache of all. Why, she wondered, should it be that some families increased, while others declined? For she had no children. Neither had two young cousins, buried where they fell— one with Braddock in '57 near Fort Duquesne, the other in Quebec with Wolfe, in '59. Already, their faces were a blur in her memory. Now, of her own generation, only she and her younger brother remained.

But the family farm continued to thrive under her hand, allowing Jeremy to go on with his studies across the Atlantic, in Edinburgh. They had agreed that the land, while left to him, was hers to care for, as long as she chose to live there. And he meant to visit as often as he could. These two thoughts gave her frequent pleasure, as well as a life-sustaining sense of purpose.

Fingering a twig of cherry leaves, Charlotte walked on toward the front lawn and its broad view, admiring the flaming golds and reds of the maples that ran down the road from Boston, and into Bracebridge. The town itself was spread out below.

Just down the hill was the property of her closest neighbor, gentleman farmer and scientist Richard Longfellow. Although some considered him peculiar, she thoroughly enjoyed Longfellow's company. In the fields yesterday, he'd worn a broad-brimmed straw hat he'd recently brought back from Italy, and wielded an iron sickle with the strength of one possessed, next to his hired men. She knew he sometimes toiled extravagantly for hours, until his strength, or his mood, played out. Then, he would go inside to brood or to plan, and eventually set his hand to something new. This afternoon, however, the cleared field was empty, and Richard was nowhere to be seen.

Almost across the road from Longfellow's front lawn stood the Bracebridge Inn, with stables and a yard behind. Farther on, placed among bright trees and hedges and lanes, Charlotte looked over a few dozen houses, some she knew with shops in their lower rooms, one with a schoolroom run by old Dame Williams. The Common with its rectangle of tall elms lay just before the wide-arched stone bridge that spanned the Musketaquid River. On its grassy southern edge stood the white meeting house, next to Reverend Rowe's somber house of hewn granite.

Through more distant trees, she could just see the top of the gristmill on the opposite side of the river's span. There was the crossroads, and the old Blue Boar, a country tavern for the rough-and-tumble. It got much of its trade from local farmers, and those traveling the north-south road that went with the river current to the town of Concord. The same road's southern aspect was quickly lost to the eye as it climbed past the mill and up into abrupt hills, on its way to Framingham. On the north, though, one could study several miles of a plain filled with plowed fields that were set apart by stone walls, as well as squares of fruit orchards bordering thicker wood lots. Bisecting all of this was a green strip of flowing river marshland, where wild ducks and geese fed and chattered among the reeds.

Charlotte continued to watch through the afternoon haze for occasional signs of distant movement. The playful air had finally taken the smell of cooked fruit from her substantial nose; in its place, it left more subtle scents from the drying fields and water meadows, and the woods across the road where birds called.

The weight of her memories began to lift. Happy to be free, she tilted her head back to admire the greens and golds, crimsons and oranges of the rustling leaves above her, and the deep blue of the sky beyond. And then, at a hint of a whimper from Orpheus, she looked to see a scarlet movement nearer to the earth.

A lone figure came walking down from the road's crest, leading a tired old horse. Both were odd enough to make her stare. The old man was especially startling. Crabbed and shrunken, he was draped with a long, full cloak of brilliant red. His head was covered with a heavy wig and a spreading, tricornered hat. Had he been younger, she thought, the full town costume on his buckled frame would have been unbearably hot for the sunny afternoon. But he appeared not to mind as he and his horse stepped cautiously, leading their shadows westward, down the dusty road.

The odd gentleman at first appeared to turn away when she took notice of him, but then he stopped and faced her squarely, with a curiosity that seemed to match her own. Without thinking, she reached down to smooth her skirts, and it was only then that Charlotte realized she still held an apple in her hand. When the old man bobbed his head in silent greeting, she instinctively held the apple out to him, coloring as his eyes met hers: met, and held them, and widened. Perhaps he was surprised at her forwardness. Or it could have been that he simply admired her face and figure. This was something that happened frequently enough. As a young widow, she knew she was sometimes referred to as "fair game."

"An apple, sir?" she asked, determined not to mind whatever the cause of his piercing stare.

"Many thanks!"

His voice was high-pitched and thin. But she was to have only the two words to judge by when considering it later.

A gloved hand reached out and accepted her gift without further comment. Then, he gave a stiff, old-fashioned bow that made Charlotte smile in return.

The stranger's jaws parted. He took a large bite, and she heard the crisp apple crunch. His smile grew and the white wig nodded gently. As he chewed, her quick eyes took in more about his person.

He might have been near sixty, or even older, she thought. And what she saw of his shaded face looked oddly white. Probably the pallor of a recent invalid, she imagined, or one who generally kept to his letters and ledgers—a man of business? His was certainly not the face of someone used to walking in the sun, as he was doing now, unless he always protected his features well whenever he went into the open air.

As for his clothing, she noticed a pea green velvet

coat beneath the bright cloak; below this were striking rich green velvet breeches, and white silk hose. His cloak, too, was lined with the best quality silk—once again, in scarlet. She also observed a frilled shirt of cambric, and soft leather shoes with bright silver clasps, hardly made for riding. Overall, she concluded, he was certainly a colorful old gentleman, but one out of his element in the country.

In another moment, she might have asked herself (or even him, since she wasn't particularly shy) where he had come from, and why he went on foot. But before she had the chance, the old man tossed the apple core into the roadside cornflowers and turned to pull himself with great effort onto his horse, while Charlotte held her breath for him. Finally in his seat, he touched his hat and started off toward the town.

At that instant, Charlotte felt the gentle touch of her conscience as she remembered Hannah toiling all alone, surrounded by apples. And so, taking one last look at the odd, retreating figure, young Mrs. Willett walked with renewed purpose back toward her kitchen door, leaving all other thoughts behind her.

Chapter 3

"WELCOME TO THE Blue Boar!" called the tavern's proprietor, standing in the doorway beneath a bristling azure monster with yellow eyes and a sharp red tongue. He gestured broadly to the open door that awaited all comers, including the stranger in a scarlet cloak who approached on foot at sunset.

Inside the tavern's smoky main room, a dusty twilight had already fallen. A few tallow ends glowed on rough tables flanked with benches, where country men sat talking over cider and ale. Nearby, a blazing fireplace had drawn a brace of elderly patrons who hunched like two fat quail, smoking long clay pipes and toasting themselves. To their backs, winding stairs led up to three dark sleeping rooms that offered accommodation to those who made no demands in the way of luxury, and had few expectations of comfort. To see to customers' stomachs, a small scullery below produced a more or less regular serving of game stews, pickled pork, and bought bread.

The whole of this adequate establishment was presided over by a former Salem man called Phineas Wise. The landlord now walked to a mounted barrel and drew off a pitcher with a practiced eye, magically extending its head of froth. Wise was a thrifty individual of lean face and thin nose, with a keen, calculating expression and a stubble of beard; in brief, he was a man who would be recognized as a Yankee up and down the coast.

When the cloaked stranger appeared, everyone stopped what they were doing to examine him carefully, and to speculate briefly about the brown cloth bundle he carried under one arm. He had evidently interrupted a vigorous discussion; he had heard several words of it as he approached the door. Soon, it began again. The stranger sat down and listened.

"Well, some of these bastards think they have as much right as anyone else to be here, but I say to that, think again!" This sentiment came from a giant of a man with curling red hair and a freckled skin.

"That's right—they better think twice about it," echoed a man with bloodshot eyes who sat next to the first speaker.

"Let them go back to France, and take their heathen friends with 'em!" came from near the west windows.

"But I say," said the first voice, "they'll take *no more* from us here!"

General enthusiasm rose from around the room.

It was with some uneasiness that the landlord finally drew himself away from the loud talk to ask the stranger's pleasure, which was a small tankard of local ale. Clearly, the heated discussion was being led by the massive man dressed in a loose homespun shirt and stained buckskin breeches. During a lull, this confident speaker picked his teeth with a bench splinter, while he leaned on his elbows over a pewter plate that held the remains of a greasy dinner. Two lesser companions sat beside and in front of him. The one who had recently spoken up displayed the rubbery features and rolling eyes of a man well into his cups, while the other seemed to wear a more permanent look of befuddlement on his up-turned face.

"Maybe we thought we knew the enemy before, when we mustered at Worcester six years back," the bul-lying voice boomed out again, "fighting men, from all over Middlesex County . . . men who'd heard what the savages, and the Frenchmen who paid them, had been up to along the Hudson. But by God, we knew far more after the bloody massacre at Fort William Henry! A dirty coward's trick that was, killing soldiers under a white flag!"

A loud chorus again agreed with the smooth speaker; most of them knew Peter Lynch, the local miller, well. He continued when the flood of voices ebbed away.

"They were damned fools ever to trust Montcalm. They might have guessed he'd let his redskins get at our soldiers, with or without a truce, and rob them of every-thing they had—right down to the shirts on their backs! We all know those who survived saw a good many scalps taken that day, too. Saw women stripped, and worse—watched infants' heads break open against the stockade walls! Saw more killed as they lay in their beds, burning with fever. And after that, the ones left were marched two hundred miles, all the way up to Montreal, to be sold for slaves! Well, we learned from that, all right. The whole world has learned of it by now, to their eternal dis-gust, so I don't want to hear any more damned lies about how a Frenchman can *ever* be trusted!"

"Cowards, every one of 'em!" cried the drunken man beside the miller, who went by the name of Dick Craft.

"Well, Peter, some of the things you're saying," began another, "weren't exactly as you say. . . ."

Peter Lynch lowered his voice and looked around with a meaningful squint. "But there's worse than those who fight in plain sight, as I just described. Spies, I'm thinking of now. Some of them are still in these parts, looking for mischief, and mayhem! Aye, they're waiting . . . watching for ways to get back at decent folk who let 'em be, more's the pity. Ready to go after 'em, even though hostilities be over."

"It's a terrible truth," Dick Craft shouted, shaking his wooden tankard in the air. "And I hope to God none of us forgets it in *this* lifetime!"

Several listeners fervently agreed, while a few others belched. Thus encouraged, the drunkard continued.

"If they plan to hang around, stealing what's ours, then maybe we'll help 'em up into the treetops with a rope or two! Or—or maybe we'll be having ourselves a feather party—what do you say to that, Jack Pennywort? We'll bring along our own f-feathers, and some nice, warm tar, we will! What do you say to that, now?"

The daft-looking man sitting next to him took a sharp nudge in the ribs, and nodded with a simple smile. "Might there be," he ventured, "some ale, Peter, for after?"

Interrupted from wiping his nose on his sleeve, the miller leaned over and cuffed the man with an enormous hand, as a laughing Dick Craft jerked back out of the way, almost upsetting himself. Once righted, Dick managed to fling a challenging glance over his shoulder into a corner, where a younger man sat near the red-cloaked stranger, glowering at what was being said.

Although he might have been taken by his dress for a local farmer, several details about this guest who sat in shadow marked him as something more unusual. For one thing, long black hair fell in waves down the sides of his face, without the constraint of a ribbon. For another, his smooth skin had a deep olive glow. And his dark eyes were startling in their intensity. Set almost flush with high cheekbones, they shone out in the limited light, like a cat's. Taken all together, one might have guessed that this was a Frenchman, with perhaps some Iroquois blood flowing in his veins. Though several men had glanced his way as the miller kept on, the young man's full lips remained together, and he held himself remarkably still.

Phineas Wise scratched his beard and frowned at the miller and his friends. Lynch had a few years and inches, and a good many pounds, over the youth he seemed to be tormenting. Although Peter had admittedly gone to fat lately . . . probably the result of a growing appetite for all sorts of things. As he gathered up some empty vessels, the taverner spoke cautiously.

"Wartime's one thing, boys. But now, thank the Lord, that's all over. And there's no law against being brought up to speak French, even around here! Besides, Peter, the Frenchmen you mean aren't exactly strangers. The Neutrals have lived next to us for nearly eight years now, and they've given no trouble to speak of, have they? I know the ones in Worcester as well as you. And from everything else I hear, they're decent, honest folk."

"Whether they live here or anywhere else, I say they're still Frenchmen! You can tell by their *smell.*" Peter Lynch caught the eyes of several of the others; one by one, his leer either convinced, or sickened, those who took it in with their drink.

"I don't know, though," said a man over by the now dark west windows, "if the French can be called worse than any others in the war. If you'll read your city papers, you'll see it's the Europeans all together who forced war on the rest of us—not only France, but England, too, as well as Prussia, Russia, Austria, and Sweden, and even—"

"Oh, give it a rest, Eli," called someone from across the room.

"That may be," said another by the cider kegs. "And you might even say, now, that there's honor in fighting for your own country, whatever it may be—and whatever the reason. I suspect it's some of our *own* men who ought to be ashamed, for doing business with the enemy just to get hold of their blessed sugar, and fa-la's to sell to city folk, even while the fighting was going on! Your own brother, Dick, for one. So I wouldn't be so quick to call the kettle—"

"Oh, if we're naming names, then, what about your three Falmouth cousins, Henry?" cried out a disgruntled neighbor. "Don't we all know they were sending their grain and cattle up to Cannadee, across the blockade?"

"Supplying the very ones who planned to come and lift my scalp in the night," chimed in a farmer finishing a plate of heavy stew, "just waiting to run down and burn our houses soon as we marched off to fight! Though they never did manage to get here—"

"At any road, we did *our* part," boasted another. "And with precious little help from the bloody-backed lobsters, and their prissy lords sent to teach us how to fight!"

"*That's* for certain!" came a quick reply. "They must've sent over some of their worst dunderheads, judging by what I saw with my own two eyes. Yet we *still* managed to snatch their bacon from the fire, didn't we, lads?"

Between vigorous assent and rolling laughter, several heads and chests rose and swelled.

"And took many a fort for them, too! Beausejour, Frontenac, and Duquesne, Niagara, Fort Ti, and Crown Point, then Quebec—"

"Oh, well, you'll have to admit that Wolfe was an awfully good tactician—"

"Now *that* was enough for young Montcalm—"

"And finally, Montreal!"

"Well I remember when we took Louisbourg, in '45," broke in one of the old birds roasting by the fire, who puffed with animation. "With old Pepperell, bless him. Sailed up to Cape Breton, took it single-handed!"

"The British Navy may deserve some small thanks," observed a younger man rather dryly, causing the other quail to come alive with a sputter.

"You can thank the British all you want for giving it *back* to the froggies, too, soon as peace was signed. If you'll remember, that's why the lobsters had to go up and do it all over again, and blow it to bits this time. And now, I wonder, just how long our *latest* peace will last?"

It was a sobering question. The war just concluded had often seemed won. Yet hostilities had flared up again and again, like flames from a burning seam of coal. But tonight, many seated in the Blue Boar only laughed at this lesson. And all the while, the young Frenchman continued to sit, listening silently in his dark corner, waiting for a further goad. The miller soon supplied it.

"What about your own pet frog, Phineas? When did he hop in this time? And why is it that you let him stay, when his kind is bound to give offense to all your decent customers?"

Those seated by Peter Lynch eyed the Frenchman in the shadows expectantly, while the speech drew groans from some at the back tables.

"You know, you're the very first to complain, Peter, since Mr. Fortier joined us yesterday evening."

"Maybe you can explain what brought him to Bracebridge, where he's got no proper business that I know of. And then he can tell us if he imagines he's going to spend another quiet night in a bed upstairs."

"He's very likely staying here," the landlord responded patiently, "because it's cheap, as you all know . . . unlike

Mr. Pratt's fine lodgings up the hill. Show me he's a bit of trouble to anyone, and I'll have him out. Meanwhile, my guests may come and go as they please. It's still a free country. As to his business—" Phineas Wise regarded the miller with a gleam in his eye.

"—as to his business, well, I think many of us know what that might be, don't we, gentlemen? And I say good luck to him, as I would to any man trying to coax a young lady—or any other kind of female, for that matter."

"Especially a young colt like Mary!" someone called, and several of the men joined in with loud good humor.

"You know what else the ladies say about Frenchmen, don't you, Peter?" called an older man, before hooting with laughter.

For a moment, it looked as though the red-faced miller might leap over his seat. But instead, a determined look crept across Peter Lynch's broad features, while his great voice softened to a syrupy growl.

"Oh, he's not afraid to walk in here, bold as brass, and sniff around—as long as I'm off trying to get custom for my mill. I suppose he saw me riding into Worcester on Monday, and came running here to try his luck. But I'm back now; and I'm only saying God's truth when I tell him he'd be better off keeping to his own kind. I'll just add what we all feel—that any of his kind that hope to get half-breeds by our women will soon be escorted *straight to hell!*"

At this, the silent young man jumped lithely to his feet, throwing out a curse and nearly overturning the table in front of the red-cloaked stranger. The miller, too, rose up and spit on his hands in preparation, followed by a wobbling Dick Craft. While others braced themselves, the two old men silhouetted against the leaping firelight spun their chairs around eagerly, hoping for a new tale to add to their threadbare stock. And Phineas Wise hurried to the back of the bar to pick up a stout ash stick he'd often found handy in a brawl.

It was in this final moment of relative calm, when calculations of positions and odds were swiftly being made, that a sound—not a very loud sound, but one that is frequently found to be commanding—gained the attention of each and every one of the Blue Boar's inhabitants, calling an immediate truce.

Its cause was simple. The old stranger, who had been in the process of rising when the excitement began, had taken a purse from an inner pocket of the scarlet cloak he wore. In the confusion, he'd tipped the open bag until its contents fell in a glittering stream onto the table before him. There, more than two dozen pieces of gold sang out loudly as they danced and reeled against each other, and finally settled down before an audience that was as fascinated as a swaying cobra hearing a snake charmer's horn.

The stranger bent his head quickly. He picked up the coins from the table, then dropped them back into the leather pouch, one by one. Around him, eyes narrowed in speculation.

Phineas Wise quietly set his club against the wall. He bent to retrieve a few more pieces that had skipped to the floor. While he held them, he was surprised to see that they were Dutch gold—guldens, from God knew where. He stood and gave them up a little wistfully. Then he retreated a few paces, to be well away from the circle of staring faces.

Slowly, the men sat down to their tables again. But they continued to watch the stranger as he produced a dull coin from another pocket, and put it by his empty tankard. After that he gave a nod to the landlord, snugged the brown bundle up under his arm again, and made his way carefully toward the open door.

Gabriel Fortier was in the doorway ahead of him.

The young Frenchman stopped to look back with a frown, then drew his foot over the frame and disappeared into the evening.

The old stranger seemed to hesitate, but soon followed, and the tavern let out its breath.

Candles again flickered quietly, and conversation, when it resumed, was subdued. Several times, one man or another looked deeply into the dark recess that now held only a table and two empty chairs.

Who was the old man in the scarlet cloak, they asked themselves and each other, and how had he come by all of that money? Everybody knew that gold and silver coins were scarce throughout the colonies. Spanish silver dollars—"pieces of eight"—were sometimes seen, as well as British sterling. But most silver received was sent straight back to England, to help pay for the flood of goods the colonies required—or else it was melted for plate, or other items. So it was with gold. And the odds of seeing Dutch coins? They were very, very slim.

Where had the stranger come by it? And more to the point, where was the frail old man going with his gold, out on the dark road at night, and all alone?

The two quails by the fire (whose names were Tyndall and Flint) relit their pipes, and issued the first of several dire predictions involving footpads, demons, and wolves. Meanwhile, Phineas Wise shook his head as he went to stand on the doorstep and jingle pockets full of copper. He peered out and saw that the chilly night was less complete than it had appeared from inside the lighted tavern. A bit of bloodred twilight still clung to the western horizon, while the sky overhead was a deep blue dotted with small, pale clouds, and several points of twinkling stars.

A breath of cold flowed down the hillside that the stranger had just begun to climb. Eventually, the road the old man followed disappeared near the crest in dense forest, with a wide stretch of old burned-over meadow coming before. As he continued to watch, the land-lord heard the lonely voice of a whippoorwill calling out from nearby woods. It cried, it was said, for lost souls who wandered in the night. The practical man listened, and half believed. Someone would die soon. The cry of a nearby owl joined that of the other bird, echo-ing Phineas Wise's own unasked question in an eerie staccato.

Whoo-who-whooo?

Where was the old man going, Wise wondered, watching him climb slowly past dark fingers of a bending hemlock that overhung the road. There was no other tavern to stop in for a good five miles. Ahead, there were only a few isolated farms nestled in a hilly stretch of for-est, and unprosperous ones at that. Was there something wrong with him? Didn't he know how to tell direction? Beyond that, did the old man feel no fear? It was a puzzle, but in the end Wise turned back to his own hearth and business, and shut the tavern door firmly behind him.

Inside, it was as if his customers could still hear the happy ring of the falling gold coins, while they called for more of the same. Now the miller, too, seemed con-cerned for the old man's safety.

"I only say," maintained Peter Lynch, "that he'd be far better off investing it, than carrying it around."

"Investing it with you?" Dick Craft asked with a wink. The miller did not return his amusement.

"Better than to lose it somewhere in the night," Lynch intoned ominously.

"Myself," Dick continued, "I've lost more money in broad daylight than in the dark. But that's rarely called stealing, is it? Not when there's signed notes, and all, to make it right—"

The miller's glowering face soon made Dick bite his

tongue, and remember that he spoke to a man quite used to doing business.

The third of their party, Jack Pennywort, had less to say on the matter. His own concern was that he should be getting home, and that his wife would scold him properly if he came in late—or do even worse. This led to the usual comments from his heartier friends who feigned surprise that Jack should care. Undoubtedly, they joked, he had become accustomed to his punishment. What of it, if he should be locked outside his own door to sleep where he might? There could be unexpected pleasures in such a system, if a man knew where to look, and what to do about it. So then, why not stay a little longer?

But Jack got up, found a copper or two for the landlord, and made his way somewhat unsteadily to the door. It should be added that this clumsiness was not entirely the result of drink. Jack had been dragging a clubfoot behind him all of his life. It was generally considered by his friends and neighbors to be quite a humorous appendage.

Eventually, followed by loud laughter, the shuffling little man gained the door. His departure allowed the tavern to concentrate on an entering party of thirsty new arrivals, who jostled Jack rudely as they passed him on the sill.

Chapter 4

At tuesday's twilight, Richard Longfellow, the eccentric neighbor of Charlotte Willett, sat alone in his paneled study. As the light faded, he contemplated an object on one of the walls. The object was a portrait. Its subject was Eleanor Howard, a young woman with direct eyes, and hair that fell in dark ringlets.

Longfellow continued to gaze, but he no longer saw the portrait. Instead, memory had taken over, giving him the only other images he would ever have of her striking beauty—for the original had been tragically lost.

From time to time, he still imagined her sitting there beside him, sometimes rocking a cradle. But Eleanor Howard had been taken when an illness settled in her throat and choked the breath and life from her, as it had done to others nearby. His own grief at the loss of his fiancée had been shared by her sister Charlotte, who soon endured more sorrows of her own. Unlike Eleanor,

Aaron Willett had refused to be bled, but in the end it had made no difference.

Longfellow turned to the window, to find most of the sky's color gone. It was lucky, he told himself, that he had learned long ago to enjoy a bachelor's life. At least, he still had Charlotte. He had admired her from the first. Her features were nothing as special as Eleanor's; he was reminded of the fact as he turned back to stare at the portrait once more, through the gloom. But Eleanor's older sister had her own quiet charms, with an intelligent spark grown strong in a soul that had always been loved, and kindly treated. Charlotte, too, was capable of thinking eternal thoughts, possibly almost as capable as he was himself.

Uncurling his legs, which had a habit of becoming entwined, Longfellow sprang to his feet, determined to buoy his mood by lighting a candle. Eleanor had frequently experienced bouts of feverish imagination and activity, coupled with an exciting lack of restraint. Charlotte's mind was quieter, more even, but still quite curious . . . although it did sometimes seem to him that she tended to plod.

Curiosity about the larger realities of the universe, things outside one's personal life—that was the secret of lasting contentment! But when Longfellow felt the urge to philosophize, he imagined the scheme of things to be chaotic, and nearly unsolvable. He certainly held little hope for any rational system of order that tried to alter the petty obsessions of most of humanity, who did their best to ruin the world for each other. Wryly, he watched Charlotte perceive a natural harmony all around her, while she noticed human discord as a force of only minor importance. It was a rare turn of mind, he thought—possibly even one to be envied.

Whatever the truths of the cosmos, her bright moods invariably spilled over onto his darker ones when the two sat and talked. She sometimes made him laugh out loud. Besides that, she listened well. And his neighbor had often helped him weather his frequent melancholia. She made him feel necessary . . . as her steadfast supporter, and as a good companion. He knew this to be a rare thing for a man whose quick, passionate nature had lost him nearly as many friends as he had ever claimed.

Not that he minded having few friends. He was, after all, respected. And as long as there were new ideas to explore, experiments to be conducted and studied, seeds to plant and stars to ponder, who could be bothered with courting admiration? Let others fear loneliness. The cup offered up by the physical world was filled to overflowing.

Energized by a new idea, Longfellow picked up the candlestick in front of him, and strode away from the fire toward a gold-framed mirror that graced one side of the simply appointed room. As he did so, he felt the pleasant flap of the long linen trousers he'd recently affected (taking the style of certain Italian peasants), which he wore outside his boots to further confound custom. The trousers were cool and comfortable, and they didn't constrain him at the joints like common knee breeches, with buttons that bit into you when you sat. They also concealed lower legs he found quite adequate for the most part, if they did not bulge enough to meet fashionable standards.

Lighting two more wax tapers that stood in brass-backed sconces on either side of the Venetian mirror, he peered at his own image. It was less beautiful than the one he had been contemplating on the wall, but it had the advantage of being alive. By the light of candles and fire, the mirror revealed a pliant, if solemn, face. It could have been a trifle underfed, but it had full lips, and now it experimented with a pleasant smile—nothing like the pinched, aristocratic sneer so popular in his former home by the Bay. Longfellow saw that false token all around him when he rode in to Boston to visit. It was enough to make a parson growl.

Further study brought to light the presence of new gray hairs among the dark mass that fell down his back—tied, but neither pomaded nor powdered. Still thick, by God, for a man who could no longer call himself young. And the eyes were certainly distinctive—the rich color of hazelnut shells. It was fortunate, he told himself, he was not a vain man by nature.

Moving away, Longfellow tapped the glass barometer that hung on the wall. For the moment, it held steady . . . steadier, he thought ruefully, than he felt himself. Would the evening *never* end?

He knew he had become dangerously mercurial again. Right now, he had the urge to argue about something—anything. Perhaps Locke, or Rousseau, or some other misleading and overblown fool. Cicero would take whatever side was left in an argument, and keep it up until they were both worn out with it, run down like clocks and ready for sleep. But Cicero was late returning home.

Longfellow sat at the pianoforte for a while, picking out a tune on the cool ivory keys, considering fate's rude manners. In his father's time, in Boston, Cicero had been far more than an adequate servant—in fact, he had nearly run his father's city house . . . especially after Richard's mother had died. He had also assisted the members of the family he'd "adopted" in delicate matters, often requiring a certain amount of finesse. At Jason Longfellow's death, his will had ended the black man's bondage, providing him with the legally required funds to remain free. But Cicero had agreed to stay in service to Richard Longfellow (who else, he asked, would have the job?) and had moved with him when the aging young man, in love, purchased the house next to the Howards four years before.

Tonight, Cicero was down at the taproom of the Bracebridge Inn, imbibing news with his wine. Like his Roman namesake, he enjoyed society even while he frequently objected to it, and it to him. Since he was no longer a slave, he had a right to sit with the others. But for several reasons he preferred a warm, hidden nook around the chimney corner. Jonathan Pratt served him Madeira there, often bringing him stories as well. And as the evening progressed and the wine and rum flowed, Cicero frequently chuckled at what was meant for very few ears (and certainly not his own), coming from patrons warming themselves beside the fire.

Bored again with his train of thought, Longfellow shifted, and started a new tune. "Maybe I'll have to get a cat to talk to," he muttered to himself, sulking while he cocked an ear at something in the distance.

Abruptly, the front door opened and shut, and quick feet sounded in the hall. In another instant, Cicero stood before him, bent almost in two.

"I came . . ." he gasped, "because I supposed . . . even in your mood . . . that you'd be interested in what I've heard . . ."

Overcome, he again lowered a head that appeared to be topped by a gray, tailless, fashionably short-curled periwig, although it wasn't.

"Difficult for me to say," Longfellow replied, waiting for more. It was not forthcoming. Cicero still fought for breath and equilibrium. Longfellow tapped his fingers on the piano lid impatiently. "And difficult for you, it seems. Another secret?"

"No. Better hurry, though . . . the rest of the town's . . . probably there already."

"Really."

"It seems Jack Pennywort . . . over at the Blue Boar . . .

started walking up the Worcester road, following an old man who's a stranger in these parts—aaaahhh! . . . and the old man . . . it seems that the old man . . . well, he caught fire! Ignited all by himself . . . nobody knows how."

There was quite a long pause, and the ormolu mantle clock chimed the hour.

"He *what*?" Longfellow inquired, squinting with impatience.

"They say . . . he . . . went up in flames."

Catching his breath, Cicero studied the effect his news had produced. He had been aware of his employer's black humor since suppertime. He believed this new event would be able to change it, and perhaps provide them both with amusement for several days.

"What—on the road? And who, if you don't mind my asking, are *they*?" Longfellow queried, taking several steps to peer out of a window into the darkness. There were lights on the opposite hillside, where none should have been.

"Over the bridge, up past the tavern. Jack Pennywort was the only one to see it. Some already say it's the Devil's work. Or witchcraft, at least. Jack claims there's nothing left of the fellow at all!"

"Ah, Pennywort. There's an opinion to value," Longfellow retorted. "And witchcraft, too," he ventured with slightly more interest. "What won't the undisciplined mind get up to, on a dull evening."

"An interesting story, though, especially for Jack to make up by himself."

"True. Especially for Jack. Although he might have remembered—"

"The reason I ran was because I thought you'd like to go over and take a look for yourself, while the thing was still hot."

"A look at what? I wouldn't imagine there'd be anything left to see. Not if the Devil made a real job of it."

A jumble of voices could be heard coming from the direction of the inn. But Longfellow had a stubborn streak, and would not be easily moved from a mood.

"Well, you might want to observe everybody *else* going out for a look!" Cicero cried, falling into a chair. "It would be a shame to have to listen to it all tomorrow, secondhand."

Finally unable to resist the urge to go, Longfellow bolted toward the hallway. "Are you coming?" he threw back behind him.

"Not just yet I'm not," Cicero said with a sigh, bending closer to the fire.

"Then I suppose it's up to me to watch the curtain rise, and take in the show . . ."

The declaration had barely stopped ringing through the hallway when Longfellow, still wrestling with his coat sleeves, slammed the heavy door behind him, leaving the lion's head knocker to pound out a final farewell.

ONCE THROUGH HIS front gate, Richard Longfellow paused, faced with a dilemma. If he "forgot" to go and ask Mrs. Willett to view with him the scene of whatever had occurred, she might think the oversight was intentional. She would also ask him endless questions, probably well into the next week.

But if he turned and went to find her, while all Bracebridge was tramping across the river (she might even have gone ahead of him already!) then he would miss the beginnings of what promised to be a ridiculous entertainment—the sort of thing that pleased Longfellow more than most social events. Undecided, he stood with his feet pointed downhill.

When he finally did turn, he saw Charlotte's cloaked figure coming out of her yard with a lantern, walking so that she was unable to see an enormous yellow face with a toothless grin coming up behind her. Longfellow waited and watched the timeless spectacle of a rising autumn moon, noting how the eastern blackness had turned blue again around the luminous disk with its heavily pocked surface.

"You'd make a fine Diogenes," he offered pleasantly as she approached.

"It's less an honest man I'm after than an answer to what's causing all this noise! Did someone ring the fire bell?"

Longfellow shook his head as she took his arm. Soon, they hurried through inky shadows that lay across the road.

"No ... but flames of a kind were involved." He smiled to see her face, lit from below by the horn box she carried, take on the look of a jack-o'-lantern.

"According to Cicero," he went on, "there seems to have been a case of what's been called *spontaneous human combustion* here. Not unheard of, although I believe it is the first time it's been managed in this part of the world. At least, it's the first I've heard of it."

"But can you tell me what it all means?"

"There was a strange story from New York in the papers last year, which was widely repeated. It seems a very respectable and well-liked Long Island farmer, sitting in his chair on a Sabbath morning, smoking a small pipe, was seen to be quickly and thoroughly consumed by a mass of flames that came from within him. At the same time, the chair in which he sat was scarcely charred."

"Oh!"

"His wife was in church, but the event was witnessed by a young female servant. She became hysterical, of course, and finally called for help. It was said she was so unnerved that she fled from the place the same day."

"Poor girl!"

"Later, the man's wife unhappily admitted that the

husband had been fond of blasphemy, and that she had recently heard him repudiate a solemn oath he had made to the Almighty—on what issue, I don't recall. That satisfied the local magistrates as to both the agency and motive."

"It was called an Act of God?" Charlotte's eyes widened with surprise.

"Apparently. A blow for the Deists and their mechanical universe. But then, who knows? Who actually saw it happen? One simple child—a pretty thing who lost her wits, they say—and, of course, the Lord himself. While I'd accept in perfect faith anything He cared to tell me directly, I'm not sure the ravings of the only other human there guarantee us an accurate account."

"So what *do* you believe took place?"

Longfellow took a moment to form his answer. Ahead of them, through the darkness, a string of bouncing lights ended in an undulating circle.

"A hearty Sunday breakfast, most likely with plenty of fermented cider. Then a seizure of the brain or heart . . . a quick death, one would hope . . . a hot coal dropped onto the waistcoat . . . and finally, a great deal of exaggeration by the press." Longfellow shrugged eloquently. "One more martyr to tobacco! Or . . ."

"Or . . . ?"

"On the other hand, the natural world is full of surprises, and no one yet knows the cause of many events we call unnatural phenomena. If, in truth, he did burn down to nothing, it would be very interesting to know exactly how, and why. It's a shame there wasn't a reliable witness."

"But you said the girl saw what happened."

He waved the idea away.

"It's one thing to *see* something—another to *observe* and discover the actual truth of a matter. Observation, of course, requires a proper perspective. It can't be done hastily, or with the emotions. The first part involves using your eyes—the second, using your brain. Rational men will tell you there's no place in Science for feelings of the heart. And Science is the place to look for explanations that will stand the light of day."

Charlotte seemed to consider all of this quietly as they increased their pace. At the time, it was unclear to her companion how much of what he'd said she had truly taken in.

SOON AFTER CROSSING the bridge, they neared the torch-lit group of milling people. Here, Charlotte considered, the road went uphill through brown, grassy fields with knots of dark firs and pines, and a few clusters of ghostly white birches. The roadbed at this stretch had been raised a few feet by the local citizens years before, to stand above the spring torrents that melted down on either side from the woods above. Once, these floods had brought rocks and pine cones to the track, which then eroded until it was full of small, winding gullies. Now only occasional wheel ruts impeded one's progress through much of the year; tonight, these were filled with a fine, dry dust that muffled every step. There wasn't much else to see.

"Do you suppose," Charlotte asked her neighbor as he eyed the crowd, "that he was a pleasing man?"

"Who?"

"The husband in your story. You said he was well liked."

"Pleasing? A farmer? He was hardly a strict church-man, from what his wife tells us. And he probably had good land to farm, living on Long Island. So yes, I'd imagine he was pleasing enough."

"And his wife . . . was she very young, or of the same age as her husband?"

"Hmmm. If she had been young and comely, the New York papers would have remarked on it, as I recall they did in describing the girl."

Charlotte looked off across the sloping moonlit field.

"And you say a similar thing might have happened here? On this road?"

"I only know what Cicero overheard and told me, and that it's close to Allhallows Eve. When the dead walk," he whispered, opening his eyes in pretended horror.

"Well, I wonder," said Charlotte as they began to make out words from the crowd in front of them.

"What do you wonder?"

Longfellow gave her only his nearest ear now, using the other to decipher some of the noise that rose up into the night air.

"I wonder," said Charlotte, who knew something about human nature, if not a great deal about Science, "whether the widow on Long Island really was a widow, after all."

Chapter 5

THEN," LITTLE JACK Pennywort went on, working sweeping gestures into the retelling of the amazing story, "as I followed along, there was a pale sort of flickering just up around his shoulders. Just before I saw the yellow gleam . . . and then I tripped over a stone, and fell down in the road."

"Not an unusual event in itself," Richard Longfellow said in a low voice to Charlotte, as he began to weigh the elements of Jack's story.

"That's only the beginning," an old hand assured newcomers who had missed the first telling at the Blue Boar.

"But as I looked again, the flames came right up out of him—all around! They rose with a *roar*, they did—rose up and danced like Satan himself, all around the old man right where he stood, waving his arms up in the air before he disappeared! Black smoke, first, black as night . . . and when the wind took it off, all I saw was a white mist rise up, and a spot of blue fire, *damme* if I didn't! There was heat enough to water my eyes, and the Devil's stink of hellfire and brimstone!"

"Sulphur, most likely," Longfellow commented quietly.

"There was an old woman burned up once," began one of the two quails who had come with the rest of the tavern men, "down in Baltimore, I believe it was—"

"And after that he was gone," Jack continued, raising his voice to be heard by all, "*disappeared*, from what I could see! Though to make sure, I turned myself complete around, and round again." He demonstrated by hopping about on his good foot, holding out both arms for balance.

"He might have run off into the trees," mused a skeptical new arrival.

"Ain't any, as far as you can throw a rock," Jack retorted, pointing.

There was murmured agreement. That much of what Jack said was true. It was at least sixty paces to the woods near the crest, with no other growth between high enough to hide in—not even a large boulder to stand behind. Back along the road to the last clump of firs was another hundred paces. Jack had already assured them that this, too, was out of the question, and most seemed to believe him. Which created a logical puzzle, unless a man *could* simply catch fire on a rare October evening. Or unless, of course, Jack Pennywort was telling a tall tale.

"—until only a kneecap and a foot were left of her," concluded the story from Baltimore, during the lull. "Nobody ever knew why."

"So I stood and looked as far as I could see," Jack insisted, "but there was nothing at all—naught of his red cloak, no body, nothing so much as a shoe buckle. This is all that's left right here!"

Looking like a curiously diminished Mark Antony on a stage, in Longfellow's opinion, Jack extended an open hand dramatically toward the dark patch on the ground before him. A lantern was lowered so that all could see for themselves a thin, gummy mass about the size of a cartwheel, under the pool of light. It was the only sign of anything unusual on the road.

On the face of it, Jack Pennywort wholly believed his own story. Among his audience, gooseflesh rose on the limbs of more than one.

"Say, Jack—would you know what happened to all that gold?" called out drunken Dick Craft.

This time, only an owl in the woods replied.

Charlotte didn't understand the question, but the mention of a red cloak gave her a start. She thought back to her own afternoon walk, to the bent old man, the offered and accepted apple. She looked up at Longfellow, but found him wholly engrossed in examining the reactions of the crowd.

A chorus of voices rose up again, repeating not only the last query, but also asking who the old man was, where he came from, and what he had been doing out alone, on foot, in the road at night.

"He's stopping over at the inn—I know that much," broke in a deep voice. "Came today. Saw him there before supper." Charlotte recognized the large head of Nathan, the inn's blacksmith, towering over those around him.

"Maybe he's there now, then," reasoned another. "Maybe somebody should—"

"If he went up in smoke, I say it must be *witchcraft*!" cried a voice that exploded into a screech. This new idea was met by a rustle of misgiving from some of the listeners, while others responded with clucks and whistles of disapproval.

"In that case, ask Phineas Wise," somebody else yelled.

"He was born up the coast, where they know all about such things."

Phineas ignored the barb that had been old even in his grandfather's day. Amidst more laughter, his sharp eyes continued to measure the strength of the gathering, looking for the first sign of any plan to turn back to his tavern for a warm mug of new cider, or something stronger.

Meanwhile, the beginnings of scattered arguments showed that some conclusions had already been drawn, and sides taken—a natural thing among men and women raised on political talk and sermons, and quite used to examining and judging their fellows.

Charlotte recognized several of her neighbors, lit strangely by their lanterns, or more broadly from above by pitch torches that flickered in the rapidly cooling night breeze. There was Peter Lynch, the miller, next to Nathan, who himself stood solid and quiet, with folded arms as strong as barrel bands. Near the center of the wide circle she saw Tinder and Flint, as they were sometimes called, the two old fixtures of the Common bench and the Blue Boar's fireside. And crowding in next to them were three boys—young men, really. She could name one member of the trio: Sam Dudley, who lived along the Concord road.

She was surprised to note that the Reverend Rowe was absent, then remembered that Hannah had said he'd gone to Boston for a day or two. (Hannah was probably already asleep, along with her husband and oldest son who had lately been wearing themselves out with haying the Willett farm, and helping at others.) If the preacher *had* shown up, Charlotte thought, something dogmatic would surely have been heard by now.

As it was, she did hear some of Reverend Rowe's flock whispering uncharitable things in the darkness— ideas they would have been ashamed to repeat in church, or in the light of day. The sound of it made her heart beat faster. But it was a question of economics that was being discussed in the most lively tones.

"Even if the gold's melted down, shouldn't it still be here somewhere?"

"There's nothing like it in this muck," said a man with a stick.

"Maybe it flew away," joked another. "That's often happened to me!"

"Or ran, with a little help," another replied ominously.

"Well, Jack was only gone for a couple of minutes."

"Could've taken the gold—I'm not saying you did, Jack—but he *couldn't* have hid a body anywhere near here, could he? Or carried it away himself, either."

Several men again looked around carefully, while Jack began to squirm. Finally, he voluntarily turned out pockets which contained nothing unusual.

"What about the Frenchman? Didn't he lead the old man out the door?" Peter Lynch called out harshly, casting his eyes about for support.

But before anyone could say more, an edge of the crowd swung open to make way for the hurrying figure of a short, portly man.

Everybody knew Constable Bowers. Hiram and his wife kept a notions shop in their home near the bridge, besides farming some land west of the millpond. Constable Bowers had few duties to perform beyond collecting and recording taxes levied by the Bracebridge selectmen, the ones who had picked him the past January for the twelve-month job. For nearly a year he had attended their meetings, where he generally dozed until they adjourned to a nearby house for refreshment.

Although the crowd made way for Constable Bowers tonight, it expected little of Hiram's brain, and only a bit more from his ear. He had dressed in a great hurry; the cuffs of his shirt were caught up inside his coat, his bulging waistcoat was buttoned one off the mark, and his neck cloth was entirely missing.

Several spoke, or shouted out the few facts known at the moment, for the constable's benefit. Meanwhile, Charlotte again surveyed the faces around her. Most were masculine—of course, at this hour—and weather-stained to a warm mahogany. But she was surprised to see, bobbing behind the others, a lighter one that really shouldn't have been there at all.

What was Mary Frye doing here, apparently all alone? The girl sometimes came to Charlotte's door to fetch extra butter or cream. Originally from Worcester, Mary had been bound over by her father for three years to Jonathan Pratt and his wife Lydia. For two years more, until she was seventeen, she was expected to do what-ever was asked of her at the Bracebridge Inn. Tonight, by torchlight, her wild eyes and tangle of black hair showed she had escaped Lydia's influence for the moment. And she was clearly in search of something, or someone. Charlotte wondered who, and waited to see.

The wattles under the constable's chin shook as he held up his hands for a chance to speak. Tomorrow, he told them, he would take down testimony at the inn from anyone who had something to say. To that end, he would remain there for most of the afternoon. After that, he would report to the selectmen to see if anything more should be done.

If, by that time, joked a wit hidden by darkness, Hi-ram was capable of seeing anything at all. Others imme-diately insisted that the Reverend Rowe be consulted as soon as he returned. From his vast reading and experi-ence the preacher would know if a man could be kindled by human design, or by craft with witches or devils. Some already guessed the stranger had been lifted up and set down elsewhere on earth . . . they'd heard older folk speak of such things. Then again, he might have been removed to some far more unpleasant part of the cosmology.

"But what," shouted Peter Lynch with determination, "has become of the Frenchman? Find *him* and ask what happened! He left the Blue Boar right before this stranger, didn't he? He's the one we should go after!"

Dick Craft opened his mouth, as was to be expected. But whatever he had to say was stopped by a piercing scream. Mary Frye's terrified cry shocked the air; before it died, the girl swooned and fell back lifeless. As luck would have it, her limp body was caught up by an extremely strong arm, extended at the nick of time. The crowd gasped, then let out its breath in relief. All, that is, but one man.

"Take your dirty hands off her!" the miller spat fiercely. Peter Lynch's face was red as a roasted beet, and his eyes bulged with fury. Several men who stood between Lynch and the smith, who held young Mary, stiffened. Charlotte saw Nathan look to Richard Longfellow, and watched Longfellow ease his way around the circle.

"Of course you realize, Peter," Longfellow began as he approached the miller, "that Nathan would be the best one to take Mary safely home. I believe Mr. Pratt would expect it of him . . . to return a maid who probably has no leave to be out in the first place. By the way, I'm glad I found you here tonight. I've been meaning to talk a little business, when you have a moment. My men tell me I have some hay acres I might sow next year with grain, but much depends on both the yield and the price of the milling, so I wanted to consult with you first, to ask you about a possible contract for grinding that I might pay for *now*, which would entitle me in future to a set price of, oh, say . . ."

When Charlotte looked around again, Nathan was already escorting a recovered but trembling Mary back along the road toward the bridge. And in a few more moments, Jack Pennywort and the rest were returning to the Blue Boar, where they might find means to counter the evening's growing chill.

"The miller was anxious enough to earn a dollar," Longfellow remarked when he returned to Charlotte's side. "It seems Peter Lynch is a man with two loves."

"Love, you call it?" she returned with a grimace.

"I'm afraid it passes for that, with some. I suppose 'lust' would be a more precise term."

Charlotte turned her flushed face into a cold wind, away from the moving crowd. Several questions leaped and fought for place in her anxious mind. What had happened here? And what was likely to happen next? It was possible that an old man had disappeared from the road. According to Jack, he had quickly burned to a blackened mess, in a way some explained as a freak of Nature. Others were already calling it the Devil's work. According to the miller, the stranger might have been murdered for some gold he carried, perhaps by a Frenchman who had also disappeared. From the laughter around her, it was clear that at least some of the townspeople were unconcerned, believing that the whole thing was a Halloween prank.

One thing seemed to be agreed—nobody knew where the old man with the red cloak was now. Hiram Bowers couldn't be expected to reach the heart of the matter any time soon. And until someone did . . . someone else might be in for trouble. Crippled, henpecked Jack Pennywort would certainly be teased, hounded, and accused. Of what, though? Possibly, only of telling a good story. But if it were proved that something had really happened tonight, a few among them might decide Jack was responsible.

And this Frenchman . . . She was well aware that feeling against the French was still running high. If Peter Lynch insisted that one of the old enemy had something to do with stealing, and possibly murder, she knew of several who wouldn't rest until more than one person had paid. It was a disturbing thought.

But broader horror hid in the first feeble cries of "Witch!"

People could smile, now, when they talked of the withered belief. Charlotte had reason to suspect that *the Devil's work* might still become a terrible rallying cry in New England, especially at a time when fear and anger divided neighbors. Oh, town folk might quickly assure you that things had changed since the days when suspicion had led to tragedy up and down the coast. But she herself remembered recent talk, when Aaron had been called worse than "Quaker" by men and women who were suspicious of anyone from beyond the village they were born in. One or two of them were on the road tonight. Were her neighbors all so different from their ancestors of seventy years ago?

If the village concluded the stranger's disappearance was due to a quirk of Nature, there would be interest in discovering how it had happened. But if witchcraft was suspected by more than a few, the *how* would become unimportant. Then the only question likely to be asked was *who*? Who knew enough to call down fire and brimstone; who would be held responsible? While other possible explanations of what had happened tonight could result in some kind of justice, this last one, if it were believed in Bracebridge, promised nothing of the sort. Charlotte shivered at the idea.

Still, one could hope that the old man would turn up again soon, with an explanation of his own. And certainly, Jack Pennywort—like the young girl on Long Island—might not be the most reliable of witnesses. It was an odd time of night to take the air, but it *was* possible that that was all the man in the red cloak had in mind. Jack could have made up the rest, especially after an evening at the Blue Boar. And yet . . .

Had anyone walked to the hill's crest to see if the stranger had gone down the other side? Or perhaps he'd doubled back, and was settled in his bed at the inn even now. She could think of several other questions Hiram Bowers might ask, if and when he thought of them.

Coming out of her own world, Charlotte was relieved to see a dark, familiar face beside Richard Longfellow's.

"You might ask Cicero," she quickly proposed to her escort, "to walk me home, after he's seen enough here. Then, Richard, you could go on to the tavern and hear what's being discussed. You know I'll look forward to hearing your opinion of the whole matter in the morning," she said sincerely.

It was a speech designed to flatter as well as encourage him, but it hadn't been necessary. Longfellow, too, had read the crowd and was uneasy. As a selectman, he felt it his duty to watch the mood of those he represented, and to see what might develop. He was also anxious to see if anything in the tale Jack told might stand up to the scrutiny of a logical mind.

"But you'll have to wait a little longer for my opinion," he added, after he'd agreed to go on without her. "I'm off early for Boston. Diana has decreed one of her country retreats should take place. I'll go in with the chaise and bring her back . . . followed, no doubt, by a wagon full of necessities."

"Dinner, then? I'll make a fricassee. And we'll drink syllabubs," she added with a ghost of a smile.

On that expectant note, they parted.

A few minutes later, Cicero ushered Charlotte Willett homeward among the last of the observers. In the forest behind them, the horned owl continued to laugh at the curious ways of mankind, and the pines sighed in soft surprise at the rising of the autumn wind.

Over the broad valley, the moon shone down on the black reaches of the Musketaquid, turning the river to winding strips of silver. And walking just ahead, the three boys Charlotte had noticed earlier playfully pushed and challenged one another. From the talk that drifted back to her, it was clear they were alive to the possibilities of the night: elves and goblins that could be expected to move through the electric air, and strange lights that might dance in woods and bogs.

One by one, each dared the others to stay and find out what kinds of things lurked in the deepest shadows. But before long, the boys branched off onto different paths through the fields, headed home, while Charlotte and Cicero kept to the Boston road.

Despite his protests, Charlotte left Cicero at Longfellow's gate, and walked the last of the way by herself. While the lantern cast its warm light on the ground in front of her, a colder light frosted the trees that had begun to writhe in a boreal wind, under brightly twinkling stars.

By the time she reached her front yard, the ground seemed to dance under moaning branches. Remembering that she'd bolted the main door early in the evening, she continued around the house to the barnyard, and entered through the kitchen. Inside, banked coals gave out a welcoming warmth, and Orpheus thumped his tail in greeting.

Charlotte went to the pantry, brought out some bread and cheese, and sat by the hearth to share it with her companion.

As the room retreated to a familiar, spice-scented background, she went over what she'd heard and seen. But she made little progress, and finally decided, with a yawn, to go to bed. Before leaving the kitchen, she went to the door. The old dog slowly rose, shook himself, then padded up to the open portal. And there he stood perfectly still.

Charlotte saw the hair between his shoulders rise before she heard the low, uncertain growl. Orpheus took a step forward, sniffing, and one step back again, careful to stay between his mistress and the night. Outside, the rushing sea-sounds of the leaves and the tortured creaking of bough on bough left her own ears unable to distinguish anything closer. But the old dog, whose nose was even better than her own, suspected something was in his path. He finally ventured through the doorway and went on for a few feet, as if carrying out a duty. Within a minute, he had retreated back inside, still growling softly to himself as he watched the dark.

Charlotte closed the door quickly, deciding that tonight she would set the heavy crossboard inside its iron brackets. Surely, it was only the wind. But an evening like this might frighten a Berkshire bear!

Taking up a candle, she went out of the kitchen through one of two doors that flanked the fire, into the main room of the house. She walked toward the tall clock at the bottom of a flight of steps. Pausing as she had done on most nights of her life, she patted its burled sidewood, before ascending the narrow stairs.

In the upper hall, her candle guttered beside a partially open sash, to which she reached out and brought down with an unexpected bang. As her heart pounded, she gasped at something that lurched against her skirts. But it was only the furry body of Orpheus, who had followed her silently on her way to bed.

The old dog jumped away when she whirled. He, too, looked around, wondering what was wrong. It was enough to make Charlotte laugh at the state of her nerves, but at the same time, it brought home to her how Jack Pennywort's curious story might be affecting her own mood—as well as encouraging fear in others. Apparently, even she was anxious to believe the worst on this windy, moonlit night.

When she was in her nightgown, she pushed back the covers, sat on the edge of the large feather bed, leaned to pat Orpheus's head, and slid her feet between the cool smoothness of trousseau linens.

It was then that she recognized a familiar scent—a sweet, medicinal aroma that came to her at odd times, and for no earthly reason. She felt the hairs on her arms rising. But this time, instead of knowing fear, she felt a sense of wonder and relief.

Horehound had been Aaron's favorite candy. Every autumn, she had made the lozenges he enjoyed whenever he had a cough, or when he worried about his throat after a day outside. Although she no longer made them, their scent was as vivid tonight as if Aaron stood by, clattering the candy against his teeth.

She knew it was impossible. But it wasn't the first time she'd noticed the penetrating aroma in this room.

She hoped it wouldn't be the last.

Blanketed by a feeling of protection and love, Charlotte settled back, closed her eyes, and slept.

Chapter 6

⌒ Wednesday

THE YOUNG MAN finished his breakfast at a brisk pace, slowing only to pour more heavy cream over the remainder of his porridge.

"You didn't hear anything before you went to bed?" Charlotte quizzed Lemuel Wainwright from a low stool, as she toasted two more pieces of bread by the fire. He thought, then shook his head. Lifting his spoon again, he remembered one thing.

"A ton of acorns fell on the roof, when the wind rose."

Charlotte handed him a piece of the hot bread to butter. "Nothing woke you later? Did you hear me coming home?"

The boy shook his head. As the sun crept into the yard, he watched the blue bolt of a diving jay, and heard it squawk. They'd already finished milking Mrs. Willett's cows. Before long, he would walk them out to pasture, through the crisp morning air that was just starting to warm.

The two had made their bargain when Lem still attended the village school run by Dame Williams, where he'd learned to read the Bible and to cast accounts as all boys were expected to do. His large family lived only a few miles away, but a brood of hungry mouths had made their oldest look around for another place to board, as soon as he could. All the noise at home had shown him the joys of solitude, so he had slept happily in Charlotte's barn for more than a year, coming inside only during spells of bitter cold.

Lem was still learning. But at fourteen his duties were nearly those of a man. On most days, he left the cows where he'd led them, and walked back across the meadow to see to the poultry, haul water, and take care of odd jobs, and to make sure the firewood was piled high. At day's end he gathered the herd back in, helped milk them once more, and then returned to the kitchen for supper and a look at a borrowed book—often with Charlotte nearby ... always after a disapproving Hannah had gone home. Her own sons had better things to do than read, as she'd told him herself more than once.

"You didn't happen to see the old man on the road yesterday afternoon, wearing a scarlet cloak and leading a horse?" Mrs. Willett now asked gently.

Finished with his breakfast, Lem continued to cast dreamy eyes at the window while he shook his head. Soon, Charlotte told him what he'd missed by going to bed at sundown, as usual. She waited for his comments. He offered only a question.

"Should I take them to the river today, or back behind the orchard hill?"

"The hill, I think," she answered.

In another minute the boy disappeared, and soon

Charlotte heard the bell of the lead cow as it swung away into the fields.

Strange, how events that left one person unmoved could act like a burr on the mind of another. But then, people rarely asked Lem what he thought of anything. Maybe one needed practice, to answer. She would have to think about that.

Today, Charlotte took morning coffee to her south facing study, where sunlight and shadow from the maples outside leaped over polished wood, and along walls painted the blue of a robin's egg. Looking around the place she'd made into a sort of private nest, she ticked off her latest tasks on her fingers, listing them out loud.

The apples were finished; most of the herbs were gathered in and drying; the root cellar was well stocked with potatoes, turnips, and parsnips from the garden; the bees and their hives had been seen to, although they might need to be fed a little sugar water again, before the hard frosts. And the hay had provided more than enough winter fodder for the dairy herd—she was relieved at that.

No other areas seemed to need her immediate attention, so she turned her mind eagerly to what her neighbor had called the second part of observation. As she did, the miniature portrait of Aaron on her desk, the one painted before he left Philadelphia, seemed to stare directly into her eyes. Whether he would have liked it or not, she knew what he would have expected her to do. Charlotte leaned on the brocade-covered arm of her chair, and thought.

The old man had been there, and now the old man was gone. But was he really gone from the earth, or only the Boston road? Maybe the whole occurrence was nothing more than an involved jest—though it certainly seemed a poor one. This, she thought, had been Longfellow's first opinion. She wondered if he still stuck to it.

A further possibility was that Jack Pennywort, never

the most sober of men, had "decorated" (knowingly or not) whatever it was he really saw. But what *had* Jack seen, and *why*?

The stranger might, understandably, have taken fright at being followed up the road from the tavern. Perhaps somehow, cleverly, he had diverted Jack's attention before slipping away. But how? Unless . . .

Charlotte's next idea seemed even more fantastic, at least at first. The old gentleman might have *planned* to give a dumb show. What if he wanted people to believe he'd gone up in smoke and flames? What if he'd chosen to leave his past behind, to start a new life? Hadn't that been her conclusion as soon as she'd heard the story of the Long Island farmer and his servant? (She would have guessed that the figure she'd seen herself was well beyond affairs of the heart—but one never knew for sure.) Still, how fast could the bent old man have trotted off? And exactly *how* had he fooled the wary Jack Pennywort?

On the other hand . . . Jack wouldn't have had to be fooled at all . . . *if he had been a paid accomplice*. Or it could even be that Jack, perhaps with someone else, had actually done away with the stranger.

Steeling herself to the last unlikely possibility, Charlotte thought on. While Jack returned to the tavern to tell a story that might have been carefully planned, a larger man (perhaps this Frenchman they talked of?) could have taken the body, and the gold, and hidden them somewhere. But this really didn't seem plausible, either, considering what she knew of Jack's character. After all, here was a man who rarely did *much* wrong, and who lived in fear even of his wife! Nor could Charlotte imagine anyone else trusting Jack to share that kind of awful secret for long. But for a coin or two, Jack Pennywort *might* have gone along with something *less* than murder. . . .

Another possibility remained. There could have actually been an extraordinary occurrence of some kind, a phenomenon that had caused the stranger to be entirely consumed by internal flames. Some believed it possible, at least on Long Island. Spontaneous human combustion, Richard had called it. Was it credible? She knew that numerous forces in Nature were still largely unexplained. And some of them *were* deadly. For instance, even though Dr. Franklin had recently coaxed lightning down from the clouds, it still had a mind of its own, and might take a life in an instant.

Thinking hard, Charlotte recalled having once heard from Aaron's brother, Captain Noah Willett, about something called Saint Elmo's fire. Reportedly, this could turn a ship's entire rigging blue with an eerie, dancing flame that sometimes played on seamen. That sounded more like Jack's story. But this phenomenon rarely caused harm to those it touched . . . and she'd not heard that it made anybody disappear.

The bright morning sunshine had turned a tray of cut-crystal glasses on a sideboard into several miniature suns. For a few seconds, Charlotte stared into their brilliance. Then, realizing her thoughts had run away with her reason, she looked down to open a drawer and search for paper and ink. At first, because her eyes were dazzled, she saw nothing within. Just like the night before, in the kitchen doorway, when she'd been unable to see anything outside—

Light? Could that be the answer? Coming from the lighted tavern into the darkness would have made it difficult for Jack to see clearly. Further, blinding flash could have kept him from seeing the stranger in the scarlet cloak jump off the road and run away. Thinking again of lightning, she recalled there had been nothing like it in the sky the night before—just steady moonlight, which should have shown Jack what he expected to see . . . an old man running away. Still, if the stranger carried a source of light *with* him . . . it might be part of a reasonable explanation. The thing simply called for more thought, and more questions. At least, it was something.

Now, what about the other show, the one put on by Mary Frye? Could her fainting have had anything to do with the evening's first act? At any rate, it was probably fortunate for Mary that Nathan had been there to lead her out of harm's way. She wondered what excuses Mary had made, while the girl and the smith walked back to the inn. Well, she could soon find the answer to that easily enough.

Finishing her cup of coffee, Charlotte decided on a course of action. She wrote out a list of tasks for Hannah, who would arrive before long.

After that, she embarked on a journey of her own, not knowing that it would raise far more questions than it would easily, or safely, answer.

THE FRAGRANT HALLWAYS of the Bracebridge Inn were quiet when Charlotte Willett entered softly through a side door. No one, she was glad to see, was about.

Unlike the Blue Boar, the Bracebridge Inn was a refined establishment that frequently housed distinguished guests . . . patrons who would appreciate a good wine, a meal of several courses, and a bed without bugs. Its landlord was both tolerant and pleasant. He was also insightful, well informed on regional gossip, and more than a little fat. Together with his wife, Lydia, he was quite able to maintain the atmosphere of safety and comfort demanded by his clients.

Jonathan Pratt took a pocket watch from his protruding vest when Charlotte knocked on the door of the tiny room where he kept his accounts. At his urging, she came in and sat delicately.

"You're very early this morning, Mrs. Willett. Especially considering the hours I hear you've been keeping.

"I came to see if you could spare me a sack of coal," she began innocently.

"A sack of coal," Jonathan repeated slowly, pinching his nose.

"I ordered some to be delivered next month," she replied, "but the nights are already so chilly—"

"That you need some coal today. Certainly. We wouldn't want you to freeze. Would you care to go and make the arrangements with our smith, or shall I speak to him for you?" The innkeeper already knew the answer. He also knew that it could be extremely tiresome for a single woman in a small village to follow convention, but that it was often necessary if she wanted any peace. This was especially true when one entered the home of a stickler for propriety in others—like Lydia Pratt.

"I think," said Charlotte, after considering, "that it would be just as well if I spoke to Nathan myself."

"It would be a great deal simpler," the innkeeper agreed with a nod. He had met this grown and respectable woman as a forthright girl of ten, when he was the inn's new owner. In those days, Charlotte Howard came and went as she pleased, bringing pails of cream, butter, and honey, and taking home sugar, tea, or coffee beans for her family. Sometimes, she walked over just for news and conversation. Often enough, their talks supplied Jonathan with more information than he had to give. Over the years, he had watched his pretty young friend train her ears and eyes well, although not everyone was aware of her skills . . . probably because she refrained from using what she learned to her own advantage, unlike so many others.

"I hear you and Longfellow were taking the evening

air across the river last night, along with half the town," Jonathan offered now in the way of conversation.

Charlotte watched the large stomach in front of her rise and fall more quickly, while the landlord began to wheeze rapidly, in the manner of a concertina.

"What you say is quite true. I wonder, though, which of your many friends happened to pass this information on?"

"Nathan . . . coincidentally."

The landlord shifted his round figure, and settled back into his chair. "You wouldn't be after Hiram's job, would you? We all know he isn't much good at it, what with the thread and button trade to look after. And you know he only has a few months left."

"It's charming, Jonathan, that you'd consider a woman as your next constable. And surprising."

"I don't know why. This isn't the first time a woman's extra measure of curiosity—and your snooping specifically—has captured my attention. And that's perhaps the foremost requirement for the job, wouldn't you say? What surprises *me* is how someone can think her fishing expeditions appear innocent, when her intentions can be read as easily as the *Boston Gazette*. I believe I can be trusted. Is there anything you would like to ask me, before you go? Perhaps about one of my guests?"

"Did he come back in last night?" she responded immediately, perching on the edge of her chair. Jonathan was forced to smile, a little proud that with him Charlotte would still expose the exuberant nature she'd been born with.

"If you mean Mr. Middleton, who took a room with us yesterday, he doesn't seem to have spent the night. I believe he rode in around three or four, bringing only a small valise. His full name, by the way, is—or was, depending on which story you believe—Duncan Middleton. Of Boston."

"What about his horse?"

"Still here."

"Did you have any kind of feeling about him?"

"He seemed nothing special to me. Actually, we hardly spoke. I'm afraid I paid very little attention to the man."

"Then you probably wouldn't know why he was here."

"It isn't something I generally ask, being none of my business. Let's say I assumed he was taking a break in a short journey, since he made no inquiries about anyone in town, that I know of, and brought very little with him."

"I see. Do you suppose he may be dead?"

Jonathan sighed and regarded her more seriously.

"This morning, I sent word to his house in the city, letting them know that something might have happened to him. I expect to have a reply this afternoon. That's all I can tell you."

"Did he take any meals here?" Charlotte asked after some further thought.

"He arrived too late for breakfast, of course; no, I don't believe he took any dinner, either. And he certainly wasn't here in the evening."

"Jonathan—where do *you* think he is now?"

"On that, my dear, I will not comment. I have enough troubles, so I leave it to you and the other ladies to supply the most likely answer. You might ask Reverend Rowe for his help; he seems to enjoy that sort of thing. All I know is that I have everything that's left of Mr. Middleton, locally at least, and I wish that I did not."

"Oh! Jonathan, show me what you have!"

Having fallen into a hole of his own digging, the innkeeper groaned, then scuttled behind a familiar breastwork.

"Unfortunately, I don't believe my wife would approve."

"No, I suppose not. I wonder where Lydia is now? I would guess she's in your kitchen, making life difficult for your excellent cook. I only hope it doesn't affect the pudding, or the pie, or whatever you were planning to enjoy for your dinner this afternoon."

"That's probably what she is doing," admitted Pratt, after sucking in his breath. Then, he began to work his lips with annoyance at the thought.

Ponderously, he lifted himself from his squeaking chair, reflecting uneasily that here was a woman who enjoyed dangerous entertainment. From such a person, no one was safe—not even an innkeeper with the best of intentions.

Chapter 7

FURTIVELY, JONATHAN PRATT led Charlotte over a path of polished boards and dark Turkish runners, up the whitewashed back stairway and along the hall to a highly lacquered door.

"The Jamaica Room," the innkeeper whispered, while he turned the brass knob.

A glow of reflected light, along with a scent of beeswax and lemon polish, seeped out of the room as they entered. Pratt quickly closed the door. The morning sun that had warmed the air inside played on a multi-colored quilt spread between the bed's four turned maple posts.

The overall effect of the room was soothing. Late roses stood in a blown glass vase, sprigs of lavender peeped from beneath the pillows, and a watercolor of a bright Caribbean scene hung on one wall. There were several things that might have told someone something about the inn's owners and its staff. But there was very little of a personal nature to help explain the room's most recent occupant.

A traveling valise made of the best quality leather stood on a painted chest across from the bed. Charlotte at once crossed a figured carpet, and paused over the bag for only an instant before reaching down and undoing its clasp. Little inside surprised her. As Jonathan cleared his throat and modestly looked away, she lifted out a shirt, a pair of white silk hose and some undergarments, equipment for shaving, a box of peppermints, and a shoehorn. Duncan Middleton had apparently been a man careful of his things. Not many took the trouble to travel with a shoehorn.

"That's all," Pratt concluded nervously, "that, and his horse. By the way, one of my other guests told me the man is a merchant and a shipowner. This same guest took my message to Middleton's household this morning. Now, as I believe that's all that could interest you . . ." But before she could take his offered arm, Jonathan flinched at a footstep in the hall, though it soon passed away harmlessly.

In that brief moment Charlotte, too, was shocked by something unexpected—a bright flash of light from a place she thought odd. It had come from behind a small cabinet that stood between the chest and a corner. The cabinet held a large china wash set on its marble top. She moved closer, and pulled one edge away from the wall.

The innkeeper moaned softly when he saw the broken mirror. A few splinters reflected the daylight, while its thin wood backing showed through in spots where the glass was missing. More lay on the floor.

Charlotte bent and picked up a large shard with an edge of her skirt. An accident, hidden quietly away? She straightened as the innkeeper continued to voice his dismay.

"I've *told* her not to cover mistakes, but to just come and tell me when something goes wrong, so that it can be fixed! You'd think I made a practice of beating my household daily, when you see the lengths some of them go to. Some day, I pray she learns to trust someone, somewhere."

"Mary?" guessed Charlotte, setting down the jagged fragment.

"She's had difficulties learning her duties here, coming from a house where everything ends up on the floor. It's certainly not the first thing she's broken. And that's not all. What, in your opinion, is to be done with young women who are in love?"

Knowing no good answer, Charlotte simply smiled, and changed the subject.

"Jonathan, did Middleton give you anything on account?"

The innkeeper looked slightly embarrassed. "Now that you mention it, he did leave a piece of gold. A Dutch gulden, actually. I plan to give it to Reverend Rowe for his fund, as soon as I see him. In return, I'll ask him to send up a prayer, for a poor soul beleaguered by women."

Another show of gold! It seemed to Charlotte that Middleton might have taken more pains to hide his wealth in a small place like Bracebridge, where he was a stranger. In fact, the man seemed to have enjoyed displaying it. It was something to consider.

THEY HAD NEARLY made the top of the stairs when another door, next to the one they'd passed through, abruptly swung open, and a bespectacled man with a body like a sapling backed into the hall. He had a canvas pack slung over one shoulder and was dressed in a jacket and breeches of faded tweed. Looking up, he gave them a casual salute.

"Mr. Pratt!" The rich, full voice made the landlord wince and look about. "I've just come back for my spyglass. I was glad to have it with me last night—training it on the full moon. Quiet a performance!"

Pratt bowed silently, as if he'd had something to do with the lunar display, and seemed more than ready to move on. But Charlotte held him back. Sighing, the landlord did his duty.

"Mrs. Willett, might I present Mr. Adolphus Lee, of Cambridge. Mr. Lee calls himself a naturalist. He is writing a volume, so he tells us, on animal life in our region."

That, Charlotte observed with an inclination of her head, explained his robust complexion, the collapsing telescope he was securing, and two thick books that stuck out from between the laces of his knapsack. His eyes also told her he had a knavish nature. Here was a man who might enjoy spending some of his time peering into the lives of his own species as well as others, she decided with an interest of her own. And she especially wondered what news of Bracebridge Lee's telescope might have brought him lately.

"I'm always very pleased to meet a man of Science," she began with only partial honesty, for she had in fact met a good many with widely varying results.

"I'm honored, Mrs. Willett. Have you an interest in these things, too?" asked Mr. Lee. His spectacles sparkled, but he seemed to stare above them as he regarded her freely; quite carefully, he looked his new acquaintance up and down in a most methodical way which, scientific or not, made her ears feel warm.

"In some things. I was fascinated to hear what happened last night, across the river. Did you happen to see the mysterious fire yourself, sir?"

"Alas, no," replied Mr. Lee with a look of genuine

sorrow. "I went out walking, it's true, but toward the east ... well over the next hill. They tell me now that I only returned after the thing was over. At the moment," he explained, "much of my work involves observing creatures who are most active at night. I got up early to go across the river this morning, though, to see what I can see; they say it isn't much after all. Frankly, I don't know what to make of the story."

"You're not alone there," remarked the innkeeper. "Your room, you know, is next to the one Mr. Middleton occupied."

Mr. Lee gaped with delight at the door to the Jamaica Room, as if it might still hold a potential conflagration.

"Did you ..." Charlotte asked with polite hesitation, "speak with old Mr. Middleton yourself?"

"Oh, no—no. In fact, I hadn't realized! I did notice him when he arrived yesterday. Well, with that red cape, it would have been difficult not to. I'd come in for my lunch and was examining some of my findings, before taking a nap. That's when I saw him, through the window. I heard him, too, now that I think of it, when I awoke later. I believe he was speaking to our landlady, probably about the room—the sheets, I think, or something of that nature. As I remember, he had a rather reedy voice, and seemed a bit out of sorts."

"Lydia never mentioned it to me," Jonathan murmured.

"Well. If you'll permit me?"

Charlotte was taken by surprise when Mr. Lee picked up her hand and bent to kiss it soundly.

"Mr. Pratt," he continued after releasing her, "Mr. Pratt, I believe I will be staying for the remainder of the week, after all; I've found rather more of interest than I'd hoped for. If you'd be so good as to keep my room for me?"

He tipped his hat, twisted his lean body down the

narrow back stairs, and was soon out the side door below them.

"We get all kinds here, and I try to make everyone feel at home. But there's something I don't care for in that one," Jonathan said uneasily. "He's too sleek . . . like a weasel."

Charlotte laughed at the rotund landlord's unflattering observation.

"Something very supple, I agree," she replied, picturing for herself a high-swinging monkey in the wilds of South America. "How long has he been here?"

"Since Sunday night, this time. He's popped up before—stays a while, and then he's off again, with a few more butterflies in his bottles, or pickled voles, or whatever it is he's after at the moment. I can't say he doesn't pay me, and he certainly eats well enough, which adds a great deal to my profit. But I feel as if he might bring trouble with him, too, which is something I have very little desire for—especially now, with this other nonsense."

And with a pace far more subdued than the one used by Mr. Lee, Jonathan Pratt squeezed his way down the narrow stairway, while Charlotte stepped lightly behind.

IT WAS ONLY a few more yards to the second reason for her visit to the inn. Charlotte walked briskly back along the front of the red-painted coach house, past the stables, and on to the old log smithy.

A hammer rang rhythmically near the open doorway, as it bounced on a crescent of glowing iron. Upon seeing her, Nathan plunged the horseshoe into a pail of water where it hissed and steamed, and emerged a midnight blue. The smith set the shoe and tongs aside, and wiped his gritty brow.

Outside, Charlotte waited under a tall beech, near a thin horse grazing in the shade.

"Is this," she called, "Middleton's mount?"

"It is. And it would certainly be a piece of luck for the poor animal if Middleton never returned. Looks like he's been mistreated as a rule, even whipped to bleeding a day or two ago. Brought in tired and hungry, besides. But he's better now . . . the cuts are healing quite well. Keeping him out in the air helps."

Nathan flicked away a flake of metal from the curling hairs on his broad arm, and stood watching her run a hand over cruel ridges on the animal's side. There did seem, thought Charlotte, to be a large number of old wounds there.

"Maybe he was a bad horseman, more used to a carriage."

"Whatever his excuse, I consider it a sin to harm a good servant."

Charlotte agreed. Nathan, she thought, was a fair man, and not afraid to tell the world what he thought of it.

"Speaking of servants, have you any idea what caused Mary Frye to faint on the road last night?" she asked.

"Mary wouldn't tell me anything, but I expect it has to do with a long string of troubles. You must have heard the talk," he answered, walking out and squinting up at the clouds.

"Some. Nathan, you didn't take Mary out there last night yourself?"

The smith let out a groan.

"No, she went out alone. Probably to meet her young Leander—a lad called Gabriel Fortier."

"In that case, wouldn't she have been afraid of being seen by the miller?"

"They probably planned to walk on the east side of the bridge, down along the river path. Very private after dark, if you overlook others there with the same idea. As I imagine you might recall." He grinned suddenly, but a new idea soon sobered him. "I'd guess he wasn't waiting for her where he promised, because of the trouble over at the Blue Boar."

Nathan told her the story of the near-brawl he'd already heard twice that morning, from early customers. So that, she thought, explained the Frenchman of Jack's tale!

"I knew Peter Lynch was an admirer of Mary's," she admitted, unable to suppress a shudder, "but then, when I saw her fall into *your* arms, I imagined . . . something else."

Nathan's face grew grave again, and she asked herself if she'd touched a sore spot, or only a tender one. In his position at the inn, he'd seen Mary every day for a year now. He might view himself as her protector, from Lydia and from the occasional traveler who made overtures. Might it also have occurred to Nathan to hope for something more?

Charlotte remembered back to when the smith first made his appearance in Bracebridge, shortly after her own world had turned upside down. At the time, each of them enjoyed a new acquaintance who could talk about something besides the past. On her almost daily visits to the inn, they had frequent opportunity to discuss the town and its habits, as well as its visitors.

But all of this was before Jonathan married, late in '61. Since then, cold words from Lydia, and piercing looks when he transgressed, kept Nathan close to his forge, and away from the inn's halls and taproom. No one quite knew why Lydia Pratt treated those who helped her as badly as she did; it had simply become an unquestioned habit for them to avoid her, whenever possible.

Naturally, Mary Frye would have looked for ways to

get around Lydia, and she, too, would have enjoyed speaking with a man who had a sympathetic heart. She might even have encouraged him as a likely provider for her future. Until she met Gabriel Fortier.

Nathan was still thinking about the Frenchman, as well.

"Mary told me she met him in Worcester over Christmas, when she went home for a few days. You've seen him around since then, I expect, though you probably weren't introduced. He's a Neutral, you know."

So that was it. Fortier was one of the Acadians, some six thousand French-speaking British subjects who'd been transported from Nova Scotia. They had settled that island themselves, long before the British took over, and had remained there peacefully under British rule for fifty years. But in '55 it was feared they might turn against their rulers, especially if French troops were to arrive and give them aid. So the Acadians were offered a loyalty oath to sign. Those who refused had been sent south. Charlotte had seen one or two of a handful of families who'd settled near Worcester. They'd lived up to their name, and caused no trouble during the late war. But some of their neighbors still distrusted them because they kept to themselves, and held on to their own language and customs.

Nathan brushed at a horsefly that attempted to land on his sweat-beaded forehead.

"Once the miller got wind of it, he made quite a fuss. You know Mary's father promised her to Peter Lynch, once her indenture's over. That'll be in two more years."

"She's so young . . ."

"Lynch wanted to marry her last year, when she was only fourteen! But old Elias Frye balked. I suppose he saw more money to be made by sending her out first. Now, he's said he'll promise the next of her sisters to another of his friends, unless Mary's willing to accept the miller in the end. At least she's not beaten here," he added with a black scowl.

"Do you suppose her father hoped she'd find someone better to marry while she worked here at the inn?"

"I think Elias did hope she'd find a man who'd offer her more. With or without marriage," Nathan added, averting his eyes. "But Jonathan, and Lydia too, I suppose, have kept her from that. So there's no reason for Mary to feel sorry yet."

"Except that she wants something that's forbidden to her. Is Gabriel Fortier a decent man?"

"That's hard for me to say. What I do know is there's a good chance that if Mary runs away with the Frenchman, Lynch will try to get her back, if only for appearances. There's no telling how far he'd go if he's made to look a fool before his friends—especially the ones in Worcester. A raw lot, from what I've seen."

"Then what's Mary to do?"

Nathan shrugged. He unmatted his damp, curling hair with thick fingers.

"They'll still need her father's consent to marry, or the law will be against them. But she has time—and who knows what might happen? Even though Lynch has offered more than was paid for her bond, Jonathan won't let her go."

The blacksmith grasped a branch over his head, and shook it until a few blazing leaves fell down.

"If there's one thing I hate to see," he continued, "it's a man who gets his way by frightening people . . . especially young girls. But Peter Lynch isn't the only man who's been given a strong arm in this world." The smith looked up at his clenched fist thoughtfully. "And two years," he concluded, "is a long time."

"It might even seem like an eternity," said Charlotte. In her heart, she felt another small bundle of trouble store itself in an empty spot, without waiting to be invited.

When she left Nathan a short while later (after arranging for the delivery of some coal she didn't need) her thoughts rushed and tumbled like water in a mountain stream. And behind her, the red iron the blacksmith returned to was again forced to conform to his will—this time, under even fiercer blows.

Chapter 8

ER WAIST WAS held straight by the whalebone under the tight top of her silk gown, but Diana Longfellow managed to lean back in her chair as she yawned with contentment. It was a thing Diana wouldn't have allowed herself to do in Boston, thought her hostess with a drowsy smile.

"They say life in the country flows like cold molasses," Charlotte's guest continued. "I must admit, I do feel unusually sweet today."

After a twenty-mile ride, Richard and his considerably younger half-sister had arrived with good appetites. Foreseeing this, Charlotte had asked Hannah Sloan to kill and pluck a large hen. Later, she had done the rest. The fowl had been pan-fried, and then simmered into a golden fricassee that included onion, carrots, and woodland mushrooms. Finally, it had been graced with a gravy of stock, egg yolks, and cream. This was offered up with a

dish of potatoes and parsnips, mashed together and laced
with butter and parsley. There was a small plate of boiled
autumn spinach, as well. Everything on the table but the
service and the salt, Charlotte thought with pride, came
from her own farm.

They sat in the front room, across from a cold hearth.
However, its chimney-mate in the kitchen crackled au-
dibly, and Hannah perspired freely while she served
them. The rich air that moved between the two rooms
was further warmed by bright sunlight that had passed
through a filigree of waving leaves outside. And a small
current of Canadian air, delightfully fresh, was democrati-
cally allowed in under one of the sashes to mingle with
the more fashionable variety inside.

Entertainment during the ample meal had come
mostly from Diana, who now seemed in danger of becoming overheated. The young woman fanned herself
while she continued to relate anecdotes of city life and
its hardships, most of them imaginary. Once again, her
brother was reminded of countless English fops, as well
as certain home-grown ones, who were in her thrall, men
who dressed in enough satins and ribbons to delight the
heart of a child: perfumed men with embroidered speech,
and too little sense to cultivate any interests besides the
ladies, or food, or fashion, or possibly the regiment to
which they belonged. They saw Diana, approaching
twenty, as an heiress more than old enough to marry. But
she remained undecided, while her suitors multiplied.
Her brother imagined she enjoyed the single state too
well to choose for quite a while. After all, it gave her
an opportunity to hear a great deal of good about the
charms of her person, as well as a chance to tweak the
noses of those around her, both male and female. Not
that he blamed her for that, he thought charitably,
laughing at an anecdote she told. Still, he would have

been happier to have her settled and out of his hands . . . if indeed she ever thought of herself as in them, which he rather doubted.

Charlotte watched and held her own thoughts, while brother and sister continued to banter and exchange tidbits about people and places. It was said that Diana Longfellow had the cool, proud nature one expected in a beauty, and she *did* often hold herself aloof from the world. But in several years of visits to Bracebridge, the elegant young woman's facade had developed a succession of small doors that she sometimes left ajar, to give brief views into well decorated, if rather disorganized, rooms.

This afternoon, her eyes, at the moment almost an emerald green, danced to the varying tunes of lively conversation, exposing a quick spirit much like her brother's. Until, of course, she wanted to be certain of having her own way. Then, Diana's dark lashes fell while she turned up a pretty ear under her elaborate auburn curls, exposing a long, downy neck. It was a pose that invariably led gentlemen, if not always ladies, to see things from Diana's point of view. Surprisingly, it often worked on her brother, as well.

Hannah brought in the last course—syllabubs made of whipped cream, sherry, sugar, and lemon mixed together, and floated in wine glasses on top of hard cider. While they sipped, the talk revolved again to the disappearance of Duncan Middleton. The subject had barely caused Diana's fine eyebrows to rise when it had first been mentioned earlier. It was not, she had implied then, the kind of thing one took much notice of, in her society. But now, she had apparently changed her mind.

"So," sighed Diana, watching her rings catch the sunlight, "our country cousins seem to become more imaginative every day. What phantasmal news! I suppose bursting into flame will become a new rustic style."

"If it does," her brother replied, "remember that it was invented by one of your own. Duncan Middleton is, or was, a wealthy Bostonian, as I believe Charlotte already mentioned."

"Oh, I've heard of Middleton—though I've never received him," Diana added, settling the matter of the merchant's standing. "But what on earth was he doing here?"

"That," answered Longfellow, "is something no one seems to know. Hardly anyone spoke to the man before he vanished."

Charlotte dipped a spoon into her glass. Stirring some of the cream into the cider below, she ventured into the stream.

"*I did* . . . as he was walking down the road, at about three o'clock—"

"You didn't tell me that last evening, Carlotta," interrupted Longfellow, "when you asked me to be your eyes."

"A lady need not tell a man everything she knows, Richard," Diana countered briskly, a trace of the new radical spirit in her manner.

"Although in Boston, many ladies do try," her brother retorted waspishly.

As this was not one of her few acknowledged faults, Diana maintained a haughty silence, but her eyes flashed at his irritating comment.

Charlotte attempted to smooth the waters.

"You didn't seem to be particularly interested in him, Richard, at the time."

"I see. Well, I'll admit that Pennywort's tale did strike me as being thin; in fact, it seems to have very little meat on it now. One might even conclude, '. . . it is a tale told by an idiot, full of sound and fury, signifying nothing.' "

" 'Out, out, brief candle!' " his sister warbled with a pleased look, for Diana had her own collection of the Bard. She continued to play the Thane's part.

" *'Life's but a walking shadow, a poor player,*
That struts and frets his hour upon the stage,
And then is heard no more.'

"It sounds as if Middleton made quite a colorful candle, too," she concluded. "I believe I'd like to see where it happened. Would anyone care to go with me for an after-dinner promenade?"

"Perhaps, when I'm through," Longfellow replied moodily. He played with his glass and said no more.

"You said this all happened at twilight, did you not?" asked Diana. "It's usually a good time for imagining things. In fact, I've led a number of gentlemen to imagine things myself, after sunset. Now, this Jack person . . ."

"Pennywort," supplied Charlotte.

"Jack Pennywort. Is that *really* his name? Jack Pennywort may have also had a wee bit to drink last night, if I know my country ways."

"There's a thought," Longfellow exclaimed, and tossed back the last of his syllabub.

"And I am able to reason," Diana went on, pushing back her chair, "that he knew the old Bostonian had money. Well, you said he dropped a good deal of it on the floor, didn't you? In that case, I should be watching, if it were up to me, to see if Jack Pennywort has an unexpected windfall anytime soon. Although I suppose it might be natural for someone like that to squirrel it away for a good while, too. . . . Your provincials can be very secretive. And they normally spend so little, after all. I mean, one has only to *look* at them!"

Hannah, who had come in to tidy the table, held up her nose at Diana Longfellow's manners, and gave Charlotte a moment's fear for some of her best china. Meanwhile, Longfellow rose to his feet.

"It's your opinion, then, that Jack went out, dispatched Duncan Middleton, secured the gold, and put a sticky mess down on the road to support his ridiculous story. After that, he ran back—all within the space of five minutes—to alert the tavern. Oh, and at the same time he dragged off the body, as well. Tell me, what do you suppose has become of the corpse?"

"I wouldn't know. But if you can't find it, perhaps no one has looked for it in the right place. That often happens to me. Not with bodies, of course. I usually lose track of smaller items; but then I've been led to believe I don't have your larger talents in all things."

"*Has* anyone been looking?" asked Charlotte.

"Several men went out with Bowers this morning— we met some of them just over the hill, on our way back. Apparently, no one has seen any sign of him."

"As you'll remember, you said you would tell me your conclusions. Have you come to any?"

"I don't know," Longfellow admitted, tapping his fingers against the back of Charlotte's chair after he helped her to rise. He chose to ignore Diana, who had to help herself.

"But I would suspect," he went on, "that this merchant will show up somewhere, someday, when the time is right."

"Yes—and he'll be dead," Diana added darkly.

"What's the village view?" Charlotte asked. "Did you hear anything new last evening in the tavern?"

"The more pious believe whatever happened to him is God's will, and several agree it's probably a rich man's due. But, there was very little to go on last night.

Most suspected that Jack had imagined the whole thing, but that if he *hadn't*, it must have been some clever trick of the Frenchman's. Young Ned Bigelow, who reads, thinks Middleton is, most likely, a Rosicrucian alchemist in disguise."

"Who, and where, is this French influence you mentioned?" Diana interrupted.

"A man called Fortier—a Neutral."

"Oh, I see . . ."

"Fortier hasn't been spotted since he left the tavern after sunset, just before the merchant went out."

"Alchemy," Charlotte repeated uneasily, reaching for her shawl. "Do you think anyone might actually believe he used magic to make the coins?"

"Why not? Lead to gold is a very old idea based on wishful thinking, which is powerful stuff. And except for Jonathan, not many around here have a prayer of touching much gold *except* by magic. Curiously, still others at the Blue Boar were much more impressed by the scarlet cloak. There was some idea that Middleton was an Italian prelate on a secret mission, and that his hobble suggested cloven hooves under his shoes. By the time I left, when several rounds of rum had warmed them up a bit further, they were so carried away that even Pennywort looked worried, bobbing around on his poor foot. I thought they just might throw him into the millpond to see if he would sink or float! And they say we live in the Age of Enlightenment," Longfellow finished morosely, shaking his head.

"It seems to me that your villagers will never change," laughed Diana. She had by now collected her wrap, long gloves, fan, and a small umbrella to protect her face. Placing her veiled hat carefully onto hair that was puffed and rolled, she sent out a further appeal.

"Now, Richard, take me to the scene of this great

Happening, and I will at least be able to say that I saw the sights, when I was in the country."

It was a request delivered with admirable Boston spirit. With no more coaxing, her brother guided both of the ladies through Mrs. Willett's front door.

Chapter 9

Under a river of dust running through the afternoon haze, a good amount of traffic moved along the Boston-Worcester road. Charlotte Willett, Richard, and Diana Longfellow were met and overtaken on their way down to the river by farmers driving wagons full of hay, sacks of nuts, and pumpkins. They also saw men on horseback and one or two in carriages, as well as a strong country girl riding pillion behind a young man, the sun giving an additional coat of bronze to her round, carefree face.

Diana watched the parade at a distance, but appeared not to notice as individuals came closer and examined her own defenses against dust, light, and air. A few politely lifted their hats. Others, dressed in homespun linsey-woolsey, simply stared at her dress. It made no difference to Diana, who had often remarked that she loathed everything about the country. But, she found it increasingly difficult to appear uninterested when Charlotte and Richard went on with their discussion of Duncan Middleton, each discovering what the other had learned about him, or hadn't.

"He seems to have been dressed as garishly as young Hancock in town," was Longfellow's comment after Charlotte described her chance encounter with the merchant more fully. "And you're sure he said nothing more?"

"Only two words."

"Not much like John there! Very pale, you say . . ."

"I guessed he wasn't used to being out. In fact, he was so pale, he looked almost ill." Charlotte glanced over at Diana's rice-powdered face, and again considered the odd requirements of fashion.

"Curious," mused Longfellow. "Still, he did ride here on a horse, which would indicate reasonable health."

"Incidentally, I met another one of Jonathan's guests this morning, who said he heard Middleton speaking with Lydia in the room next to his. The man's name is Adolphus Lee."

"Interested in Nature, hair like a bird's nest, step with a curious spring to it?"

"That sounds like the same man."

"I met him in Cambridge, last year. He'd come up to study from somewhere . . . Connecticut, I think, and seemed moderately interesting. He was studying botany at the time," Longfellow added.

"Now it's animals."

"A Jack-of-all trades. I'll have to talk with him again."

"He has a rather pretty brass telescope with him."

"Does he? Hmmm. Now, here's something you may not know. It seems Middleton also carried a brown bundle of cloth with him on his last outing, wrapped with string."

"That is interesting—"

"And the gold mentioned last night was not only gold, but *Dutch guldens*, according to Phineas, who got a fair look at a few of them."

"The old man gave one to Jonathan, too."

"Did he? Then he certainly wasn't trying to be inconspicuous."

"That was a great mistake, I'd say," Diana offered. "One shouldn't flaunt money even in Boston, at least without being in good company. Not even then, if someone might produce a pack of playing cards."

"Still," Charlotte ventured, "in the country, it's usually a good deal safer—" She stopped, remembering her own fears of the night before.

"I wouldn't be too sure of that," Longfellow warned. "I will say that Jack Pennywort, at least, seems an unlikely murderer. From what I've seen, he has the mind of a child."

"But you don't believe he's honest?"

"Should I, because he's childlike? You amaze me, Carlotta. I only say he doesn't seem capable of a great deal of criminal planning. Children know what's right and wrong, and should be held accountable. But a child might also be unable to keep itself from telling fanciful stories. Let's just say I believe Jack when he says he saw *something*. His story's too involved for him to have manufactured the thing entirely on his own."

"How do you propose to separate the grain from the chaff?"

"By scientific methods, for a start. Last night, I gathered up a specimen of the burned material from the road, which I'll attempt to analyze after supper. I've already sent to Boston for the necessary chemicals. They should be here by evening."

"For the love of *heaven!* Must you always find something horrible to do, every single time I visit?" came a plaintive wail.

In the midst of further argument on the subject between sister and brother, they reached their destination.

The spot was still marked by a dark, ominous ring, for few had summoned the courage to touch it—though more than one had bent with that idea in mind. Diana glanced at it briefly with a handkerchief to her nose, and then began to readjust her apparel. Meanwhile, Longfellow embarked on a vivid description of the previous night for her edification.

During his monologue, Charlotte had some time for uninterrupted thought. She carefully observed the lay of the land around them. A running figure in a red cloak would have had a hard time escaping someone's eyes, unless they had been blinded by sudden bright light, as she'd already surmised—and, as Jack steadfastly maintained. Jack had mentioned smoke that had drifted off to his left. This seemed probable: the wind had come from the northwest for most of the last two days. He'd also mentioned that he'd stumbled on a stone. Where was it? The road beneath her feet was trampled smooth, and seemed free of anything larger than a pebble.

She walked to the road's left edge, and looked off in a line with the scorched patch. The elevated grade sloped off a little more than two feet before it met the level of the surrounding field. For quite a distance, several kinds of wild grasses mingled with goldenrod and Queen Anne's lace, and an occasional clump of weaver's weed. She leaned down to examine the nearest clump of barbed teasel heads on straight, prickly stalks, and gently pulled something away.

Several wool fibers remained between her fingers. They appeared to be bits of a coarse yarn, dyed a dull brown. Charlotte tucked the strands into a handkerchief, which she slid back into her pocket. Then, she looked more closely at the immediate landscape and its inevitable roadside clutter.

She soon identified some cheap glazed crockery, perhaps from a traveler's jug . . . a fragment of greasy newspaper long exposed to the sun, the wrapper of a sandwich, probably . . . a bit of discarded leather. But nothing more revealed itself in the vegetation.

She was about to stand, when a glimmer from something (a chip of quartz?) made her reach into the field grass, where her fingers recoiled from something sharp. She tried again. This time, to her satisfaction, Charlotte lifted up a piece of silver-backed mirror.

Unfortunately, further examination of her curious find was halted by a sound of warning that caused all three of the walkers to turn as a horse cantered up the road.

The approaching dark stallion, decided Richard Longfellow, was bred for racing. It occurred to his sister that the rider, too, was well-bred, although to what purpose would have been more difficult to say. The man appeared to be a few years younger than himself, Longfellow observed further, and under his tricornered hat he sported a finely made powdered wig, which set off his high complexion nicely, and made him look a very proper fool. Diana Longfellow thought the newcomer extremely well proportioned, particularly noticing a nicely formed thigh resting on an expensive leather saddle, and the masterful, gloved hand that guided the bit of his spirited mount.

To Charlotte Willett, the man before them appeared to be riding on a very high horse. She realized that this was a difficult position to maintain, especially should one have the misfortune to be galloping toward a fall. Or, she thought, observing him more closely . . . or, he might be a man of authority, who yet harbored a desire to dismount and walk among his fellows.

He was certainly dressed in style, in a deep blue coat with gold buttons, and silk smallclothes of canary yellow. His handsome black felt hat with a white plume completed the picture. As the rider reined in, the group on foot could see in his boots dark reflections of their own faces, while his horse pranced, snorting and foaming.

Longfellow—realizing what a dangerous thing it was to bring this nervous animal so close to the two women—stepped forward to protect them. The ladies, nevertheless, stood their ground.

The gentleman dismounted with surprising speed, to bow before the disapproval of at least two of the party below. He took the measure of the silent trio before speaking to Longfellow.

"From your interest in that mark on the road, I'd guess that this is the location of last night's curious incident."

His accent and manner confirmed that he was an Englishman, probably lately arrived in Boston. It also informed his audience that he came from the aristocratic world, especially noted, in the colonies, for its corruptions and prejudices. But there was also something more about him to hold one's interest—something that hinted at intelligence, and a character accustomed to measuring its surroundings.

"It is the place where *something* happened," Longfellow agreed. "I suppose you've come to gawk?"

"To gawk—and to find out what's become of Duncan Middleton. My name," he finally decided to tell them, "is Montagu. Captain Montagu. The Crown has appointed me to assist those who keep order in this colony and judge its wrongdoers: namely, the Superior Court of Massachusetts. For that reason, I have come out to investigate, and to discover whether this" (here he gestured to the road) "was some kind of country farce, meant to amuse your farmers . . . or whether it was something else."

"We're not particularly fond of tomfoolery in the country," said Longfellow slowly, eyeing the other's feather, "especially when there's work to be done."

"You believe, then, that this was no more than a harmless annoyance?"

"That's not exactly what I said."

"What if some say it was murder?" the captain asked boldly.

"I, for one, say nothing of the sort. If you've come to investigate, Captain, then by all means, investigate—if you can find someone who has the time to stop and talk. As I say, most of us are quite busy at the moment."

The anger in Montagu's eyes warned Longfellow that here was a man who was not only proud, but perhaps even dangerous.

"As I can see," the captain replied with a grand sneer that made Longfellow grind his teeth. "However," Montagu went on, "I have spoken to Governor Bernard, and have his instructions. You and your countrymen are required . . . *requested* . . . to be of assistance, if indeed you can be of any help at all. Perhaps, as you say, that's beyond you. Still, someone here must know *something*, if only a very little."

Diana laughed at this, and favored Montagu with a look of her own, which she was glad to see had some effect.

"I presume," said Longfellow, "that you'll be leaving us shortly?"

Montagu shook his head with a twist of a smile.

"In that case, I imagine you'll be staying at the inn."

"I have arranged for accommodations there."

"Then I suppose our further meeting is inevitable. I'm Richard Longfellow, one of the local selectmen. My house is across from what you'll undoubtedly call your 'headquarters.' Captain Montagu, this is my neighbor, Mrs. Willett—and my sister, Diana, on a brief visit from Boston."

"Captain Edmund Montagu, at your service, ladies."

Longfellow grimaced at what he considered archaic and overlong formalities, as more bows were exchanged. His sister, on the other hand, used the chance to expose herself to better advantage, while she plied her lashes.

To Charlotte, who alone had no particular ax to sharpen, it seemed that something interesting and unusual had occurred, beyond all of the verbal fencing she had just witnessed. Somehow, the attention of the government in Boston had been directed toward tiny Bracebridge. And although it was no great distance away, she had found that the people of that city were generally uninterested in the concerns of outlying places. So why should Montagu be here?

Middleton, of course, had come from Boston, and was a wealthy man. But why should the Crown send out one of its own to question them, and so soon? This captain had even mentioned murder—with no body to indicate foul play.

Montagu's eyes had now come to rest on Charlotte Willett.

"I've been to see Middleton's room at the inn, and I've looked through his possessions there. I can tell you that these do, in fact, belong to the man. Also, the report of the clothes he wore here tallies with what his housekeeper saw when he left, two days ago. But none of this leads me to where he is now."

"*Two* days ago?" Charlotte asked with some surprise.

"He left his home on Monday morning."

This, Charlotte considered—and then she wondered how much Montagu had learned from Jonathan, and if her own interest in Middleton's valise had figured in their conversation. Looking into his composed face,

Charlotte knew only that she would never be sure what Captain Montagu knew.

"Curious, isn't it?" Montagu continued. "Oh, by the way, his horse is also the genuine article—the one that's housed in Pratt's stables. I've seen it before, as well."

"I, myself, have seen Duncan Middleton before," said Diana, "and cannot explain why anyone would particularly care if he arrived late for dinner, or disappeared entirely. I can only imagine that you have some special reason for your interest. Something rather devious, I suspect. Am I right, Captain?"

"I have my reasons," he admitted. "But, unfortunately, they are reasons I am not at liberty to share."

"Not even in confidence?"

"Not even with you, my dear."

Diana's unclouded gaze turned stormy in an instant at this familiarity, coming from a man she had obviously failed to captivate. At the same time, Charlotte felt her natural sympathy for Captain Montagu growing.

"I fear the sun is beginning to tire me," Diana declared, "and I've developed a most *obnoxious* headache."

She turned to link Charlotte's arm in her own, and marched her friend away.

Longfellow watched Montagu remount his dark horse. He stood defiantly, his hands behind his back, while the nervous animal and rider turned in circles, prancing first clockwise, and then the other way around.

"After I've spoken to this fellow Pennywort," Montagu called down, "and the others who saw Middleton last evening, I would like to have your opinion. So, may I invite you and your party to supper?"

"I'm afraid we've been well filled for today."

"Then dinner, tomorrow."

Something in Montagu's tone made Longfellow agree, although he did it with a sigh.

"All right, then, tomorrow. I rarely refuse an invitation

to dine at the expense of the Superior Court of Massachusetts. I accept for the three of us—provided, of course, that Mrs. Willett doesn't object. As to my sister, no one ever knows what will capture and hold her interest next; but I believe she, too, will come."

"Tomorrow then," said Montagu, touching his hat. The horse tried to wheel once more, but its rider turned it furiously, digging his heels into the animal's flanks until it leapt away through spurts of flying dust.

"WELL, 'MY DEAR,' " Richard teased his sister when he finally caught up with the two ladies, "what do you think of our fine friend from Boston, and beyond?"

"I wish he were tied down to a plank in his chemise, and then I would have some amusement with that silly feather of his."

Longfellow's shock wasn't entirely pretended. After some thought, he relayed Montagu's invitation to Charlotte, who accepted with pleasure. Eventually, so did Diana.

"I presume Montagu won't get much help from anyone else, if he treats others in the style he's just displayed," Longfellow added, to be soothing. Diana appeared to relent slightly.

"At least it *was* a sort of style. And he appears to have enough wit to be amusing. Maybe we'll be able to play fox and hounds with him. What do you think, Charlotte? Will Captain Edmund Montagu be good sport for us?"

"What I'm wondering," replied Mrs. Willett, who had watched Montagu clatter over the bridge and past the village green, "is whether any fox could run far and fast enough to escape, with a man like that on its trail."

Chapter 10

RICHARD AND DIANA Longfellow spent Wednesday evening at home with Cicero, where they supped on broth and bread. The young woman offered a further torrent of Boston observations, which the two men followed with keen, if irreverent, interest.

Much later, Longfellow retired alone to his kitchen, from which came curious noises and a variety of unique odors, until well into the night.

Across Longfellow's flower garden and up the hill, past Mrs. Willett's beds of herbs, Charlotte and Lem shared a simple meal of corn cooked into a hasty pudding, thinned with cream, and sweetened with syrup, full of apples and walnuts. When they had finished, the boy took a book from a collection that shared a shelf with some crockery, and lay down with Orpheus to read beside the fire.

Charlotte sat at a small table by the north windows,

prepared to use what light remained to answer letters from her relatives in Philadelphia. But while trying to put recent events into words, her thoughts raced faster than her pen. Finally, she put down her quill to light a candle, and let her mind play as it would.

In all probability, the whole thing *had* only been a kind of farce—or a sleight of hand intended to inspire awe and fear, to hide some unknown purpose. She was nearly sure of it. Maybe it was the old man's own business, as long as no law was broken. But a nagging sense of injury made her reconsider. Should Duncan Middleton be allowed to come into Bracebridge and arouse suspicion and anger . . . and possibly even create blame for a crime that had never really occurred? And what kind of man was he, to expose others to danger, for his own ends?

The piece of mirror and the strands of wool she'd found by the road were now in a cupboard drawer. Edmund Montagu might find them interesting. She considered getting them out again, and half turned in her chair.

For an instant, through a pane of glass, she saw a face—a white, featureless face that pulled back and disappeared in the near dark as she focused on the spot where it had been. Quickly, she looked toward the hearth where Lem read slowly and Orpheus slept forepaws and whiskers twitching.

Charlotte blew out the candle, then leaned across wax-scented smoke to peer into the night. Long black shadows in the yard ran from the newly risen moon, which had just begun to illuminate huge sunflower heads hung to dry on the barn. Could *that* have been what she had seen, without really seeing?

She turned back toward the fire. This time, she saw Lem and Orpheus watching her. The old dog rose and padded to the door. When it was opened, he loped off into the darkness, curious but still unconcerned.

She could let her imagination run wild, Charlotte told herself, as well as anyone in the village. Maybe she'd seen her first moonlit ghost, or a goblin! More probably, it was just another trick of smoke and mirrors, this time staged by Nature. She pulled a handkerchief from her sleeve and wiped her twitching nose. The night was getting colder. She felt herself shiver. Suddenly, the powerful surge of an idea, almost a premonition, threatened to overwhelm her.

She had good reason to believe that love sometimes found ways to reach back from the grave. What, then, about pain—or even a blazing hatred? Somehow, she felt sure that the old man she had seen on Tuesday afternoon was not dead. But her intuition also told her that something sinister had entered Bracebridge. What that something was, though, she couldn't say.

Tomorrow, she, too, would have a talk with Jack Pennywort. And then she would tell Edmund Montagu what she suspected about the old merchant, the mirror, and the brown fibers. After that, the captain could continue to search for Middleton for his own mysterious reasons. She would be quite happy to return to thinking about her farm, and her neighbors, and her own quiet business.

IN THE TAPROOM of the Bracebridge Inn, Edmund Montagu sat over a superior bottle of Madeira, after a surprisingly good supper.

No matter what lack of manners might be shown by the rural clods one had to deal with, he thought, their comforts here were substantial. At least the innkeeper was bearable. Even if he did have the misfortune to possess a bitter-faced, sharp-tongued wife.

Montagu still smarted from a mistake of his own, that had started things off entirely on the wrong foot that afternoon. But it had *not* been entirely his fault. Unfortunate that the horse had shied when he rode up the road toward Mrs. Willett, Longfellow, and his startling sister. He hadn't intended to alienate them from the very beginning—but that's apparently what he had done. Regrets mixed with shame had made him more formal, more officious, more galling, perhaps, than he ever meant to be.

If he hadn't borrowed Peabody's damned horse when he left Boston—did the thing never tire? Had he been a better rider himself, more than appearance suggested, it might not have seemed . . . he might not have needed to pretend . . .

Later, he'd been unsuccessful with the others, as well. Three of the village selectmen had called on him, but each had been busy on his own farm on the previous day, just as Longfellow had predicted. Although they wished him well, they had been very little help. The constable, a buffoon named Bowers, had scratched out a written statement, but beyond this he seemed unlikely to venture. He and two others had even asked Montagu to lead their local investigations. This he had agreed to do, temporarily, to avoid more questions about why he was there, as well as to keep these bumpkins from accidentally intruding into his own plans.

After they'd left him, Montagu had reviewed the notes in his personal journal. There, accumulated bits of information from the records of Boston and other places gave him a surprisingly long and detailed account of the elusive Duncan Middleton's past. No, it really wouldn't do, Montagu thought again, for his fellow inquisitors to follow him too closely, or too far.

As for Pennywort, the little man had obviously told his story so many times that anything he said now was bound to be out of proportion. Jack had no real explanation of his own for what he'd seen. Montagu had also sent for and spoken to several others who had been at the nearby tavern on the night in question. An uncouth flourmonger had disclosed some interesting things about a visiting Frenchman. A few had quietly mentioned witches, speaking behind their hands. In fact, one had insisted that his cow had been made dry by the evil doings, and asked quite seriously who would repay him for his loss.

But Montagu had drawn no nearer to discovering if anyone might have learned where Middleton had actually gone, or if the merchant had employed any help in going. And that was the heart of the matter.

Someone, he thought, must know more than he, or she, had already told. Others might unwittingly have seen something that would be of use to him. So far, the only sensible people he had met in the town were the three he'd offended, but he hoped to do better on the morrow.

Montagu stuck to his conviction as he slowly sipped from a long-stemmed glass. Someone knew something. Eventually, someone would talk. In the morning, with that in mind, he would start again.

Chapter 11

$\mathcal{L}$ *Thursday*

THE YOUNG BOY who tramped the river marsh was buffeted and chilled by the night winds. But an object over his heart warmed him as he sloshed through the dark. The sun was an hour from the eastern horizon; no color yet showed in that quarter of the sky. To the west, through racing clouds, the boy glimpsed a dying moon. Its pale light was reflected on thin ice along the edges of the Musketaquid's leaden passage.

As the river mud pulled at his boots, Sam Dudley balanced his long fowling piece in one hand, and wiped his running eyes with the other. He made for a small lean-to made of stones and brush, used by village men when they were after waterfowl. It was a place where they could wait out of the wind for the light of day, and for the flights of ducks and geese that settled onto the marsh at sunrise.

This morning, Sam's thoughts were far from ducks

and geese. He had taken his gun in case anyone should be up to see him leave the house. And he had announced he'd be off early to go hunting. But it was not exactly the truth he'd told his mother the night before, while his father was still out drinking. He *had* gone hunting for something, but not for birds.

Once he was seated cross-legged in the rough hut, Sam's mittened hand reached up to the small deerskin pouch he wore around his neck, the one his mother had sewn and embellished with shell beads and given him at Christmas. If he played his cards right, what was inside held the answer to his future. It would be the first of many, he devoutly hoped. And he thought that if the Lord did help those who helped themselves, as his father and Reverend Rowe so often told him, then he was as close to heavenly assistance now as he was ever likely to get. Because it was for what he had seen and confronted on his own that he'd been paid his shiny gold piece two nights before—as well as for what he'd sworn he wouldn't tell.

Sam thought again of the way he'd doubled back and waited alone on Tuesday night, in the clump of firs just off the road, to see if goblins and witches might appear after all. He had seen someone come down from the woods, enter one of the village habitations, and converse with its owner. He had seen someone leave. Then, there had been the red gleam of the large bundle going down into the black water, weighted by a stone.

It was really all a joke, and only a matter of business . . . not life and death at all, as people had been led to believe. And *business,* he'd been instructed, was a thing that a man had to learn about firsthand . . . something he had to be on the lookout for, unless he wanted advantage to pass him by. Well, the sooner he learned how business worked, the sooner his friends would have to follow his example. He would lead all of them in building up profit, if things went well.

It was a little like a game, he decided, when you were not quite sure of the rules. It wasn't anything like education in the dame school, where an old woman taught you letters and sums. It wasn't like hunting or farming, either. There, what your parents or grandparents or uncles taught you would usually be right, and would help you do a job properly. No—this was a final initiation, he reckoned, into the real world of manhood, where you had to take things as they came and make the best of them ... even without being sure if they were really *right*.

He frowned, but realized it was too late to reconsider. From the sweeping clouds above he heard the uncertain winnowing of a snipe, like the lament of a lost child. Maybe he would take the money he was about to make and go West, to start a new life. He'd heard—

Sam turned at a crackle of ice. Walking toward him on the river path came the one he had expected to meet. Gun in hand, the boy rose with a greeting.

The two spoke for a few moments, and then Sam was asked to turn and estimate the time from the slowly spreading glow in the eastern sky. He looked and considered, appreciating the long thin line of scarlet under a blanket of dark cloud. It wasn't yet dawn, but it was the closest thing to one the boy would ever see again.

An arm reached up behind him and came down swiftly over his face. Sam dropped the flintlock, as another arm tightened around his throat. He clutched frantically through heavy mittens. But with wool-covered fingers, he was unable to find a grip.

Then it was too late.

After the boy had lost consciousness, the other dragged his limp form to the river's edge. Sam began to revive when the cold water touched his face. But he was pushed down hard into a pool of icy mud and held there, until his body ceased to move.

Before leaving, the murderer tore off the deerskin pouch that hung around the boy's neck, opened it, and dropped the contents into one hand. There was a packet of powder, some extra shot . . . and a gold coin. Pocketing the latter, Sam's instructor in life tossed away the rest, and walked off briskly into the moonset whistling a tune—having no idea that what had befallen Sam Dudley had been witnessed by other eyes.

THURSDAY BEGAN FOR Charlotte Willett when she rolled over and patted Orpheus, who sat beside the bed. Thick clouds through her window promised a morning of bleak gray.

When she made her way outside just before sunrise, she found the yard had been transformed. Bushes and trees had been stripped of their leaves. The tall oak over the barn shuddered and wailed in protest under a renewed high wind, while in front of the house, the tops of the younger maples swayed and bent in supplication. Clutching the hood of her cloak against the fierce gusts, she bent forward and hurried on.

When Charlotte opened the small side door to the dairy, it was wrenched from her hand and flung against the low building's clapboard side before she quickly claimed it back. Once she had pulled it shut from the inside, she stood gulping the sweet aroma that surrounded her.

Her eyes soon adjusted to the subdued light that came in through a line of small windows. Facing her was a long row of dark, empty milking stalls. Hay had already been put into the continuous manger, at the edge of the flagstone aisle where pails were cleaned and stored. Lem had taken care to fork the manger full the evening before, working from a pile of loose hay near the double door. That door was still barred on the inside. She removed its crosspiece from large metal supports. In a few more minutes, her young helper would lead the herd in from the barn. Then they would both begin to fill the wooden pails with warm milk for her buyers—and for their own breakfast.

This morning, Charlotte felt oddly uneasy in the darkness, despite the quiet, and the familiar animal smells of the barn. She picked up one of the empty pails, removed its lid, and examined it for cleanliness. Then, a small sound that seemed to come from the middle of the dairy made her look up. Whatever it was, it stopped almost before she could be sure she'd heard it; turning her head, she could hear nothing more. It might have come, she guessed, from the trench against the wall where the cows soon would be driven in. (Occasionally, a rat from the fields decided to move in as well, until Orpheus changed its mind.) Even though the hay inside tended to absorb noise, she could still hear the wind's sharp play. Perhaps something had fallen onto the roof. She tilted another bucket and began to examine its depths, sniffing.

And so it was a complete surprise when the door she had recently entered blew open again and banged repeatedly. Shock caused Charlotte to lose her balance and fall back. Happily, her descent was cushioned by her heavy skirts, as well as the pile of hay behind her. She had just begun to laugh, when she quickly stopped. It had taken only a moment for her hands to feel the hay she had fallen into, truly feel its texture, its depth, and above all its unexpected warmth.

Charlotte stood up with a movement almost as sudden as the one that had seated her. Quickly, she turned around to stare at the dim depression. Very recently, someone else had been on that same hay, out of the wind, hidden in quiet sanctuary.

The door banged again. She remembered the careful way she had latched it against the wind when she came inside. Then she heard a cowbell, and in another second a tall figure opened one of the double doors behind her, fastening it back so that the black and white animals he escorted could amble slowly to their stalls.

A look of surprise grew on Lem's face as he took in her dazed expression. And then, once more and with a *whoosh*, Charlotte Willett sat down.

"IT STILL MAKES me fidget," said Hannah Sloan later in the morning, "to hear of that Frenchman around here somewhere, up to no good." She pulled a pile of bread dough into another large fold, and pushed it down again into the low wooden bin in front of her. Charlotte looked over from the table where she tallied her accounts.

"But you never felt that way about any of the Neutrals before."

"We never before had such strange things going on! An old man disappears . . . and Emily Bowers says Hiram's had reports of all sorts of trouble—from a child with fits, to a horse with the staggers. Though I suppose such things aren't unheard of during the best of times. But as to this Frenchman, why, what if he *was* to lurk around, waiting to prey on a woman alone? Worse yet, what if one of the local men was to find him here?" Hannah added with a darting look.

Charlotte was glad she hadn't mentioned the unknown guest in the diary that morning. But had Hannah seen him go?

"Mary Frye seems to think Fortier is an honest man,"

she finally answered. "Good enough to marry, according to what Nathan tells me."

"When does a girl who's lost her heart have any control over her head? Oh, I don't blame Mary—she's all right. But *he's* an angry one, from what I've heard. And I'm not sure but he's got cause to be. The way they were all treated, sent off from their homes like blackamoors, by His Majesty's fine governor! If you ask me, it'll be a long time before the Acadians forgive our king. Who's to say war won't break out all over again? What if the French should decide to come back? I say I'd rather know where the Neutrals in this country *are*, and keep my eye on them."

"It's my guess that Gabriel Fortier isn't here. He probably went home to Worcester," said Charlotte, skirting complete honesty.

"He might have . . . but with Peter Lynch pressing Mary for an answer, I doubt if the Frenchman's in any mood to go far. No, he only left the Blue Boar to avoid the miller. He's still around, somewhere."

"But do you really think he's guilty of any crime, Hannah?"

"Well, he was the first to leave, just in front of the merchant that night . . . though probably all of them had the same idea of lining their pockets," Hannah said with a sniff as she thumped the stiff dough. "Still, I don't see how anybody could have robbed the old man and then made him disappear that way, without being seen. But *somebody* must be guilty of something! I hear from my boys," she continued, "the talk at the tavern, and the apple press, and the mill; and they tell me stories have come back from Concord and Worcester. Some are saying crime goes unpunished in Bracebridge, that ungodly things have been happening, and that it's not safe here anymore. Well, the way our own men are starting to talk about taking the law into their own hands, it may be all too true!"

MEANWHILE, OUT IN the barnyard, Lem drove a maul deep into a section of pine. While the report of his hammer still rang, he stooped with a practiced, easy movement to throw the split pieces onto a small mountain of winter firewood. As soon as he saw Charlotte approaching, he greeted her with a broad, lopsided grin.

Admiring his work and enjoying the scent of the fresh slabs, she returned his silent greeting. More than the countryside had grown during the summer, she realized. Nearly to full height now, Lem seemed to have found a new grace, after a year or two of tripping over his feet. There was a promise of strength in his broadening shoulders, too. It was a fair trade for the sweat he put into his work.

"Autumn's the busiest time for most of us," Mrs. Willett began cautiously.

Lem agreed with a nod, wiping his face with a sleeve.

"So many jobs to take care of all at once. Do you think you could use some help this afternoon?"

He gave her a curious look through a lock of hair, and rubbed his hands over his upper arms, making no guesses.

"I only thought," Charlotte added, "that we might share some of the work, and a little food, with someone less fortunate."

He had to agree with that—and to admire again her kindly way of thinking.

"Like Jack Pennywort," she added.

Now he looked at her with plain astonishment. He shifted from one foot to another, waiting to hear more.

"I have an idea he'll be sitting in the Blue Boar, still

telling his story. I'd like you to go and ask him to come here in about an hour. And Lem . . ."

He brushed some wood chips from his sunburned arms, still listening.

". . . if you should happen to see, or hear, anything that might be interesting . . . you might tell me about it when you come back. If you'd like to talk. Over a cup of tea."

He gazed at her with new concern. Maybe he should think about asking Mr. Longfellow to drop in and speak with his mistress more often. Mrs. Willett must be desperate for someone to talk to . . . however impossible that seemed. Though it *was* pleasant to know she considered him a source of conversation. But he was apparently on a par with Jack Pennywort there. Lem wished he knew what he should say.

"I know what I'm asking may seem strange," she went on, after trying to read his look, "but you see, I'm going out to dine later, at the inn. And I was hoping to learn more of the truth from Jack about what's been going on. More than he's thought to tell—or has been willing to! I need your help to get him here," she finished in a rush.

Ducking his head, Lem shoved long arms into his coat. He was glad she couldn't see the expression of pride on his face. Pride was a thing that looked silly enough, he often felt, on an older man's face, let alone on a younger one's, who should know better. That his mistress might consider him a man now, too—that she had even asked him to join her in a conspiracy of sorts—was something he'd have to think about.

I'll do my best, his final nod signified. Then he walked out quickly to the main road, to be further tousled by the gusty afternoon.

Chapter 12

WHEN LEM WAS gone, Charlotte continued through the yard, looking forward to a visit with Richard Longfellow, reasonably confident he'd be hard at work on matters of interest to them both. Under bright autumn clouds she forced her way against the wind, across the fading gardens.

She eventually found him in his greenhouse, built against a rock wall that formed the south side of his barn. Cicero sat in its small vestibule, surrounded by late roses on trellises set against the costly glass walls. He appeared to be engaged in pleasant contemplation, with his eyes closed. Through the inner door, Charlotte could see Longfellow bending over a workbench.

"His experiments with the love apples?" she asked the old man, stopping for a moment to share his limestone seat.

"He'll kill us all, before he's through," Cicero growled after a yawn.

"And Diana? Where is she?"

"Miss Longfellow is out this morning. She let it be known she didn't care much for the smell last night, and that she was going to the inn to recover herself."

"Ah," said Charlotte. Diana's current visit was proceeding along the lines of most previous ones.

The glasshouse was a breath of July in late October, due to the rich soils and growing things within its humid warmth. Southern honeysuckle twined next to pots of Appalachian rhododendrons and bare stalks of South American orchids. This year, a raised bed of West Indian pineapples grew below a permanent and fantastic palm, next to an orange tree in a Spanish jar. Several other beds were generally used for starting annual vegetables, or for growing strawberries.

Near the back, a multi-flued Baltic stove sat ready to protect the tenderest plants on the coldest nights, though the stone wall behind it stored sufficient heat from sunlight to keep the frost away during much of the spring and fall. Each morning, after late September, large felt shades which were attached to the rafters were rolled up, while at sunset, they were unrolled again and overlapped for more thermal protection.

Longfellow frequently explained the workings of the place to Mrs. Willett, and to anyone else willing to listen. And many did. The building and its contents, the result of years of research and experimentation, were the wonder of the neighborhood. This was especially true during the snowy months. Then, favored guests might be asked in for a meal taken *almost alfresco*. Others had to make do with peering in from outside.

"How are the *lycopersicon*?" Longfellow's neighbor inquired with interest, joining him as he bent over clusters of dark green leaves that partly hid several glossy red fruits.

"These inside are still doing nicely," he remarked, picking back some errant stems with his long fingers, "but I don't believe *pomodori* will ever be seriously grown for food here, the way they're being cultivated in Italy— even though they're one of our own natives. I've found they make an interesting condiment, with some spice added. But I predict it will never take the place of oyster sauce."

"I seem to remember you telling me that all of the solanaceae, including these, can be deadly."

"Some parts of them . . . and the nightshades, in particular. Although even they can have their uses. I'm sure you're aware that Italian women often court love, and death, by widening their eyes with *belladonna*. Insanity is another frequent effect. In my opinion, however, it's tobacco that's the worst of the family. A wretched, dangerous thing to foist onto society. Our plantation friends are happily leading the rest of us to perdition, solely to line their pockets."

" 'It's good for nothing but to choke a man, and fill him full of smoke and embers.' "

"Hmmm! Old Ben Jonson was perfectly right. Though he neglected to mention snuff! However," Longfellow went on more cheerfully, "the potato of the same genus seems to be a more healthful success." He dropped the tomato shoots he held into a basket of clippings meant for the compost heap outside, and sniffed at his fingers.

"And so, we conclude that this family is both dangerous and beneficial, like so many others. Which reminds me . . . is Diana enjoying her stay?" Charlotte asked politely.

"About as much as she ever does. If my sister can find something to gossip about, or someone to admire her silks and scents, she's reasonably happy. If she's forced to live simply like the rest of us, however, she dies a thousand deaths—and few of them are quiet ones. Still," he added, reconsidering, "she's certainly good at creating amusements."

"As we'll no doubt discover tonight. Do you think she'll bite Captain Montagu, or will she be content simply to mumble him?"

"We'll have to wait and see. But let me tell you what else I've discovered, through my scientific inquires. I've been reviewing what's known of combustion, to help you with your interest in this absurd affair out on the highway."

"And?"

"Not an easy task! No one knows the exact components of combustion. The theory of phlogiston maintains that this element, and another called calx, must be present in all combustible matter—the one escaping in the burning process, the other remaining as a residue. Although personally, I agree with the ideas expressed in the work of the Englishman Boyle, and his pupils Hooke and Mazori. They believed that the mixture of air and the volatile sulphurous parts of combustible bodies causes them to act one upon the other—and, that parts of both ascend during combustion, generally accompanied by smoke and flame, leaving a final, unburnable residue behind."

"Oh, yes?" Charlotte commented, frowning.

"It's also known that a volume of air in a sealed chamber is diminished by the process of combustion—and that once diminished, this air will no longer support burning, if one should attempt to ignite *another* object within the unopened chamber. It's curious that the same effects may be obtained by enclosing an animal in the space, and allowing it to breathe until some necessary part of the air is removed."

"But that's—"

"This leads many to assume that *combustion* and *respiration* are actually the same thing. Although during respiration, of course, combustion is not observed. Still, if the process were to be altered by yet another cause, then the effect of actual fire might conceivably result from respiration in an animal, or even in a man—perhaps even in our Mr. Middleton. No one yet comprehends such a cause, if one does exist. The original research was done nearly a century ago, and it's high time for some additional progress to be made. Once we know exactly what this substance in the air necessary to combustion *is*—"

Longfellow threw his arms apart and breathed deeply of an unknown source of inspiration.

"But as yet," countered Charlotte, "we have no good reason to suppose that the man just *burst* into flames—"

"There are precedents, as well as similar things in Nature. For instance, we all know that spontaneous combustion of certain things can occur when they're carelessly stored, especially when damp—and that they will sometimes explode into flames after smoldering for a while. Hay, coal, logs—it's not uncommon. A farmer considers this to be a naturally occurring process, without truly understanding the cause. That is why he dries his hay before storing it in his barn."

"I think we can assume, though, that Mr. Middleton was neither damp, nor confined in any particular way."

"But *something* might have altered his original state, in a way that could be repeated in a similar situation, at another time—something *perhaps* linked with his natural respiration."

"Then you do believe it's likely Duncan Middleton was consumed in some kind of fire?" asked Charlotte cautiously, fingering a stalk of rusty chrysanthemum tied to a stake of cane. Longfellow smiled his sweetest smile, and let his true conclusion out.

"I believe nothing of the kind," he said firmly.

"None of this is actually relevant to the matter we're looking into. I find it much more likely that substances far simpler than the bodily tissues of Duncan Middleton were burned on Tuesday night."

"I've wondered myself if it might not have been something like Greek fire."

Longfellow stared at her blankly. He had planned to explain the rest of his idea after Charlotte had been suitably impressed with its beginning. Instead, he was forced to pause and admire the fact that she'd reached his own conclusion without him.

"My library isn't a very new one," she reminded him gently, "but it's well stocked with the classical authors, and I do find some time to read."

"Come with me."

"I've read of its historical use, of course," she managed as he towed her by the arm past a startled Cicero, and then on toward the house. "The Byzantines created Greek fire for warfare, didn't they? And it was later taken up by the Crusaders, I think who used it against the Saracen. But whatever the secret formula was, I seem to remember it was activated by contact with *water*, so I don't quite—"

"Sometimes it was," Longfellow shouted back over the wind. "But with the substitution of phosphorus, which burns when exposed to *air*—"

"—a kind of land bomb could be made! Oh! But what exactly is phosphorus?"

"A highly unstable element, isolated in Hamburg in the 1660s, derived from . . . well, at any rate, isolated. It burns first with quantities of white smoke—very useful for camouflage, by the way—and then with a clear blue flame."

He slowed for breath, and looked up. The faint cries of Canada geese filtered down from the sky, as a flock passed overhead like hounds running after prey.

"Phosphorus may be kept," Longfellow continued, "in a vial of turpentine, or even water. If the vial is broken and pieces of phosphorus exposed to air, they should burn very nicely. If you add to this a bit of charcoal for a base, some pitch, sulphur, and a dash of saltpeter, then you have a fine, portable package full of fire, smoke, and the smell of Satan at your disposal, waiting to be tossed down. The intense heat would of course cause the glass to melt while the rest burned, making the entire thing *appear* to have occurred without a natural source!" Reaching the house, he opened the kitchen door.

"I tried it last night with the materials I had delivered. And here you see the results. Nearly identical with what I removed from the road."

Charlotte stared at kitchen surfaces scattered with glass dishes and tubes, and at a large, flat rock covered with black material, on the floor in front of her feet.

"So that's how the effect was created," she finally managed, while her nose wrinkled at the lingering stink of combustion. "I certainly hope *your* information, with what I have to tell you, will bring us close to a solution."

"Then Captain Montagu will be forced to conclude that there are more than roots and vegetables inhabiting the country! But, I'm still in the dark, Carlotta, when it comes to explaining how Middleton managed the *rest* of his trick. How do you think he kept Pennywort from seeing him, as he ran away?"

"I do have a few ideas—"

At that moment there was a banging of the door, and the sound of silk brushing along the hall. Diana Longfellow flounced into the room, the fashionable hoops at her hips causing her skirts to swing barely within the bounds of safety. It was eminently clear that the morning had seen another triumph, and that it, too, was soon to be related.

· · ·

"YOU SHOULD BOTH be glad," Diana began vigorously, "that *someone* cares for the safety of your little village. I've just come from expressing my thoughts on recent matters to Captain Montagu."

"Captain Montagu?" her listeners asked together. Diana paused to examine a fingernail.

"Could it be," inquired Longfellow, "that you've re-judged the man, and found him human after all?"

"As I say, Captain Montagu—who, by the way, was particularly glad to speak with someone respectable, and intelligible. I've been making myself very useful . . . unlike, he informs me, certain others in the neighborhood."

Charlotte and Longfellow waited for more.

"He's apparently having trouble discovering the facts from the local rabble, so I related to him what I had heard of this monster Pennywort, stalking innocent travelers and then covering his crimes by spreading tales so *absurd* that your rustics were bound to believe them. I convinced the captain that this blackguard Pennywort should be arrested immediately, and locked up somewhere until he can be tried."

"Diana," her brother asked at last, smoothing back his hair from his forehead, "have you ever seen this character you describe so vividly?"

"No," she had to admit. But she kept her chin high, inviting a challenge to her powers of intuition.

"Well, Jack Pennywort is shorter than you, he has a deformed foot, his mind is about as active as that of a possum that's been hanging at a cider bung—and to lock him up would deprive a wife and four small children of the rather dubious livelihood they now enjoy. While it may be fashionable for some in your world to ridicule and torture Nature's unfortunates, following perhaps the great courts of Europe, it will hardly do to taunt such victims of misfortune *here*. We should all, I think, have a little more compassion than that."

Much of what Longfellow said was, of course, a lie; laughing at Pennywort had been a sport enjoyed by a good portion of the village for much of their lives, although it was not especially popular among the more enlightened. But Diana's eyes lost some of their snap as she listened, and considered.

"Besides," her brother added, "Charlotte and I have already concluded it's very likely Middleton isn't dead at all, but only gone away. It seems he himself was the inventor behind his rather theatrical demise."

"What! But how? And *why*?"

"Why? How should I know? But the fact is that you are out to hang an innocent man. My experiments, which you objected to so heartily last night, prove that the merchant *planned* to disappear. And so he did."

"Yet doesn't it seem strange," Diana asked very slowly, savoring each word, "that Middleton, a prominent, wealthy merchant, would leave everything behind—even his ready funds?"

"Do you happen to be acquainted with the man's lawyers? Or have you acquired a crystal ball?"

"No, I heard it from Edmund— from Captain Montagu," she corrected herself, smiling at the memory of his confidence. "The captain informs me that his own inquiry leads him to suspect foul play, as none of the man's wealth has been touched. He's clearly dead, Richard."

"Middleton probably arranged to have his property sold by an accomplice. Or else he plans to claim it himself, when he's good and ready."

"Then we'll see," was all he could get in reply.

Charlotte, though surprised by Diana's information, also remembered suddenly that she had something else to attend to.

"Shall I call for you around four?" Longfellow asked as she lingered for a moment at the door.

"No . . . you go on. I'll join you at the inn. Right now, there's someone—well, I'll tell you about it later."

Leaving her neighbors to continue their family fray, Mrs. Willett made her way back across to her own safe and ordered kitchen. She felt greatly in need of a strong cup of tea, as well as a few moments for quiet thought.

Chapter 13

HANNAH SLOAN WAS peacefully shredding cabbage for pickling when the kitchen door burst open and Charlotte bustled in, with Lem trailing close behind.

At first, the young man only stood, and gulped. Then, quite abruptly and to the amazement of both women, he began to pour forth a description of his visit to the Blue Boar. While she listened, Charlotte filled a green glass goblet with buttermilk, from the jug on the cellar steps. It was as if, she thought, a lava cone had been lifted up, and a new Vesuvius born.

"Right away, I found Jack Pennywort sitting there, the way you said he'd be. When I told him you'd offered to give him work for a day, and food, he called for another pint of ale. I doubt," Lem added, pausing in his narration for a moment, "if we'll get much work out of him when he comes, or if he'll have much money left from what you pay him, after Mr. Wise collects what he's owed."

"Why on earth do you want Jack Pennywort coming *here?*" Hannah cried out, her cap shaking. "The man's liable to make off with anything that isn't pegged in or nailed down! The last time he worked for Julia Bowers, and her husband the constable, no less—"

"Don't you think offering a kindness to someone in need is worth our taking a chance?" Charlotte interrupted softly, a quiver of unclear origin in her voice. Hannah swallowed a further protest for the moment. But her expression showed that she was far from convinced.

"Then," Lem leaped on, apparently enjoying the new exercise, "there was a noise at the door, and Peter Lynch came in with several others, who could barely keep still while the miller spoke. He told Mr. Wise that he'd been harboring a thief in Mary's friend, the Frenchman, and then Peter and the rest demanded to see the Frenchman's room."

At this, Hannah stopped her muttering to listen.

"And did Phineas agree?" Charlotte asked quickly.

"They pushed Mr. Wise aside before he could even answer, and started climbing the stairs. I went up behind, and when I got to the door, the farthest one, I saw Peter Lynch rise up from behind the bed. And he was holding a gold coin! It was a Dutch one, too, he said, a gulden; then he passed it around for all to see."

"No!" Hannah breathed softly.

"He made Mr. Wise admit it was exactly like the ones he'd picked up from the floor on Tuesday night, when the old man dropped his purse."

Abruptly, Charlotte felt her neck begin to tingle. Jonathan Pratt had been given one coin. She'd already guessed there was a second one about, and would soon see if her theory was right. Yet here was a third! And this coin promised to do far more harm than the others.

"After that, the miller shouted here was proof Gabriel Fortier killed the old man for his money. He said when the Frenchman came back to get his clothes, Providence made him drop a piece of the treasure he'd stolen. Some of the men talked about finding the Frenchman and giving him a taste of the whip, before they gave him over to the law. But since nobody knew where to look for him, they finally settled on going to hand the coin over to Mr. Bowers."

"It's clear what Peter Lynch thinks to gain by it," Hannah interjected, her face livid with indignation. "It's the girl Lynch wants, and he's out to get her, no matter what he has to do!"

Charlotte felt the color drain from her own cheeks, and put her hands to her face to warm them again. Neither she nor Hannah believed the miller's accusation to be true. But how had Peter Lynch come by the coin? Could it be that her recent conclusions were wrong? What if the merchant really *had* died after all—been killed, or at least abducted? If his gold had been taken from him by force—but in that case, where could the body have gone? And why would a man like Peter Lynch risk suspicion by producing such a coin, *if he had actually killed Middleton for it?* No; it was all too ridiculous. Especially when she herself could offer an even simpler explanation for the appearance of the second coin—and show there *was* no third.

"The main thing holding the others back is that no one's found what's left of the merchant," Lem finished, gingerly setting down his empty goblet. "But as soon as someone does, several of the miller's friends promised to help him turn Bracebridge upside down to find the Frenchman, and then hang him from a tree!"

It was a terrible thought. Yet it was something at least a few of the local folk, whose families had recently suffered at the hands of the French, might easily do.

"I only hope they don't become tired of waiting," Charlotte said bleakly, as she slowly brought a canister of black tea down from its shelf, and took the kettle from the hob.

THE TEA WAS half consumed when Lem insisted on going back to his hammer and maul. Shortly after that, Jack Pennywort knocked lightly at the back door. Looking somewhat the worse for wear after his few days of fame, the little man sat and took a cup with plenty of sugar, along with a heavy slice of nut loaf spread with butter.

Between mouthfuls, Jack attempted to explain again, in language suitable for his new audience, what he'd seen and done on Tuesday evening. Outsized and outnumbered by the two women, he also fidgeted, and kept a close watch on the door, even as he accepted a second piece of buttered bread. And yet, thought Charlotte, Jack managed to answer the questions she put to him with at least the appearance of honesty.

"Then you actually saw the gentleman's figure moving for a few moments through the flames. But you didn't see him again afterward?" she asked as she leaned forward on the table, while Hannah kept her eyes on Jack from across the room. Pennywort had obviously tired of telling a story he no longer dared (or cared) to embellish. By now, it was far from fresh, and had begun to shrink a little, which seemed to have caused it to lose some of its flavor. Still, as long as the ladies were interested. . . .

"That's right," he agreed, staring blankly at a pair of candlesticks that gleamed on the window ledge. "As I say, I saw a pale flash, and another gleam, like, after that. Then came the flames and smoke. After the smoke had gone off and the *blue* fire rose, I looked far and wide, but I saw no sign of anybody there at all."

"And at your feet?" Charlotte asked, watching him intently. "Did you think of looking there?"

Jack said nothing, but regarded her with a wary expression.

"You say the road was brightly lit by the flames?"

"There was light, and shadow, of course," he answered finally. " 'Twas too bright to look at the fire for long."

"And then you saw the man waving through the flames—now I can't seem to remember, did you say these flames looked to be red?"

"First regular, then blue, I said, mistress. And no one can tell me different, because I know what I saw!" he added hotly, sensing that she might be trying, as others had, to confuse him.

"I'm sure that's so," she answered with another offer of the bread plate, which Jack again accepted. "Earlier," she went on calmly, "I heard—well, they say you left the tavern on the heels of the old man, and went off in the same direction. But I never heard anyone say why you decided to follow him—"

Jack winced suddenly. Clearly, a piece of nut had affected a rotten tooth. As Charlotte watched with sympathy, he readjusted the morsel with his tongue and thumb, and then went on.

"Because I expected he might get into trouble, as the Frenchman had gone off before him, and we'd all seen that gold."

"Extremely sensible. And thoughtful of you, too." Her kind words were rewarded with a crooked, gaping smile. "But you didn't actually see the Frenchman outside, did you?"

"He could've been waiting behind some trees. Soon

as I saw the old man slip down from the road, that's the first thing I thought—"

"Down from the road?"

"He went off toward a clump of fir trees. It was the ale, and the cold—that's what I figured. Not worth mentioning. When he came back, I followed him a little longer, until I saw the rest."

"So, it's not very likely that Gabriel Fortier was in the trees, or somehow made Mr. Middleton disappear a moment later."

"Could've had a charm—maybe put a spell on him, some say. I don't know about that myself."

"More tea, Jack? I'm sure you'll wait for another cup, with more sugar? Now, I wonder if I can recall what it was I heard about a brown bundle the merchant carried. . . ." she added to herself, getting up to spoon more leaves into the warm pot.

Jack had by now begun to massage his jaw. When Charlotte poured the hot water, she saw him reach into his breeches pocket for something, probably an oil-soaked clove, which he expertly nestled into the source of his pain.

"What *about* his bundle?" Jack asked after a bit more thought.

"Well, did he have a bundle when he came back to the road?"

"I never said he had a bundle."

"But he had, before. I'm sure Mr. Longfellow told me he was seen with one earlier. Did you go back to look for it in the trees? Perhaps some time later?"

Pennywort gazed around, consulted with his crooked foot, and finally replied: "Next morning, I did. No harm in that, is there?"

"None at all. A man has a perfect right to be curious, I'd say. Even a woman. What did you find? Something mysterious?"

"All I found was string."

"String?"

"Aye, string. Only a piece of string. Not worth mentioning, you see."

Jack had ceased to see the point of retelling the story, especially its pointless details. He began to stretch on his chair, looking toward the backyard, his tongue working its way around his mouth to catch the last of his small meal.

"Do you know, Jack," said Charlotte, almost done with him, "you tell your story so well that I can practically see it happening. You first saw two glimmers of light. The first was just a pale flash. And then, a gleam. Now, I can almost see that gleam, and it looks to me like a coin catching the moonlight—maybe a piece of gold dropped carelessly onto the road? One you might naturally bend down to pick up, when you reached the place where it fell?"

"What if I did?" Jack answered, puffing himself up with sudden fright. "I'd be an honest man still, though there'd be them as would say I stole it *all*, if I said I pocketed the one! Why, I only come *here* to do an honest day's work for you. But some might say it looks like you be trying to trap me—"

"I do believe you only picked up what had been dropped . . . but dropped for a very good reason. Of course, you know the main reason I called for you is that our woodpile needs another splitter, and that's certainly warm work I'm sure you'll enjoy this cool afternoon. Only tell me one thing more—aren't you a close friend of our miller, Peter Lynch? Could it be he took the coin you'd found away from you, afterward, for reasons of his own?"

The little man had gone as white as fresh bleached linen. Whether it was the pain of his tooth again, or a fear of something greater, she couldn't be sure. But he held so strongly to his story that Charlotte was finally forced to let him go, after he'd repeated it all once more, at top speed.

"I got nothing out of it, God help me!" Jack concluded shrilly. "Naught from the miller, naught from the old stranger! Naught but *string*! I'll give you no more talk now, and no work, either! Not this day, I won't."

With that, Jack Pennywort hurled himself lopsidedly into the yard, leaving his gentle inquisitor to tap her chin thoughtfully, while Hannah Sloan put down her broom.

Chapter 14

IT WAS NEARLY four o'clock when Charlotte Willett put the final touches to her costume, and slipped a few small objects into a pocket that hung beneath her petticoat. Then, taking up her skirts, she left her bedroom and moved carefully down the narrow stairs.

Before slipping wool over silk, she stood for a moment by a long glass at the door to take stock of her appearance. The clear blue of the dress she'd chosen certainly complimented her eyes. The pinned-in square of wide lace that lay over her bosom covered it modestly, but not entirely, which was the expected effect. And although there were no preparations on her lips or cheeks, her natural high color (and steady exercise) kept her looking healthy, capable, and consequently interesting, without attracting overdue attention. It was a pleasing thought.

She gave the small stays at her waist a final, chastening

tug. Then, she swept her cloak over all, and fastened it with an ivory scrimshaw clasp Aaron had obtained for her from Captain Noah Willett. At last, she felt ready.

Pulling up her hood, Charlotte opened the door and gave a final thought to the supper she'd laid out in the kitchen for Lem. After that, she pointed the toes of her Morocco shoes (the ones Longfellow had bought on his travels) toward the inn, and braced herself as she felt a waiting hand of autumn wind come up to accompany her.

AT THE SAME time, Lydia Pratt looked into another mirror, adjusted a loop of black hair, then touched the beauty mark she had recently applied to her cheek— quite possibly to confound her husband, for Lydia rarely adorned herself at all.

"But you told me you *hadn't* spoken to him," Jonathan Pratt reminded his wife. They stood alone under the large chandelier in the front hall, watchful for interruption from without, or within.

"I told you I didn't see him arrive; *that's* what I said. As for being in his room, I'd simply forgotten about it. Don't you think I have enough to worry about? After all, it's Mary's job to see to their needs once they're settled. But she was nowhere to be seen when he called, and I remember now that *I* had to go up instead. Of course I had strong words for the girl, as soon as I found her!"

"But you did say—"

"It wasn't anything of the least importance—only something about the sheets—now where *is* that girl? I suppose she's gone off again, with dinner to serve to the captain!" Lydia Pratt's looks were always sharp. But when she frowned, the tightness of her mouth made her jaw stand out even farther, and her black eyes glinted under what sometimes looked like one thin eyebrow set atop her narrow face.

"Lydia . . . dear . . . Captain Montagu was naturally anxious to hear the details of your conversation, when I mentioned Lee told me one had occurred. Naturally, I was somewhat embarrassed that *you* hadn't mentioned it when the captain questioned you. I told him you'd probably overlooked the whole thing . . . but you might have been the last one ever to speak to Middleton, if you don't count his ordering a tankard of ale. If Lee hadn't said anything—"

"Which is another thing!" His wife seemed about to go on in the same vein, but abruptly decided to hold her tongue. "If and when I get a chance," she began again with better composure, "I'll speak to the captain. Wasn't it enough today that you brought that great green *thing* into my kitchen, to scratch up the floor and the walls with its horrible claws? On top of that, you actually seemed to expect me to dispatch it!"

"Sweetheart, it was quite chilled and slow when I left it there. Besides, you wouldn't have wanted it brought dead all the way from Boston? It might have given us all the flux!"

The sea turtle had been a bargain, Jonathan went on. It also kept him from asking more about his wife's whereabouts on the day of Duncan Middleton's disappearance, for which *she* was grateful—to the turtle, at least. If anyone should ever find out what she'd done . . .

Nervously, Lydia stepped back as Jonathan moved past her to open the door for a guest he'd seen through a tall window, hurrying up the walk.

Charlotte Willett entered with an entourage of swirling leaves. When she'd lifted her hood and unfastened the clasp of her cloak, the landlord took it from her shoulders with a flourish.

"Your two gentlemen are already in the taproom," he told her, gesturing to the familiar passageway.

"Good evening," Charlotte said formally as she made a small bob to Lydia, expecting a similar courtesy in return. Her greeting was answered only by a stiff nod as the landlady turned and walked away. Jonathan shrugged his apologies to an old friend. He was about to offer her his arm when they saw, through the multipaned window, something else that made them both stand still.

Now Diana Longfellow approached the inn. She was accompanied for the sake of convention by Cicero— who could barely keep up with the young woman's flying figure as it moved precariously across the road and up the stone walk, buffeted by sharp gusts that caught her widespread skirts as if they were sails.

Once the door was safely closed behind her, Diana's wave indicated to Cicero that he might go along. He gave Diana a withering glance as he headed toward his usual spot in the taproom, but smiled to Charlotte, approving of her quiet air and her sensible lack of hoops.

"I really don't know how I manage," Diana began huskily after the landlord, too, had retreated. She sat and bent down with a small gasp and several jingles to replace her leather shoes with silk ones, taken from a banded box she carried. There were tiny bells, Charlotte noticed with astonishment, on the upper part of Diana's costume, bells which could be flounced casually to call attention to one's bosom. She wondered if fashion (if that was what it was) had taken a backward look to the Elizabethans, or if it had simply gone mad once again while trying to change the future.

"I told Richard I'd be ready in just a few more minutes, but he insisted on coming ahead by himself, and left only Cicero to help me here. What if I'd been blown down in the road, or run over by a dung cart? I really don't believe he would have cared."

"I'm fairly sure his appetite would have suffered."

"Are you? Lord! I must catch my breath before I move." Sliding the shoe box under her chair, Diana straightened and took a small bottle from an embroidered bag. She removed its tiny cork stopper, and Charlotte leaned closer, drawn by a wonderful aroma.

"*Parfum parisien*," said Diana, dabbing a bit from finger to neck before offering the bottle to her friend. "I'm afraid the first application has been blown away."

"It's a wonderful scent," Charlotte responded truthfully. And the little container was a thing of beauty, she noted, turning it to catch the light. Made of black enameled porcelain, the bottle had the design of a red-and-blue dragon winding its way around the surface in a highly effective manner. It was one of the best of Diana's frequently presented discoveries.

"It's new, of course—Captain Harper lately brought a few in to Providence. He maintains there are only a half dozen in existence! The scent's the product of a French firm, but the bottles come from Canton, according to Lettie Hitchbourn. She brought two of them back with her to Boston a few days ago, and sold one to me. Sold, mind you. Lettie would have made a wonderful merchant. That woman has a heart of gold. *Minted* gold. Most of us have more interesting things to do, though, than to think of money all day long."

Charlotte's smile came easily. She knew that Diana played to whatever audience she had—but also that she had a great deal more knowledge, and perception, than one might think. It was a secret that by now the two women shared comfortably with one another. Unfortunately, her elegant looks and withering babble were greatly admired by many town acquaintances, and were what Diana generally enjoyed displaying. It was something that caused Mrs. Willett to be thankful for her own lot in life.

"Well, I think I can manage now," Diana said at last. The two began to walk toward the smell of pipes and wood smoke, and other comforts.

The room they entered was hardly full, but Charlotte recognized several faces that turned to watch their entrance. She smiled toward Adolphus Lee next to the fire, who dipped his shining spectacles with an energetic bow (although his eyes were clearly on the lady he had yet to meet). Apparently, it was too rough tonight even for naturalists to be abroad, Charlotte decided as she inhaled the heady aroma of spirits and foods. Two slightly rumpled and bewigged gentlemen sat beside Mr. Lee; they, too, paused in their discussion, and bowed in tribute to the ladies, causing Diana to look with some pleasure in the opposite direction.

Charlotte soon spotted Longfellow and Edmund Montagu, perched, she thought, like owls in a nest. In fact, they sat in a small area at the top of a few steps, set off by a wooden divider—much like the officers' deck of a ship. They, too, rose from their chairs as the women approached, and helped them to glasses of Madeira from a silver tray as soon as they were comfortably arranged.

It was obvious that the gentlemen had been engaged in a heated discussion. Even Diana's charms failed to divert them for long.

"As I say," Longfellow rejoined, "leaving ten thousand troops here after the end of hostilities was sheer folly. Today, most sit in New York—but where will they turn up tomorrow? You'll keep these men on short pay, and what's more important to your own interests, they'll be kept from looking for employment back in England. But the war is over. I don't see why anyone thinks we'll be happy to pay your soldiers to retire with *us*."

"They may be kept busy enough. Pontiac and his

Ottawas are setting fire to much of the West as we speak. In Virginia, Pennsylvania, New York—you must know that every one of our forts, except for Detroit, has fallen to Indian—"

"—not a great surprise, considering the quality of the officers you've been sending—"

"—predation, which leads me to suspect that even here, near the coast, you may one day be glad you help pay for British troops. And I say *help* pay, sir . . . no one expects you to assume the entire cost of their upkeep. But England has already been saddled with tremendous debt, paying for your last defense—"

"So in return, you arrange to have redcoats prowling our waterfronts."

"*And* your frontiers! We may not have seen the end of French intrigue. Your merchants might also be glad of someone with money to spend, ready to consume your truly amazing surplus of foodstuffs."

"While your customs men begin taking away our sea trade! We read lately in our pamphlets and papers that the Crown plans—"

"You would do better with a few less of those! From what I've read they're all filled with lies—"

"—to go along with this idea of Grenville's to raise further revenues with an enforcement of the molasses tax, and several new ones. Yet we have always sympathized with the king's needs, and raised and delivered our own revenues. When we are asked with some consideration—"

"Asked?" Montagu appeared to hardly know whether to smile or frown.

"Well, then, is this new way supposed to please us more? Let us levy taxes in our own assemblies, just as you do. After all, it's the right of every British subject to be *requested*, rather than forced, to supply the Crown with funds. *And* to be represented directly in Parliament, most of us will maintain."

"Do you *really* think you and your colonists here are on equal footing with the people of England—those by whom Parliament is chosen?"

"Certainly; we're English, and men too, and yet you treat us like children!"

"The analogy has some justice, surely, when you look at—"

"Do I look like a child to you?"

Charlotte had heard much of this before, on otherwise enjoyable evenings spent in her neighbor's study with a decanter of canary wine, or perhaps some old French brandy that had slipped through the blockade. Now, she looked down with more interest at the hand-lettered bill of fare lying next to Longfellow's tapping fingers. Diana, too, read it over when Charlotte placed the card telling what was to come between them.

To start, a green turtle soup—something Elizabeth, the inn's cook, born and bred in Marblehead, would know how to do to perfection. Then, roast goose with oranges and oyster sauce. (The goose would be one of Lydia's ill-natured pirates who hissed and grumbled around her kitchen door. It would not be long lamented.)

Goose was to be followed by a wood pigeon pie made with celery and walnuts—an excellent idea, Charlotte decided, for her own purse as well as Jonathan's. The cook would use not only a great deal of cream from her dairy, but a large quantity of butter as well. And a 'made' dish like this one of game birds would be, for Jonathan, mostly a matter of a little shot and powder, some seasonings, and a simple, flaky flour-and-lard crust.

With the birds would come a dish of greens and gravy, as well as one of fresh roasted beets, peeled and buttered hot from the coals. And finally, rum-baked spiced apples, and a cranberry custard. Edmund Montagu had arranged to give them a good dinner, although it was something less than a feast. Still, it was a fine offering to occupy an odd afternoon, even without the further amusements Charlotte saw ahead.

"—and this Dutch gold piece that Bowers tells me was found by the miller . . ." Montagu went on, "of course, you realize it indicates the West Indies, or Surinam. Either way, it means smuggling."

"That wouldn't be surprising, since we can't get enough molasses from Britain's islands to keep our distilleries going. And just how do you expect us to keep buying goods from you without hard currency?"

"Distilleries which in turn supply rum to trade for slaves. A very nice business," Montagu added haughtily.

Here, Charlotte managed to interrupt. She had never seen a slave in Bracebridge, but she had heard about Dutch gold very recently.

"Were you speaking just now about the coin from Gabriel Fortier's bedroom at the Blue Boar?"

"We were, ma'am," Montagu replied.

"By the way, Captain," Longfellow interjected, "are you conducting a search for Fortier now?"

"Not at the moment. But with the insistence of half the town, someone may soon have to organize one."

"I believe Mrs. Willett is about to try to convince you to clear Fortier's name. Indeed, we talked about a mutually discovered theory this afternoon, which sheds some light on your mysterious merchant. But I won't stand in her way. I'm sure she'll tell it beautifully."

Seeing the eyes of all the rest upon her, Charlotte gathered her courage, took a deep breath, and began.

"I propose a succession of events. I think they might help to explain Jack Pennywort's adventure, and the part played, I believe, by Duncan Middleton in his own disappearance."

Montagu tilted his head briefly, and again raised piercing eyes to hers.

But Charlotte's beginning was delayed as Jonathan Pratt came to inform them their first course was ready. They all rose and soon climbed the main stairs, before they were ushered into a small private dining room with its own fire, several candles, and a large linen-covered table. Here, Lydia Pratt met them as well, coming from the kitchen end of an interior passage, and carrying a heavy tray.

The party sat as a bread basket and a large tureen were transferred to the table. Then, as they broke open crisp rolls, a thick green soup was ladled into bowls. It was tasted and pronounced delectable, having just a hint of amontillado to set off its richness.

Finally, when they were settled in comfortably, Charlotte recommended the story she and Richard Longfellow had pieced together, recapping what was already known, and adding even more.

AT TWILIGHT (SHE recounted), following the tavern's usual talk and a threatened brawl, complete attention was drawn by the spilling of a bag full of gold coins. Shortly afterward, Fortier got up to leave; soon after that, the merchant followed. Jack went out as well, driven by habit, curiosity, and very possibly a touch of greed. He would provide the necessary audience for what was to come.

When Middleton saw that he was being followed, he quickened his steps, drawing away from the crossroads and the tavern as he climbed the lonely road to Worcester. It was a quiet night, and a suitably mysterious and auspicious one. Jack Pennywort must have wondered where the stranger could be heading as he left the safety of the village—wondered, too, if he himself would be seen following. Unexpectedly, Middleton left the road and made his way to a cluster of nearby fir trees, presumably to answer a call of Nature. This left Jack with more time to think, and to grow afraid.

When Middleton returned to the road, the brown bundle he had been carrying had vanished . . . because it was now worn under his cloak! The brown "bundle" had actually been a second long garment which he had planned to put under the first, covering that garment's bright red lining. The merchant again hobbled uphill, followed by a limping Jack, who vowed to himself to return later to examine those trees. (When he did, he found only a piece of string.)

"Excellent! Something I hadn't thought of," Longfellow interjected.

Before long (Charlotte continued carefully), Middleton approached a clear spot he'd already chosen in the elevated road, where nothing obstructed his view for a hundred yards to the sides, and nearly as far ahead and behind. Next, he took a small piece of mirror from his pocket, which came from the one broken in his room at the inn. (Although he himself broke the mirror to obtain the useful fragment, he knew it was almost certain that a servant would be blamed.) Now, he used this fragment of mirror to look back, and saw Jack still there. It was the reflection of the rising moon in this glass that Jack saw as a first faint flickering, up near the old man's shoulders.

Now, Middleton held something else in his hand—a gold coin. This he dropped into the road; then he took several more steps. In his mirror, he saw Jack stoop to pick up the shiny object. It was time to bring the performance to its conclusion.

Here, Charlotte paused for breath and took a sip of

wine, while her audience waited in silence with anticipation. Thus fortified, she continued.

"Perhaps pretending to stumble on a stone, in case
anyone was watching, Jack bent to pick up the coin.
This gave Middleton a chance to twirl his cloak so that
the dull brown inside was on the outside. Then, he threw
a small bomb, previously concealed in his bundle, onto
the road. It was filled with specially prepared ingredients;
Richard can tell you how it was made. As it burst into
flames, Middleton waved his arms and leaped about behind the fire. When enough smoke came to hide him
completely, he jumped down onto the south slope of the
road. He lay flat in the weeds with the dull cloak over
him, knowing Jack would be partially blinded by the
smoke, the light, and by the tears that heat, and fear,
brought to his eyes.

"After he recovered from the first shock, Jack looked
far and wide, but could find no one. He was still unable
to see what was under his own feet! Then even the blue
fire that followed the first began to die away, and before
long, darkness returned. This time, it brought even more
than its usual terrors. So Jack turned and ran down the
hill to alert the tavern, and to find safety again among
his friends. After a few more moments, Middleton got up
and went about his business, probably making for the
woods to watch the further proceedings—apparently no
longer under the constraints of an earthly body, and yet
not quite ready for heaven, either!"

In hindsight, it was a simple and effective plot.
Charlotte was pleased to hear her explanation immediately declared quite likely, even before she took from her
pocket fibers from the brown cloak, and the piece of mirror, which she'd found beside the road. She also took
pains to point out that if Lynch had wanted to get his
hands on a gulden with which to incriminate Gabriel
Fortier that afternoon, he had only to look to his smaller

friend, for Jack Pennywort would likely have told him he had "found" such a coin.

Longfellow next gave them a recipe for the making of something like Greek fire, which Edmund Montagu followed closely. Against all expectation, the British captain felt a growing respect for these new country acquaintances. Not only did he appreciate the methods of Mrs. Willet and her neighbor, but he had to agree with Longfellow that in one or two ways, at least some Americans *were* something more than children—even though their political opinions might still be those of innocents.

He had information of his own to add to their story, which he knew would surprise them. He also saw a rare chance to join in an amusement with a fair amount of safety, without risk to his own mission. Perhaps it was the combination of the quantities of sharp cider he'd taken earlier, as well as the wine, and the warmth, and even the company, that led him to feel an unaccustomed glow in this cozy place. He would have to remember to be careful.

At this juncture, the soup was removed while a crisp-skinned goose was brought in, along with the dishes of vegetables.

"All of which probably means," sighed Diana as she helped herself, "that I was wrong about Pennywort. And that you, Captain Montagu," she added with obvious satisfaction, "were misled by the merchant into believing him dead, when he's not dead at all! But *why* did Duncan Middleton go to all of this trouble, simply to disappear? And more to the point, where on earth is the irritating old man *now*?"

Chapter 15

"THAT'S WHERE I begin my tale," Montagu started, laying down his knife while the others gave him most of their attention.

"If I may," he continued, "I'll tell you the story of a young man intended for the army, who found that company not entirely to his liking, once he'd bought his way into it. While there, he met too many other 'second sons' who were at loose ends, engaging the enemy rarely, gaming, drinking and fighting each other far too often. Understandably, many of these fine young men got themselves into trouble. A few others, like myself, pulled them out when we were able—smoothed over the rough spots . . . hid what sins we could with appropriate compensation—and were rarely seen or thanked directly.

"It has for some time been my way to follow those who find themselves in trouble. More recently, I have watched those who may be *creating* it . . . against the Crown's interests. Which is why I came to Boston."

"Then you are a spy," Diana breathed softly, with a dazzling smile.

"If you like, although if I were, I'd scarcely tell you so. At any rate, I assume that we are all on the same side! Let us say that I'm the tax collector's helper, at least temporarily."

"That should make you a popular fellow," Longfellow commented, after barking out a dry laugh. "Why *do* you want to tell us about your business?" he asked point-blank, staring hard at Montagu's unreadable features.

"Largely because you seem to know a great deal about one part of it already. I'm sure I needn't ask you not to broadcast what I've said, or am about to say. Why make my life more difficult than it is?" the captain asked rhetorically. "But I believe this affair will soon be over. Until it is, I can tell you something about Middleton that could help you settle things in your own little community, when I am gone away tomorrow."

Pausing, Montagu glanced at Diana, but she only picked delicately at a wing joint with her teeth. He went on, addressing her brother.

"I've been watching Duncan Middleton for six months. He is a shipowner, as well as a merchant who deals heavily in cargo taken to and from the West Indies. And I, too, believe that he is very much alive!"

"But you told me . . ." Diana began to object. Then she saw Montagu's smile, and knew that he had toyed with her. With a cold calm, she settled back to listen to the rest.

"Middleton recently met with one of his captains who had returned from Curaçao, which explains the pocketful of Dutch guldens he was seen carrying about," Montagu continued. "Our merchant is a notorious smuggler—like a great many others who avoid payment of duties on certain listed goods which they import—and who buy and sell foreign commodities directly, thus bypassing His Majesty's home ports, and pockets. None of this is what one might call news; enough people know it to fill a prison. Let's just say that these things may not go on quite so freely, in a short while.

"Happily, at least for us, Middleton has recently devised a novel and even odious scheme to cheat his fellow man. By diluting the rum he ships with other substances . . . mostly cheaper turpentine, as well as a bit of black powder . . . he is hoping to make money on the frontier. Mysterious death at the edge of civilization is still rather commonplace, and he believes his poisonous brew will be overlooked as its occasional cause. But as soon as it can be proved that his drink is deadly, we will be able to stop him."

"I should hope so," said Longfellow thickly, wiping goose fat from his chin with his napkin. "But what was it that got you to focus your attention on the old reprobate in the first place?"

"In most criminal affairs, local officers know a great deal before they have proof . . . or before they're allowed to use what proof they have, against those who break the law. It's simply a matter of asking them what they know. And, with the new interest in colonial controls, some of them will soon be authorized to take to court what they, and I, have learned. At the moment, Middleton seems a prime candidate for prosecution. In fact, your merchant has already been tried for holding improper manifests, but this was done by a judge and jury of his own peers— which, oddly enough, didn't seem to do much good. This time, though, it will be the Admiralty Court. Without a jury of his fellows, and especially with his new sins exposed, I believe Duncan Middleton will have very little hope of remaining a free man. He'll find he has an enormous fine to pay, as well. He should be an invaluable cautionary example to others who might have similar plans in mind. This will be doubly true when government begins to confiscate the goods of all those who benefit from cheating it out of its due."

"So—taxes are one thing, but tainted spirits quite another," Longfellow concluded at the end of Montagu's rather long speech. "A man indeed goes too far, when he becomes a threat to civilization."

"I'm glad you agree. I had hoped I would be able to *appear* to believe in his death here, so that Middleton would feel safe in taking further chances. Toward that end, I encouraged your sister to carry misinformation back to Boston," the captain admitted, still addressing Longfellow, "but I see I can no longer use that strategy."

"But you feel sure he's gone on from *here*?"

"What would keep him in a backwater like this? No, I'm fairly certain he's off to take care of other affairs— although the fact that he's left so much in Boston for us to seize does indeed surprise me. He must have had much more hidden abroad than we ever imagined . . . perhaps in Curaçao, or Aruba. At any rate, a close watch is being kept for a wagonload of his rum we have reason to suspect was sent west from Providence on Monday night. An officer who had . . . delayed, shall we say, the post from there to Boston on an earlier day was waiting for him, though he somehow missed meeting Middleton on the road."

"Lost him, did he?" asked Longfellow with a trace of scorn. "Until we found him in this little backwater. Too bad you didn't have one of our local lads with your man in Providence, to help you track the fellow. Most are quite good at it—apparently, better even than some from England. Do you hunt, Captain?" He was gratified to see Montagu stiffen slightly.

"As most gentlemen do."

"I'm sure you've followed many beasts in your time, and dispatched them. Although it's always seemed to me there's generally so little harm in those poor old foxes, it's a puzzle why you'd want to dress up in a red coat and run after them, when you could be doing far more helpful things about the countryside."

"I still don't understand," interjected Charlotte, hoping to at least delay the squall that blackened the Captain's brow, "why Middleton came here to stage his disappearance in the first place. I imagine it's likely he thought we were 'bumpkins,' as the Dutch say. Or possibly, small potatoes," she added, smiling. "I know the world thinks life is slow and backward here, which is a thing that can sometimes put our people's noses out of joint. But why Bracebridge, in particular?"

Montagu approved of the lady's modesty and tact, as much as he felt her neighbor's attitude rub against his nature and breeding. For Mrs. Willet, at least, he found it necessary to add a warning.

"It's probable that Duncan Middleton came to Bracebridge because he has an accomplice here. He hasn't taken his own horse away, nor have I heard of him buying another. And it's a long walk from here to Boston, especially for a man crippled with gout. So, someone must have obtained one for him. As I've said, I'll go after him tomorrow, and I'll send word when we have him in custody. But until we've had a chance to question the man thoroughly, it might be wise to keep watch for any other unusual activities here. Middleton plays a dangerous game, and so might anyone he's chosen to help him."

"You think, then," Longfellow said gravely, his barbs forgotten, "that someone among us might be planning to do more harm."

"I really can't say," Montagu admitted. "But I think it would be prudent to assume that could be the case.

CONVERSATION WAS ABRUPTLY arrested by the arrival of the pigeon pastry. This time, the new dish was brought in by Mary Frye.

The girl's tense features reminded Mrs. Willett of other matters at hand. As Richard Longfellow cut open the steaming, egg-glazed crust, and Mary gathered the previous course onto her tray, Charlotte decided it was high time to clear the name of Gabriel Fortier.

"Captain Montagu," she began with a look of hope, "I believe we can assume the coin Peter Lynch found this morning is likely to have come from Jack Pennywort, who picked it up on the road—"

"I'll enjoy roasting Pennywort later this evening for lying to me, after I've had him plucked," Montagu assured her.

"Yes, well, then don't you think you might tell the village that you've laid to rest any reason for suspecting Mr. Fortier of committing a crime? I believe he has friends who would be relieved to hear he's no longer being sought."

A grateful look from the serving girl was quick in coming.

"Everyone certainly seems upset when they talk about him," Diana agreed. "In fact, I wonder if it might not *still* be a good idea to find him, and watch him for his own good."

"Why, exactly, do you say that, Miss Longfellow?" Montagu asked gently, perhaps hoping to mend a fence or two.

"From what I hear, it's more than stealing or murder that they accuse the Frenchman of now. He's being talked about as some sort of hellish magician."

"Where have you heard this?" her brother asked.

"From Cicero, of course. For instance, they say it's because of Fortier that one of the local men injured his arm at the cider press this morning. It seems they were all standing around as usual, and one man's eyes suddenly grew as big as saucers, like the dog in the children's tale. Then he began to speak in tongues to the owner's cat, which of course instantly became a witch's familiar in the opinion of everyone there. After that, he knocked down several of the men like ninepins, before he fell against the gears and did himself harm."

"I've heard something else quite recently, about a boy who may have disappeared . . ." Charlotte added quietly, as Diana continued to laugh at her own story, and Mary left by the passage door.

"They get together and drink themselves silly," Longfellow muttered through his napkin, as he worked a stray piece of shot out of a mouthful of bird. "Then they blame anything but themselves when the inevitable happens. One would hardly think they needed magic for that."

"What's this about a missing boy?" Montagu asked Charlotte.

"Two men were discussing it by the gate outside . . . they greeted me as I came in. I didn't think very much about it, knowing how some young men have a way of getting lost, from time to time. Now, I wonder . . . They asked me if I'd seen him, thinking, I suppose, that he might be with Lem Wainwright, who lives with me. Oh—the missing boy's name is Sam Dudley."

"Sam?" Longfellow responded, alerted as much by her tone as her words. "Where was he last seen, and when?"

"They said he went out to hunt some time before dawn. No one remembers where he planned to go, but as of four o'clock, he hadn't returned. His family, or at least his mother, is quite worried."

They followed Montagu's gaze as he stared toward the steamy window. The faintly illuminated branches beyond showed that the wind was still very active, while the darkness had fallen completely. As they watched, beads of rain appeared on the glass, then flew against it as if thrown in handfuls, before racing down in gathering streams. Behind them, the fire beneath the wide chimney hissed a warning.

"It's hardly an afternoon to stay outside, is it?" Diana ventured, a little uncertain.

"How old is this boy?" Montagu asked abruptly.

"Fifteen, or sixteen," Charlotte answered.

While his sister returned to her portion of the pigeon pie, Longfellow leaned back with a blank look. "He's probably found someone to visit—possibly a young lady," he suggested at last.

"And the Frenchman's still missing, too," Montagu mused, pushing a piece of carrot across his plate. "If he weren't, I'd have his hide or the truth," he added, plainly worried about the possibilities before him.

Quite suddenly, a gust of wind blew every flame on the table sideways.

Then, as if by some form of magic, a silent form appeared in the dark mouth of the kitchen passage.

"THE FRENCHMAN WAS missing, *Capitaine*. Now, he is here."

The new voice that broke the silence caused heads to swirl, and in an instant, all eyes took in the man who stood before them.

On closer inspection, there were two figures standing there, one behind the other; Gabriel Fortier stood to the front, while over the Frenchman's shoulder, Mary

Frye's pale face could just be seen. Clearly, she had known where he was all along, and had brought him in from nearby.

"I hide no more," Gabriel stated flatly, looking around the room at all of them, but letting his glance rest on Diana longer than on any other. He seemed to see something to address in her eyes, while she returned his look with unconcealed interest. Her evident approval, thought Charlotte, could not have been lost on anyone present.

"I have come, also," he continued boldly, "to claim my Marie. We are in love. We would run away together, but she is bound here. I respect this ... I respect Jonathan Pratt for giving her his protection. It is for this reason only that we wait—not for any fear of a *tyranneau*," he said bravely, barely refraining from spitting on the floor to drive home his point in the time-honored way.

Edmund Montagu put down his fork and knife, and dabbed his lips with a damask napkin.

"I hope several questions will be answered before *either* of you leaves this inn tonight," he said. But Montagu made no attempt to rise; he had seen Gabriel's hand go toward his belt, half hidden beneath a billowing shirt. It was not unlikely that Fortier, clearly a woodsman, carried a weapon of some sort, concealed but within easy reach.

"I may answer questions for you, *Captaine*, but I am protected by the rights of an Englishman. I know that you are unable to hold me without just cause. And I remind you that you have no legal body behind you, as well."

"Is everyone here mad?" Montagu asked the company at large. "The rights of an Englishman? Who'll claim them next—Louis Quinze?"

But Fortier went on in language that was well chosen, if delivered with a distinct accent.

"There are witnesses, you know, who will say that I was not there when the old man in the red cloak disappeared. Jack Pennywort saw no one else, as he tells everyone. On that night, I was by the river, regarding the moon. Mary and I were to meet, but I saw all the people, so I waited. Later I heard them return, calling out my name. Many of them were angry. I saw the smith, Nathan, give Mary his arm, and take her home. I only returned to the Blue Boar at midnight, through a loose window. No one saw me but for Phineas Wise. He warned me to go very early in the morning, and I followed his advice."

Gabriel Fortier paused and glanced back at Mary, who again seemed about to faint. Silently, he took her hand and helped her to sink gently into a chair that stood against the wall. The girl looked up into the Frenchman's passionate face. Charlotte saw with interest that Mary was still unused to such tenderness.

"There is really no need for an alibi now, Fortier—" Longfellow began.

"Did you see anyone else by the river?" Montagu interrupted.

"No—no one."

"What did you do with yourself after that?"

"Most of the time, I watched from the woods. The next night, I slept in Mme. Willett's *laiterie*—her dairy. This morning, she nearly found me. I hope she was not afraid."

Charlotte only smiled in reply. That explained, she quickly reasoned, why Orpheus hadn't growled last night, when she thought she saw a face at the window. The two had probably been introduced by Mary some time before.

"The Devil, you say! And no one told *me*?" Now it was Longfellow who interrupted, realizing that Charlotte might have been injured—at the very least, by sharp tongues of the village.

"But why do you stay, away from your family and your work, when you believe Mary is protected at the inn?" Montagu demanded.

"If Peter Lynch were to force Marie to—" Fortier swallowed hard before he summoned enough calm to continue. "If he can get her into his bed, then she will be made to marry him, even against her will. That must not happen. So, I spend my time watching him, or her. What else can I do?"

It was an answer that affected them all, and made Mary lower her eyes to hide tears that filled them. Was it love, wondered Charlotte, or shame? Or perhaps hatred, for Peter Lynch?

"It is difficult to hide, when you are poor—though the fault is not your own," Gabriel went on practically, possibly to draw their attention away from Mary. "Even when you begin to know a place. Much of the time, one can only live like an animal in the woods. It is very difficult, with men and boys coming to hunt, or looking at the birds in the trees; even little girls arrive, picking up nuts and nearly finding you. It is not a position for anyone to admire. And it is cold at this time of year, and very wet. So I have decided to come inside again."

"Where will you stay tonight?" asked Jonathan Pratt behind him. Gabriel turned.

"I am a free man. I do not need to answer," the young man finally replied, reminding Charlotte of the rooster who ruled the roost of her hen house.

"I suppose not," the innkeeper said. "I was about to offer you a place here. I had an idea that I might need some heavy chores done before winter sets in. Since my help is mostly female, I thought I could make use of another man's hands."

While Gabriel considered, Pratt brushed by him

with the tray holding the party's baked apples and a red custard, which he set down.

"Stay in the stable then, for now," Jonathan continued. "It's dry, and reasonably warm. Later, we'll arrange for something better."

First Gabriel, and then Mary, seemed ready to speak. But the landlord looked severely at them both.

"If you're finished, this is a private dining room. I'll finish serving the guests myself."

"Two lost, one found," Charlotte sighed softly as the relieved couple left the room, and the desserts were set upon the table. But the peaceful finale that Jonathan Pratt expected for his guests was not to be. Only moments after they had started on the fruit and the pudding, an explosion of sound came from the direction of the kitchen. It was quickly followed by Elizabeth the cook, who burst into the room with her plump arms flying.

"It's the miller—full of rum, and come to take our Mary!" she cried.

Then, she turned around and rushed back out through the open doorway, and down the reverberating hall.

Chapter 16

BY GEORGE!" SHOUTED Jonathan Pratt, following at the large woman's heels.

Chairs immediately scraped as all four diners rose to pursue the cook and the innkeeper down the dark passage. Because Charlotte and Longfellow knew the miller's ways, as well as his strength, they hurried on with trepidation. Diana was only glad for some exercise to counteract the dulling effects of a large dinner. And Edmund Montagu thought, as he followed Miss Longfellow's swinging skirts, of Tom Jones's preposterous inn at Upton—though he suspected this situation might prove to be far more dangerous. The scene they found in the kitchen did little to allay his fears.

Elizabeth stood facing the scowling Peter Lynch with a butter churn paddle, while several feet away, Mary wielded a wickedly sharp boning knife—not, Montagu noted with interest, in the usual way of women, but low and underhand, as one who had witnessed this sort of fight before. Trapped against a table near the far wall, Fortier could only watch. So far, he alone had been unable to find a weapon. The whole scene was lit by the glow from the long fire, where meat continued to roast on an unturned spit while its attendant, the cook's young daughter, cowered in the warming nook.

"I need no one else to tell me my business," Peter Lynch roared, shifting away from the two women and making for the Frenchman. Gabriel picked up a bench and held it like a shield before him. He had not been carrying a gun or a knife after all, thought Montagu, while he watched Longfellow walk bravely between the miller and his intended victim.

"Since you're careful of your own affairs, Peter," Longfellow soon suggested in a remarkably dry tone (considering the circumstances), "you might want to consider this: Captain Montagu represents the law; in fact, he has been sent on the king's business by Governor Bernard. Perhaps you know that the governor takes a dim view of the murder of his subjects, be they court or country . . . or even Frenchmen. He's also fond of taking their persecutors to court, because it gives him a chance to make someone's possessions his own. Or, let us say, the Commonwealth's. This sort of thing also helps keep many lawyers busy and well exercised, which in turn keeps them out of trouble—at least as much as can be expected.

"After considering the evidence, Captain Montagu sees no reason to charge Fortier with any crime. So you can see, Peter, that it would be in your interest to stop now, turn around . . . and leave."

"Leave her to lie with *this*?" the miller snarled, flinging an arm at the corner. "Why, for all I know he's already—"

Abruptly, a new thought struck Peter Lynch, causing

first a grimace, and then a grin. Slowly, he lowered his clenched fist, and soon a heavy chuckle could be heard coming from his straining, casklike chest.

As Lynch relaxed, Gabriel took the chance he'd been waiting for. With the scream of a panther, the smaller man raised the bench he held up into the air, rushed forward, and brought it down hard against the miller's head. The whole thing was done with such force that the two soon found themselves lying on the plank floor, in a tangle of limbs and boards.

At the same time, Mary bent and crawled closer, as if to better see what damaged had been done. But as she began to rise, Montagu came up behind her and clapped a hand onto her wrist. Then he took away the deadly knife. Her face in her hands, Mary fell forward and wept. Gabriel saw, and his face reflected her anguish. Peter Lynch looked, and grew a cruel, lopsided smile. Thrusting himself up and back onto bulging haunches, the miller rose to totter unsteadily on his thick boots, and finally broke into an ugly laugh.

"She's promised to me, innkeeper, as soon as you're done with her. And no brat of a boy is going to stand in my way! Let him follow me like a pup, and starve if he wants to. It won't change the way things are with you or me, or with Elias Frye, either. Her father's given me his word, and I intend to see he keeps it! Sooner or later, the girl will be mine."

Finished with his speech, he turned to go, but Charlotte Willett's clear voice surprised him into stopping. In fact, the ringing tones startled even her own ears.

"Remember, Peter Lynch, there's still a matter of bearing false witness against your neighbor."

"Why should any of us listen to a woman who hides criminals . . . especially one who's being sought by the whole village?" countered Peter. "We know you sheltered the Frenchman, and it won't soon be forgotten, I can promise you that! They burned his kind for witches, in years gone by. Remember, mistress, they hanged Quakers, too, in the town of Boston—and not so very long ago!"

"Friends," Charlotte corrected him without rancor, while Gabriel Fortier defended her in more bitter tones.

"She knew nothing! If you do more against this lady, or mine, I swear that I will come for you, Lynch, and then I will *kill* you!"

The hush that fell was brought to an end by the miller's drunken laugh.

"It could be that one of you, or all, might disappear first, one fine night. Poof!" Lynch exclaimed, exploding his bunched fingers in a startling gesture. And with another gale of scornful laughter, he slammed out of the kitchen and into the rainy night.

Mary rushed to shut and bolt the door. Then she flew to Gabriel's arms, while Elizabeth pulled her child from the hearthside and hugged her tight, for the little girl had begun to cry. Montagu laid down the narrow, horn-handled knife he'd taken from Mary. Everything was again moving toward harmony . . . at least for the moment.

The four guests had barely agreed to go back and finish their dinner, when they found their retreat blocked by a scurrying Lydia Pratt. Her eyes were bright, and her breath was short. Lydia looked all around; then, her glance rested questioningly on her husband. Jonathan calmly played down the recently concluded drama, as he thought how to approach a delicate subject.

"Lydia, my dear . . . I have offered to give Mr. Fortier a chance to do some work for us, in exchange for his keep and a little something more. It strikes me we could use another man about the place, for a while."

His wife seemed ready to argue. But quite suddenly

she drew up short. It appeared to some of the others that as she looked at Mary, she eyed the girl with something beyond her usual disdain. Lydia had never had any true cause to dislike her servant, as far as anyone knew. Still, her refusal to favor Mary in any way had been marked—until now. To her husband's pleasure, Lydia only nodded at his latest suggestion, keeping her lips tightly together. It was an unexpected triumph.

"I thank you," Gabriel said quite simply.

"Prove yourself useful then," Lydia finally responded grimly, leading Charlotte to wonder again at the woman's motives.

"I think I'll retire to make some small repairs," Diana decided, walking around the landlady. "Mary might be of help. Shall we withdraw upstairs, Mrs. Willett, while the gentlemen start their coffee and brandy?"

Charlotte agreed at once, and Mary followed them up to a small pair of rooms set aside for the immediate comforts of the inn's female guests. While Diana sat at a table and removed several items, including her new perfume, from her bag, Charlotte watched Mary pour water from pitcher to basin, then arrange two embroidered towels.

"It looks as though you, too, have triumphed over a dragon, like St. George," Charlotte suggested to the girl, once she decided they would not be overheard. But Mary's face looked back from the mirror with its usual solemn expression.

"I won't believe it. No matter how willing she seems."

"If Lydia really means to help you and Gabriel—"

Mary laughed briefly, and dabbed at her face with a dampened corner of her apron to remove the remains of her tears.

"You *must* know better!" she replied bleakly, looking away from the mirror. "She's only agreeing now because . . . because of something I know, although she's not sure I know it. Something best left unsaid, as long as I still have to live under the roof of a witch! It may be that something will come out, when I leave—or it may not," she considered, offering both women a smile that was at once mysterious, and a little sad.

"Well," said Diana, resetting a curl, "this is one of the most dramatic evenings I've had for months! I'd no idea life in the country could be so full of passion, and danger! What do you suppose will happen next?"

With one little finger, she rouged her lips from a tiny pot on the table in front of her, and then reapplied a dab of scent from the Oriental bottle.

"If it were up to me," she continued, "I'd choose something comic to end the evening, and send everyone home in high spirits. Although I'm not entirely disposed to laugh after such a large dinner, with these stays!" She stood and twisted her torso in several different directions, causing her hoops to brush against the vanity table. It teetered alarmingly, until she stepped away.

"Let's go back before the gentlemen forget we exist. I'm sure they've already begun to bore each other with their political views again," she concluded, waiting for Charlotte to finish a brief appraisal in the small mirror. After she had cleared the tabletop, Diana's rustling skirts led Mrs. Willett down the hall, while Mary stayed behind to tidy up the room.

Only when she was sure the two women had gone did Mary take a small enameled bottle from her pocket. For a moment, she looked at it with great curiosity, watching the way the dragon caught the candle's light, as she turned it round and round in her work-rough hands.

Chapter 17

I THOUGHT THE Court of St. James's less impressive than it might be," Longfellow said languidly to his new acquaintance, as they both sipped well deserved brandy, after their bold encounter. "One could wish it had more brain and culture attached to it, and a little less pomp and powder. It might be wise for the gentlemen of the upper classes to try breeding not for wealth, as they do now, but for brighter children—*that* would be progress."

They saw the ladies returning, and Longfellow rose to pour for them, as well. But the conversation continued much as it had gone on during their absence. Richard now waited for Captain Montagu to take the next shot.

"One can hardly disagree with your . . ." Montagu cleared his throat, wondering if a word existed to describe them. ". . . your *antic* observations. Of course, from your own dress and habits, sir, I'd already guessed that you might prefer the company of, how shall I put it? People who work with their hands? But then, you Americans have many origins, which allows you to choose your fashion from a very great diversity of tinkers and farmers."

"Ah, yes, we do enjoy the styles of many countries here, and many occupations."

Apparently, thought Charlotte, noting an absence of ill humor, their exertions together in the kitchen had begun to form a bond.

"That, to my mind," continued Longfellow, "is preferable to relying on the tastes and foibles of a crumbling elite in a moribund capital—although your Old World does have notable *architectural* remains. But as you've said, Captain, we have admirably simple tastes here. And our colonies are even more widely admired for having men of inventive minds, like Dr. Franklin, whom I imagine you've heard of by now. I expect that's also true of most countries of the Old World, however—in their *general* populations. I've been impressed by a great many things I've seen throughout Europe, both in science and the arts," he finished, pleased with himself for the fairness of his argument.

"Then perhaps you've also seen the way the Continental peasants struggle to survive outside the gilded capitals your wealthy young men tour and overpraise. Have you visited the less lovely sections of Paris? At least we English rarely starve *en masse*, the way they do now throughout France. Englishmen all enjoy certain rights, as Monsieur Fortier pointed out. Rights developed, I might add, solely by your English ancestors, and upheld by the government they alone created!"

"A greater pity, then, since you're so proud of them, that you don't extend all of these rights to Americans!

But we 'children,' I assure you, must soon grow larger and stronger than you or your ancestors . . . as children will, when given a superior diet. As the proprietor of a dairy, I'm sure Mrs. Willett agrees."

"Well, I—"

"I hope, at least, that we can *all* agree on the benefits of the British parlimentary system?" Montagu asked the table.

"Of course," Longfellow assented, "despite the fact that the body *you* elect is filled with men who would prefer neither to see nor to hear us, and who rarely do anything in our interest at all . . ."

"It's allowed you to enjoy what you call your 'liberty' this long! But it may be that you Americans should start a united Parliament of your own. Then you would know *real* trouble. And don't forget to include the ladies among your revolutionary representatives!"

Both men, along with the women, soon found themselves laughing together at the idea—although the Americans laughed less than their host, and for different reasons.

"Have you seen conditions across the Channel yourself?" asked Charlotte of the captain. Montagu became serious again.

"It's an increasingly hard life in France. While most struggle just to exist, a very few enjoy everything money can buy. I suspect that in a dozen years, the French will have problems at home which will keep them from fighting with us, or with you."

"I have read in the *Gazette*," said Diana with new energy, "that children in London can still be put into prison for debts, and hanged for stealing a loaf of bread— while royalty continues to think up new fashions and diversions."

"Ah yes, the *Gazette*," Montagu replied. He picked up the bill of fare and slowly fanned himself, rather than saying exactly what he thought of that newspaper, or any other touted as an honest, unbiased source.

"Yet here," he continued, gazing at Diana's clothing as he spoke, "many of your ordinary citizens choose to wear silk and lace, rather than less costly attire, even though they live far from any court. Wouldn't you agree with my earlier argument, Miss Longfellow, that people like these, able to pay more than a poor weaver or a plowman in England, should at least pay the Crown for *some* of the cost of their own protection, or be thought ungrateful . . . perhaps even disloyal? No one here is truly poor, after all."

That point, too, would soon have been debated, but for the reappearance of Jonathan Pratt.

"I'm sorry to interrupt—"

"'Jonathan, what's happened?" From the landlord's somber face, Mrs. Willett feared she already knew.

"What, indeed," he answered hesitantly. "Sam Dudley's been found. He seems to have drowned in the river, just to the north of the footbridge."

"The boy drowned?" Montagu inquired sharply. "How?"

"No one knows for certain. It could be that he slipped in the early darkness. Startled by a deer, perhaps—or simply lost his balance. It's likely he was stunned, he fell, and drowned in the shallows. At any rate, he was found in the marshland, and was taken home to his mother."

"Most unfortunate—I'm sorry for her. I presume a physician has been called to examine him," Montagu added, somewhat to Pratt's surprise.

"Oh, he's been dead for some hours, by all appearances. No need for a doctor. Anyway, there's none here in Bracebridge. When we have a serious need of one, we send word to Cambridge. If there's time."

"I'll go and have a look at the lad tomorrow, then, before I leave. Where is his house?"

Still somewhat mystified, the innkeeper gave him directions. Jonathan hadn't heard, Charlotte realized, all that they'd been discussing before, nor did he know of Montagu's warning of possible danger to come. She felt her emotions welling as her throat tightened, and she imagined the quiet body stretched and tended by his mother for the last time. Sam Dudley! She'd seen the boy for years, hurrying here and there. Sam Dudley, one of the youths she had seen, and heard as well, walking home on Tuesday night—

This final thought decided her. She would pay a visit to the Dudley farm in the morning. It would be a call of sympathy, and something more. But she would be sure to go early, before Captain Montagu arrived. At the moment, she had no desire to encounter any more of his disconcerting stares.

Richard Longfellow had risen while Mrs. Willett considered. Silently, he left the room after the innkeeper. In the hall he caught Jonathan's arm.

"Have you still got Timothy about the place?"

Timothy helped the hostler look after the horses, and sometimes did other jobs. Often, the boy ran errands, or took assignments from the inn's guests when they needed messages delivered. Tim was a devil in the saddle, especially for the right price.

"He's around somewhere," Pratt replied, trying to think where he had seen the young fellow last.

"Well, if he's not otherwise engaged, I'd like you to give him a letter."

Saying this, Longfellow took the landlord's candle, forcing Jonathan to follow him as he made his way to an alcove desk where he knew paper, ink, and quills were to be found. While Jonathan watched, Longfellow sat and quickly wrote out a note, folded the paper twice, put a name and a Boston address on the outside, and sealed it with a drip of wax.

"Where, by the way, is Nathan? He'd have been interested in what went on in the kitchen earlier."

"If he were here, I'm sure we would have heard from him."

"Out of town?"

"No, at the Blue Boar, I imagine. He's been there quite often lately."

"Has he?" Longfellow returned the candle, and leaned back while the landlord went in search of the boy.

Soon, at the approach of the alert Tim, Longfellow rose and gave him the letter and some copper coins, shook his hand solemnly, and then went back to rejoin the party with at least one new question in mind.

"I propose," said Edmund Montagu as Longfellow re-entered, "that each of us escort a lady home through the storm—for the wind is strong enough to blow either off to Providence. Rhode Island, of course," he added, winning at least one smile with the ancient joke that was still new to the Englishman. "Mrs. Willett," he concluded, "may I offer my arm?"

Charlotte was quick to catch the look in Diana's eye. She replied gracefully, but firmly. While she appreciated his offer, there were tiresome proprieties in village life, she told him, that had to be considered. Perhaps it would be better if Mr. Longfellow, a family friend and neighbor, were to escort her. As he and Diana were both residents of Boston, she continued, rather than Bracebridge, and thus probably considered to be odd already, they would have little to lose by going together. The captain might even escort Miss Longfellow home in an official capacity, while her brother was otherwise occupied.

Montagu smiled at the transparent refusal, but readily agreed. Before long, the four left the inn and passed through its outer gates with wavering lanterns, then turned to go their separate ways into the driving dark.

• • •

"I'M CERTAINLY GLAD," said Diana, once they were safe inside her brother's house, "that Richard keeps a good cellar, although he has a strange prejudice against tobacco. But I suspect you take no snuff. May I offer you a glass of something?"

Montagu watched her toss her cloak onto a stand in the large entry hall, and again heard the small bells over her chest rustle.

"Thank you, no. I believe I've already had enough tonight to unsettle my brain."

"Then a cup of Dutch chocolate, as only I can make it. Please, take off your cape. You won't leave me all alone? My brother is sure to be away for an hour or two. And an empty house is so dreary. Besides, there is something about which I'd like to ask a man's advice. I have been struggling to understand a poem," she continued, walking through a doorway.

This came as quite a surprise to Edmund Montagu. He'd hardly thought the colonials the sort of people likely to appreciate Milton, Pope, or even Gray. It was especially odd, he thought, to be asked for such advice by Diana Longfellow. Here was a lovely woman indeed—yet he wouldn't have guessed this particular female concerned herself with inner beauty, or spirit in general.

He followed her through a passage and into the kitchen where he stood, watching and recalling. When they had been together before, the talk had been of fashion, then intrigue, secrecy, and others things she appeared to find increasingly exciting. Since then, he had used her rather shamefully . . . even admitted it over dinner. Not that she hadn't deserved it, in return for subjecting him to her own flirtatious fictions. Now, she wanted to talk to him of poetry. Was it simply a ruse to get him to speak to her of love, for her own amusement— or even, possibly, for revenge? For all he knew, that brother of hers might be waiting for a chance to challenge him to a duel—probably with pitchforks, or even manure shovels.

Montagu had no way of knowing that Diana had taken care to ask Mary Frye earlier if the captain had brought any books with him. Had she noticed, while arranging his towels and tidying his room? A book of collected poems had been Mary's answer. No—Montagu only knew, as he followed Diana into the kitchen (and saw the enchanting way she looked about for materials and means to prepare him a cup of cocoa, leaning and reaching) that his own reserve was beginning to thaw beneath a shower of smiles, to the music of those maddening bells.

"Please, sit there in that comfortable chair by the hearth, while I just—"

He sat. Now that her curls and clothing had become disheveled by the wind, she had a look quite unlike that of the lady he had met only yesterday on the Boston road. This new unbending, even an unraveling, might lead to further surprises. Herrick had put it well, back when men and women were keenly aware of the truths of life under its various costumes.

> A sweet disorder in the dress
> Kindles in clothes a wantonness.
> A winning wave, deserving note,
> In the tempestuous petticoat,

He drew a breath as Diana, climbing a short kitchen ladder, kicked one foot into the air, and steadied herself—

> A careless shoestring, in whose tie
> I see a wild civility,

Hoops that hid a figure, he now realized, might lead to other possibilities as well. He averted his eyes as her skirts lifted, but soon looked back again.

Do more bewitch me than when art
Is too precise in every part.

Gad! Had the strange mood of the little town transformed *him* now, as well? When in London, or Boston,
for that matter, he found it easy to maintain his sense
of place and order. Under the eyes of men and women
besotted with themselves and their positions he, too,
could appear stylish and self-absorbed, and would be accepted. But in this place, he seemed to be held suspect
for the very manners that had earned him entry to the
best houses in Boston. And now, he was teased with
their opposite, by a lady of that town! Could she have
realized his secret—that he longed to enjoy life without
its many artifices—life that was good, simple, even po-
etic, thanks to the rural influence? How he would have
enjoyed seeing the lady before him in simple country attire! Yet even with this strong urge, he knew from experience that life was never *really* simple, not even in the
country . . . not even here.

Montagu wiped his brow carefully with a handkerchief, pretending that all he wiped away was a lingering
drop of rain. Thank heaven, he thought, he would be
leaving in the morning. He seemed to be under some
kind of spell—but was the bewitching agent Diana
Longfellow, or his own frustrated hopes? This might
prove to be, he warned himself, a very dangerous cup of
cocoa. He would have to be on guard.

"Fie, fie, fie, Captain Montagu," his companion gently chastened, turning around on a step with a tin of
dried fruits in her hand, "only watching me move about
this chilly room, when you might be down on your
knees, coaxing the embers of our fire. A warm country
kitchen, in rain and storm, is an appealing place to be—
even a desirable one on a night like this, don't you
think? Now, if you will rise and hand me down . . ."

• • •

LATER, SITTING IN his room at the inn, Edmund Montagu suspected he would have gone a great deal further, had not Cicero chosen that moment to enter through the kitchen door. Odd, he thought at the time, that the expression on the rain-slick face of this country servant should remind him of quite a different face—one he'd stared at somewhere else quite recently. Where had it been? Well, at least it had diverted his attention from Diana Longfellow!

Finally, as he lay in bed, he had it. Curiously, the unusual smile he remembered had been on a woman's face, in a small, dark oil he'd seen hanging in an enormous palace in Paris. It was a painting that had some indefinable magic about it. It had been painted by the old Italian . . . what was his name? Oh yes, he thought as he drifted off. Leonardo. Vaguely, he wondered if the man had known anything about poetry.

EARLIER, A LAMP across the way had moved from house to barn, as Lem left Charlotte's kitchen for the sweetness of his bed of new straw, next to warm and quiet bovine companions.

On their own, Charlotte and Richard Longfellow sat for another hour, watching the dying embers with Orpheus between them. The dog sighed while Longfellow curled and spread his fingers into the old fellow's silky coat, working out a cocklebur.

Longfellow, too, had been offered refreshment, and had settled on a cup of mint tea, hoping it would help his digestion. He'd watched carefully as his neighbor prepared it for him, admiring her straight form, her country woman's quickness, her efficiency of motion as she performed a familiar task. If only Diana had some of Mrs.

Willett's natural desire to please, framed in a domestic setting of her own, he thought with little hope.

"I wish we could think of something between us to improve Mary Frye's future," said Charlotte after she had poured out the tea. "I know it would be difficult to go against her father directly. But Richard, you're a well-respected man; if you could find something to tell him against Peter Lynch as a husband—"

"Would recent threats against another woman's life do?"

"I don't suppose we need to take much notice of that. After all, he hardly knew what he was saying."

"He knew well enough, since the same threat had just been made to him! Whatever way he has in mind to carry it out, *that* was a warning."

"But why? Lynch must know I have little influence with Mary. As for bringing up the coin—"

"Yes, now about that coin. As you so kindly pointed out, he could be blamed, even sued, for making false statements against Fortier, since he knew they *were* false. With lawyers as thick as hickory in the woods, our miller may yet find himself in a trap of his own making. Lynch has valuable property to lose, too, which seems to be a major attraction for the legal mind."

"And Mary? Do you believe she'll be safe now?"

"My guess would be she's safer than the miller. The Frenchman seems to have a grand passion, and a short fuse. It's a triangle of the oldest kind, and one that no one else should try to alter," he added, waggling a finger in her direction.

"Am I to take two warnings in one night?"

"You are. I know gossip is not your worst vice, but the desire to find things out for your own satisfaction is a thing I've seen you carry to extremes. In this case, it might be unsafe, as well as unwise."

Charlotte spread her fingers on her skirt, then

looked up with a toss of her hair which, Longfellow thought, looked surprisingly like honey in the firelight.

"Do you want to know what really piques my curiosity at the moment?" she asked him abruptly. "I'd like to know what's come over Lydia Pratt. Mary said that Lydia *had* to go along with Jonathan tonight, because of something the girl could tell us, if she chose to. Which she did not. I'd like to know what Mary uses to keep Lydia at bay. The girl sounded as if she might consider blackmail as a weapon—although the word is probably too strong."

"Blackmail, and Lydia Pratt the victim? That would be a satisfying twist. For someone who calls the tune as often as she does, a little enforced behavior is a delightful thing to contemplate. Ha! But what do you think this charge against Lydia could be? Is she keeping the profits of her geese from Jonathan? Great Heaven, she might be the leader of a local coven! She does have the face for it. She could even be the chief thinker of a criminal band ... highwaymen who hide their plunder in her linen chests. Which will it be?" he asked, rubbing his chin with enjoyment.

"Did you know," asked Charlotte solemnly, "that Lydia Pratt was the last person to speak with Duncan Middleton, and that she failed to mention it to anyone? She happened to have been overheard by your old friend Mr. Lee. At least, Diana overheard Jonathan telling Captain Montagu about it, and told me. So tonight, when the captain mentioned an accomplice—"

"You don't think that *Lydia*—?"

"What if Lydia knew Middleton before, and drew him here? After all, we've known her here in Bracebridge for barely three years."

Longfellow couldn't be sure what lay behind Charlotte's look, but he allowed himself a chortle, nonetheless.

"You take none of this too seriously either, I see," she finished with a small laugh.

"Some of it I do. And so should you," he warned again, getting slowly to his feet. "When I go, I'll check to make sure you've bolted the door behind me. And you might go to your study and watch my lantern—or Jonathan's, at any rate, which I'll take with me—until I'm safely through my own back door."

He gazed out at the thrashing rain. His eyes became vague, even grave, filling Charlotte with new apprehension.

"The miller made no threats toward you, Richard," she said, puzzled by the sudden change.

"No, he didn't. But then, it's not only the miller I'm worried about," he replied, just before he gave her a quick brotherly kiss, and disappeared into the swirling night.

Chapter 18

G OD'S WILL," SIGHED Rachel Dudley, indicating the body of her son. A mother came to accept that the Lord worked in mysterious ways, her early visitor concluded, and that heaven answered few questions. But exactly how the young man had got to heaven was a question that might still be answered on earth, Charlotte Willett reminded herself as she stood in the doorway.

Sam Dudley lay on his own bed in a room he had shared with his younger brother, Winthrop. Now, Winthrop could be seen through small glass panes, sitting by the woodpile and holding on to a fowling piece that had come into his possession only the day before. What had become of Sam's father, Charlotte could only guess—though John Dudley's jug today might be a welcome consolation, she thought with some sympathy.

Charlotte stepped forward to examined the motionless figure. Sam's chestnut hair had been carefully combed.

He was fully dressed, except that he wore no shoes. But his mother had covered most of the body with one of her quilts. A quilt in progress, on the stretching rack in the main room, was made of finer remnants; probably, it would be sold to pay for necessities, while Mrs. Dudley's own family made do with rougher work. Sam's loss would surely be felt as they continued the struggle to "get by."

"He was so stiff with cold, it took me till this morning to lay him out proper."

Somehow, she'd managed. Charlotte had half expected to see signs of a fight for life. But Sam looked as if his last day on earth had ended in peaceful sleep. The only odd thing to be seen was a scrape on his forehead. Had it been, after all, a simple misadventure, a misreading on the boy's part of some known danger? Or had it been something far less common, and far more horrible?

Charlotte reached to touch a beardless cheek. Then her fingers took the quilt away from the long neck. Now, she saw a small bruise at the front of the boy's throat. And the throat, she speculated uneasily, seemed not quite as round as it should have been.

Meanwhile, Rachel Dudley had taken up a beaded deerskin bag from the bedside table, to explore it with fingers tired from clutching. She spoke proudly, through trembling lips.

"This was a gift I made for him last Christmas, right after his father gave him the musket to hunt with. He told me he needed something to hold powder and shot. I made it as pretty as I could, and he always wore it under his shirt, right next to his heart."

Her voice caught, and she stopped to whisk away a new tear almost angrily. With a determined motion, she sat and took up the cold hand lying next to her. Then she pushed the bag into its limp, curled fingers. Only now did Charlotte notice that the little bag's knotted leather thong had been broken partway up its rawhide length. "I guess it caught on something when he fell . . ." the woman went on, seeing the question in Mrs. Willett's eyes. "I don't know if he tangled himself in some bushes in the dark, or just exactly . . . what. They found it lying not far away, next to his gun. Winthrop's got that now. I hope he'll be more careful. . . ."

Rachel Dudley suddenly shuddered, and she gave in to harsh, dry sobs. Charlotte's own thoughts were far from calm, but she hid them for the sake of the grieving woman whose arms she held, until they stopped shaking.

In a little while, Rachel took up the cold hand once again. Then, as the mother became absorbed in memories, Charlotte offered soft condolence, and left the room.

A little girl with pigtails like braided corn silk stood just outside the doorway. She politely escorted her guest through the large room that served as kitchen, storehouse, and living area. There was a small cot next to the fire. It must belong to her tiny guide, Charlotte decided.

"Would you take some cider?" the child asked, as she'd certainly heard her mother do. Charlotte sank onto a low stool by the hearth. She shook her head as she adjusted the young girl's homespun dress, which had lost one of its wooden buttons.

"Your name is Anne, isn't it?"

"Yes—"

"Have you had your breakfast?"

"I had some with Win. We had porridge and syrup. Are those your combs?"

Charlotte's eyebrows rose as she saw Anne looking at the top of her head.

"Yes, they are." She stopped, recalling the warm spring day when Aaron had brought them home.

"I guess they're made of real shell."

"From a very large tortoise, I should imagine," Charlotte agreed.

Anne drew in her breath to think of it. "My brother

Sam was going to get me a comb, when he went to Boston. That's what he told me."

There wasn't much to say in reply. Sympathy would mean only unwanted pity to a serious girl of six or seven. The child had simply stated a fact. But now, the full sadness of the lost promise seemed to strike Anne, as she looked wistfully past Charlotte to her brother's room.

"He told me he would, just like when he brought me back my ribbon." Reaching up, Anne fingered the ends of a grease-spotted grosgrain band she'd tied around her neck.

"A very pretty ribbon. Golden, like your hair," Charlotte said gently.

"Yes, but not as golden as *real* gold. A gold coin—"

The child suddenly gasped and dropped her eyes. In her open palm, she traced a circle the size of a small coin with the nail of a stubby finger, frowning. Then she sighed, and her eyes closed briefly with the effects of a night of fitful sleep, taken while others were weeping.

"Gold is pretty, isn't it?" Charlotte agreed quietly. "Have you seen very much of it?"

"The only time I *ever* saw it," said Anne, leaning closer, and lowering her already small voice, "was the gold Sam showed me. But he said I shouldn't tell. I've seen silver before. After the harvest last year we had some, for a while. I got to hold it. It shined, by the fire, and there were crowns on it, too. The gold was prettier, but Sam wouldn't let me hold it as long. He said it was a secret, after I spied on him and saw him pull it out," she confided.

"From his neck pouch?"

The girl nodded.

"Did Sam tell you where he got the coin?"

Anne shook her head and pulled on a braid. "But he said if I didn't tell, he would bring me a comb, the very next time he went to Boston. Like those." She let go of her hair to point again, then let her hand fall back to her side.

The combs—one of Aaron's gifts. One of many. Slowly, Charlotte reached up and pulled them from her hair, hoping that several pins would continue to hold most of it where it sat. She looked at the combs seriously for a moment, and then handed them to young Anne, whose fingers were already outstretched near eyes wide with disbelief.

"I think these are just like the ones Sam would have brought you from Boston. But promise, if you take them, that the gold coin you saw will still be a secret, until I tell you otherwise. Will you promise?"

Anne bobbed her head vigorously.

"Good. Now I have to go . . . but you'll have more visitors before very long—"

"Thank you!"

"You're welcome . . . and you're to tell Mr. Long-fellow, when you see him, that you're very fond of crowns, especially on silver. He'll enjoy speaking with a little girl about coins, I think—and then you might have a piece of Spanish money to look at, at least for a little while. But you mustn't tell *anyone* about the other coin—remember!"

"Sam says a lady wouldn't want to talk about money, anyway. Sam says I'll be a lady someday, too." The child watched with a look of hope, lost in a world of imagining.

"With combs to spare," Charlotte soon answered from the doorway, as she sent a farewell glance past the happy little girl, to the boy and his silent mother in the room beyond.

ALTHOUGH RAINDROPS STILL wept from the black limbs of the trees, gusts no longer rattled the thinned woodland borders as Charlotte walked home. The storm appeared to be over. She paused along the way to admire rainbow prisms within a thinning tangle of blackberry vines, while the gray clouds above made way for patches of blue, high and to the west. It was a day, as well as a season, for abrupt changes.

She left the Concord road and followed a path to a narrow wooden footbridge, crossed the river, and walked through field grass toward her own pasture. She was glad to have escaped meeting anyone when she hurried away. It was only when the path began to climb that she turned and saw three figures walking north along the main road she had just come from, making their way toward the Dudley home.

Charlotte squinted into the distance, trying to assist her imperfect eyes. One of the men she knew by height and gait to be Richard Longfellow. A second, with wig and winking gold buttons, was Edmund Montagu. The last, pumping behind the others, was Constable Bowers. It would be his duty to go along and examine the facts surrounding any surprising death. Not that she believed he would be likely to actually look for any problems— unless someone forced him to.

After the three men disappeared through the door that opened for them, Charlotte turned and resumed her lonely walk. In another moment, she had to brush back her hair as it began to fall down in front of her eyes in wisps and strands, then locks—and finally, in something like a cascade. She was taken aback to be so far from comb and mirror, but was amply compensated by the memory of Anne Dudley's delighted face, and her small, open hands.

But this was no time for pleasant thoughts. Instead, she forced herself to concentrate on questions of a darker nature—of exactly what was so, and why. It had first seemed possible that Sam Dudley, out alone in that dark morning of cold and wind, had stumbled and fallen. Had his brain been stunned by a quick meeting with a rock, death could have come even in those shallow waters. Charlotte wondered if she should have examined the scalp under the thick hair more closely. But it hadn't seemed necessary, especially after she had seen the throat. Most would have said it was not her place to pry any further. After all, others would soon see what she had noticed. But the mention of gold again—that was a question almost heaven-sent, for her alone to consider.

Small Anne had described a highly unusual object, something rarely seen at the Dudleys', or in any other house in Bracebridge. Assuming it was another Dutch gulden, wouldn't logic dictate that it most likely came from the same source? Jonathan had received one coin, and was waiting to give it to Reverend Rowe. Bowers now had another, the one she supposed Jack Pennywort picked up on the Boston-Worcester road, and later gave to Peter Lynch—the same coin Lynch had pretended to pick up in Fortier's room at the Blue Boar. Lynch turned the coin over to Bowers yesterday afternoon—but it was yesterday *morning* that Sam Dudley had apparently died.

She felt as if a chill tide were rising around her. Couldn't the coin she believed came from Jack—the one Peter Lynch claimed was dropped by Gabriel Fortier—as easily have been taken from Sam's body? But if that was true, how had Sam come by it originally? Had it been given to him by Duncan Middleton? If Sam had come upon the merchant sometime after he had "gone up in flames"—

It was barely possible. But—what if the miller had taken the coin from the boy, knowing Sam had it because *he* had given it to him, some time after he'd received it himself from Middleton, who then left the village? Her mind swiftly made a further leap. Could Peter Lynch have been the reason Duncan Middleton came to Bracebridge in the first place? Edmund Montagu had already explained Middleton's scheme to sell tainted rum. Wouldn't the miller, who made frequent trips to Worcester and beyond, make a useful accomplice? Maybe the old man carried his gold to Bracebridge to pay for stores, as well as the miller's future service. If so, Peter would have been the one who found the merchant a horse on which he might quietly leave the village. But why would Middleton want to make such a spectacle of himself, and disappear so *obviously* in the first place? That was still a question she couldn't answer.

And just how far would Peter Lynch have gone to keep up the pretense of the merchant's death, if Sam had stumbled onto the truth? Worse yet, the miller could have *truly* killed Middleton, to remove the merchant from the scheme Peter planned to carry on himself. What if *that* was what Sam had realized? Peter Lynch might have given one of the coins to Sam for his silence . . . knowing he could reclaim it soon—and end the boy's life in the process!

She fought against the whirl of her thoughts, determined to calm her mind and methodically examine its quick conclusions. So far, these were all mere suspicions, without solid foundation. And surely, not all the gold in the world belonged to Duncan Middleton! What if Sam had gotten the coin somewhere else, and been envied by a friend who clumsily tried to take it from him? Or, he might actually have stumbled and fallen by accident, as his mother believed.

One never knew what fate held in store. That's why, thought Charlotte as she continued on her way, all days had to be cherished, like precious jewels. Or gold coins—Dutch guldens that could mesmerize and enthrall even a small girl, let alone a hardened, twisted soul full of jealousy and greed, and capable of the worst crime imaginable!

It was an awful thing to ponder. To accuse the miller would be a most difficult thing. Yet her conscience told her that men and women were not put on earth only to enjoy goodness and innocence, nor should they refuse to see or hear the evil around them. And so she continued to screw her eyes into a fierce squint. But they were focused on the muddy ground now, rather than on higher things. And they saw very little that was uplifting along the winding trail that guided her feet.

SO DEEP WERE her thoughts that Charlotte barely heard the first quick calls of a familiar voice, as it began to peal through the open air. Her concentration was finally shattered when she recognized it as the sound of the brass bell that hung over the meetinghouse. On the Sabbath, it rang out in a joyful manner. Occasionally, as on the evening before, it tolled more ponderously to announce the death of one who had belonged to the community. But now it rang with a clamoring that was nearer to its third purpose, that of summoning folk to a fire. Yet she could see no smoke coming from the village houses. Certainly no flames threatened from the wet forest, or the thoroughly dampened fields.

Still, someone rang the church bell with a great deal of determined energy. From both sides of the river, she saw people hurrying toward the meetinghouse at the edge of the Common, some arriving with buckets and tools in hand, others with their skirts and aprons and petticoats lifted out of the new mud as they looked around in puzzlement and alarm. Charlotte, too, hurried over the hillside's slippery grass and down onto the Boston road. But before she could reach the meetinghouse, she saw several of the same people who had just gone in come back out again. Leading them was the unmistakable figure of Reverend Christian Rowe. So he was back! Apparently, the preacher had summoned them all with the now-silent bell to his (and God's) house.

And then the reverend began to run, leading his flock with an animated face framed by flashing white collar ends. His black coattails flew out behind him like witches' weeds, while his white-stockinged legs twisted and bent like a spider's, as he attempted to look around and move ahead at the same time. Where could they all be going? Charlotte saw the crowd cross the stone bridge over the river. There wasn't much of anything on the other side, except for the tavern . . . and the grist mill!

Sure enough, they turned south on the road to Framingham. But instead of heading for the mill's wide doors, her neighbors turned off and went around to one side, back to the millpond. And there they stopped, flapping and buzzing like a disturbed hive with something decidedly ominous in mind.

Chapter 19

EVERYONE IN THE village knew the still reaches of the millpond that took its water from the river. Overhanging branches were reflected on its black face, ringed with pickerelweed, arrowhead, and water lilies. It was a fine spot to spend an hour in meditation, or to walk with a valued companion, or even to throw stones at the flat surface of the water in the hopes of rousing a frog. It was a sheltered, peaceful place loved by many—even by the Reverend Rowe, who might be seen following its encircling path while he searched for inspiration.

Perhaps that was what he'd been doing this morning, thought Charlotte as she caught up with the rest near the water's edge. He might have been trying to shed the taint of Boston in this quiet haven. Had the reverend received a startling message from above, or been given divine commands, like Moses?

What the Reverend Rowe had to show for his early

morning walk was something far more down-to-earth, Mrs. Willett realized when she joined the gasping crowd. At its head, deep voices and weed-draped arms had joined to negotiate the removal of a sagging, dripping body.

There was little question how the miller had met his death. Peter Lynch's face and forehead were horribly cleft in a gaping line that ran for nearly five inches, light pink and clean, its edges resembling the flesh of a large pike ready for the pan. Behind this peeped something else that would also be familiar to a frugal cook—something convoluted and gray.

All in all, it was a terrible sight. If the wound had not been so fascinating, thought Charlotte, who was by now encircled and supported by the crowd as it swayed collectively—if it had looked less awful, it would have been impossible not to gaze first and overlong at Peter Lynch's eyes. For they, too, were ghastly—open, staring, bulging from white sockets. The eyes were surrounded by puffy folds of skin, some of which showed what looked like a reddish rash. Other parts had already helped to sustain the pond fish.

There was nothing to be done for Peter Lynch, except to lift him. As the corpse came up, a rush of dark water dropped onto the shoulders of several men, who turned their faces away. Then, getting firmer grips, they began to convey Peter toward the meetinghouse, where he would be lowered directly onto the coffin boards, to wait until a box could be made. These boards had held many other corpses in their day, in a dim alcove just off the unheated building's entrance. But the miller would no longer care about the cold.

Clutching her cloak for warmth, Mrs. Willett was very glad to have more air and room as the throng spread out and moved away, following the body. Up to this point, most talk had been in the form of short and sharp reactions, or brief, necessary orders. There had been only one or two simple questions. (What there had been none of, she noticed, were tears for the miller.)

But by now, numbed minds were beginning to function again. Charlotte watched with quiet concentration, reflecting on many of her own recent thoughts, while voices rose up around her. It seemed to her that the crowd had begun to steam and swell, like a pie without a vent.

"How could it happen?" one of the village women asked her husband, who gave no immediately answer. "How could a man as big as a tree be hit in the head like that? There's no one *here* large enough to do it—not that I can see!"

"I'll bet he was robbed, too," threw in Phineas Wise, speaking his own worst fears.

Dick Craft, too, found his voice, which showed less sympathy than one might have imagined. Yet he, too, seemed puzzled.

"The miller was no ordinary man to be fooled, as we all know. He'd fight, by God—unless whatever came after him had more than mortal strength . . ."

"Oh, come," began another, soon stopped by a chorus demanding that he and all the rest let the man speak.

"First, a rich old buzzard disappears," Dick went on. "Then a young boy dies, and now a man in his prime is clearly *murdered*. I say, it looks like someone trying out his powers, until he's sure of 'em. Someone who doesn't belong here, and doesn't care *what* in hell happens to the rest of us! It looks to me as though the Frenchman came to Bracebridge to practice his evil arts, until he got good enough to overcome his rival, Peter Lynch, face to face!"

"With black magic!" and "Witchcraft!" joined in several voices at once, to a furious wagging of heads.

"The French themselves are extremely nervous on that subject," began Tinder from the Blue Boar, and Flint immediately began to reflect on witchcraft in the Pyrenees, which he had visited in his youth.

"Done with his own hatchet," called a voice panting behind them a minute later. "The one Peter kept buried in a post, inside by the big stone. It isn't there now. But there's blood there! Dripped onto the floor!"

"Most likely the hatchet's in the pond," someone else ventured, to more nods and shouts.

The Reverend Christian Rowe watched the growth of discontent and fear with lofty pleasure, holding high his head with its astounding halo of flaxen hair, waiting for the right moment to take command. Before long, it came.

"I tell you," began the Reverend Rowe severely, causing some to stop dead in their tracks. Unfortunately, the preacher continued to walk, and so they had to hurry after him again.

"I tell you something foul has been happening here in my absence, but now I mean to get to the bottom of it! Certain members of our church came to me late last night to talk of these matters, and to ask me to set things right. And that is what I intend to do! I have also heard there are those from Boston who've come to our village to give us their opinions—with no good result. I tell you it is time for the people of Bracebridge to take their own business in hand, and root out the cause of their own trouble!"

Strong approval from every side greeted this idea, but again the reverend held up his hand, and this time he *did* stop walking. The few behind him who thought they had learned their lesson kept on until they bumped into the men carrying the miller's corpse, which added a few new snarls to the general confusion.

"What news is there of the whereabouts of this Frenchman?" Rowe called out. "Who is sheltering him?"

Several voices spoke up at once, but one rang above the rest.

"He's gone over to the inn! Peter came and told us so, back at the Blue Boar last night. Jonathan Pratt offered Fortier work—and this even after the Frenchman threatened to kill the miller!"

"Threatened to *kill* him?" Rowe repeated, glaring from left to right.

"He's not the only one who's made threats against him, either!" came a rejoinder.

"That's right! Peter told Mistress Willett he knew she'd hidden the Frenchman on her farm, when we were looking for him—"

"He did! And she accused him of terrible things—"

"Mrs. Willett!" Rowe's voice thundered. Then it turned to honey, as he spied her in the crowd. "Mrs. Willett . . . *why* have you given refuge to this unwelcome stranger in our midst?"

"It's true he told me he'd slept in my dairy," Charlotte began, speaking loudly enough to be heard by the reverend across several heads. "But I know him to be innocent of anything to do with the first—"

"Innocent! And how is that for *you* to say? I would have thought you would have plenty to do just now, madam, without the help of a man on your large farm, without even a man to protect and instruct you, and with harvest time upon us. And yet, you come here and tell us that a fugitive whom we all seek is *innocent?*"

"Reverend Rowe, there are things known only to Captain Montagu which—"

"Ah, Captain Montagu! The man sent here to assure our safety. The man whose presence has done nothing to prevent one certain murder, and possibly even two!"

A worried rumble rose around the preacher as the others considered his bold statement. An official from

Boston was, after all, a voice of authority, and one to be heeded rather than annoyed, if such a thing were possible. But could the death of the miller, and that of Sam Dudley, now somehow fit together? And *would* Montagu do anything about either of them?

"Mrs. Willett," Rowe added, his voice softly menacing again, "how is it that your hair has fallen down in a most unusual manner? Could it be that you've had no time to put it up after some recent . . . *rendezvous*? It would be well for you to remember that what's often overlooked in Philadelphia, or in Boston, will not be tolerated here! Go home, and look to your own person, and to your own business!"

This barb met with derisive laughter that caused Charlotte's cheeks to flame—though little enough of it was meant for her. More than a few of the men and women present thought Rowe had gone too far in his personal attack on a neighbor. Phineas Wise, for one, disagreed with Rowe. After all, he asked several of those around him, weren't the Quakers plainer folk than most of those now living in Massachuetts? And didn't Charlotte Willett take pains to follow many of their ways? Hardly a brazen woman, she—though certainly comely, one might admit. Even so, he couldn't remember there being any scandalous talk about Mrs. Willett's virtue before. (At least, nothing that she could be blamed for.) And as for adequately running her brother's farm, well, what was wrong with that?

"An interfering woman has hidden the source of our contamination, and led to murder," shouted Dick Craft, using a biblical turn of phrase that astounded more than one person in the crowd. "Let's go and search her farm, to see what else someone might have hidden there. Maybe that's where the gold is!"

For a moment, the crowd held its breath, and considered.

"First," Reverend Rowe jumped in, "we'll go to the inn and find this Frenchman." It seemed to Charlotte now that even Rowe wondered if he had overstepped his bounds, at least in the case of her appearance.

"I doubt if he'd dare to stay there if he did kill Peter Lynch," spoke up Mrs. Hiram Bowers. A few other women agreed that this was only sensible, including Esther Pennywort, who still scanned the crowd from time to time, looking for her husband.

"We will divide ourselves, for speed," instructed Rowe, "into two groups. I will lead the first to the inn, where we will inquire of this Captain Montagu what he knows, and where the Frenchman might be. The second group will escort Mrs. Willett to her farm—for her own safety—will look for the same Frenchman, and do whatever else must be done. Let us be quick and let us be quiet, lest the guilty be warned."

By this time, they had reached the meetinghouse doors. Those who carried Peter Lynch made their way inside, where the unwieldy body of the miller was deposited with little ceremony into the alcove, and the damp men who'd carried him tromped out again into the chilly morning air.

"What about Bowers?" one of them inquired, and the rest hesitated, although many were on their toes to go.

"Where is the constable now?" Rowe asked, looking around.

"Gone off somewhere this morning," his wife announced. "With Mr. Longfellow, he told me."

"I believe Mr. Longfellow—" began Charlotte, until one of the surly men clasped his hand firmly onto her arm.

"Yes, Mrs. Willett?" asked the reverend, as he would have asked a tiresome child what it wanted.

"Nothing," she replied, and left it to them to find out for themselves.

"We may not have had a body before, but we've got

a body now, by God—and a murderer to catch," thundered a tall man in the back, who beckoned to the rest. "Let's go and find him!"

At that, the crowd started out, scuttling on its way like a centipede, one undulating segment carrying along a captive woman with flying, cider-colored hair.

HANNAH SLOAN LOOKED up as she heard shouting. Before she could rid her hands of laundry water and cover a wooden tub with its lid, two men who held Mrs. Willett between them entered the low kitchen—only to find that the odds were now about even. Hannah's stern countenance, and her firm-footed stance, told them that they should advance no farther—at least for the moment.

"We've come to find Fortier," one of them said, causing Hannah to look at him closely.

"Here? There's no one here! And what do you mean, holding onto Mrs. Willett that way?"

"We've escorted her home, where she ought to be."

"I happen to know she's been out this morning offering her assistance to Mrs. Dudley. I doubt you can say as much good for yourself, Ephram Dawes. What was the bell for? And why are these men—" Hannah stared in disbelief out the window. ". . . stealing Mrs. Willett's chickens?"

"They're searching the farm, although I guess it's not going to do much good. I came here, Hannah, to keep this lady from harm. There are some who think she deserves a lesson, after what they heard in the Blue Boar last night from Peter Lynch—"

"Who is dead," Charlotte interrupted, staring hard at Hannah.

"Murdered, you mean," the large woman answered sharply.

"And just how would you know that?" Ephram

asked, suddenly suspicious. "We only found him a few minutes ago!"

"A lucky guess. Now, run upstairs, open all the doors, look where a man might hide, and then leave this house, or I swear I'll carry you both out myself. It's a child's game you're playing, and no mistake."

Shaking her head grimly, Hannah set about starting a pot of tea, while Charlotte gazed at Ephram, seeming to ask if he needed any further instruction. He did not.

The two men went into the next room and through the house quickly, then left by the kitchen door with something like an apology offered in passing.

"I think," said Charlotte, removing the last of her pins, "that they may have difficulty finding what they're looking for."

"Was Peter Lynch really killed?" asked Hannah Sloan, sitting down. Charlotte nodded thoughtfully, holding on to a twist of her hair.

"And I don't believe he's the first, either. What I have to wonder now," she added, staring at her friend, "is whether he'll be the last."

Chapter 20

THE THREE MEN visiting the Dudley farm had also heard the ringing of the bell, but had continued their examination until they were satisfied. Leaving young Sam's corpse and returning to the open air, they glimpsed a crowd in the distance. It seemed to be gathered around the meetinghouse. As the trio hurried forward, they saw it move off, heading up the hill on the Boston road.

Soon, the main body turned toward the inn, while others continued on to Mrs. Willett's gate. Longfellow felt a familiar disquiet. Taking long strides across the bridge, he wondered what Charlotte had done this time. First, she had married a Quaker. Now, she lived without a husband, or a relative of any kind. And recently, she had pulled the miller's beard. The woman didn't exactly encourage trouble, but it seemed to court her—as he wished a man of substance might do, and soon. Had the miller now come for his revenge, leading a mob?

Longfellow looked back at the thickset public servant who rolled along like a galleon behind him, fully aware of the man's limitations, as well as those of his temporary position. He knew well it was not a constable who kept order and peace, but the will of the people. And this was a will Richard Longfellow trusted only so far.

Beside him, Captain Edmund Montagu thought once more of what he had seen of Sam Dudley. Without a physician, there was no way to be absolutely sure. But Longfellow had said he'd already sent for one of the best, and that he should be arriving soon. The man would confirm what they both suspected. The bruising had been slight, but the coincidence was great—far too great to ignore. It was more than likely, thought Montagu, that the boy's death had not been an innocent one. And he decided to postpone his departure for one more day.

The sluggish mind of Hiram Bowers was also mulling over the possibilities suggested by the body, the alarm, and the crowd that had just turned toward the inn—but why were some of them advancing to Jeremy Howard's property, up and across the way? The townspeople were on edge—the constable knew that only too well! Many of them even expected *him* to set their minds at ease. If only they would learn to settle their own fears, as he so often had to do with his own. Now, something seemed to have irritated them again. Hiram thought that he would be glad when the end of the year rolled around, and he could go back to selling buttons. Now, what was it someone had said the other day about Mrs. Willett? Ah, yes. It seemed Jack Pennywort—the last one to see the merchant Middleton alive—had paid a visit to Mrs. Willett yesterday, supposedly to do some work, which he avoided in the end. Phineas Wise said he'd come back for another pint, just half an hour after he'd left in the first place. But Jack would not discuss his visit with the lady, and that in itself was very strange . . . not even after he'd been brought two free tankards. Jack had even gone home early. Very queer indeed! Well looking on the bright side, maybe the crowd that now entered the inn had found something to celebrate. It was possible. Anything could happen, and often did. Maybe the others had gone to invite Mrs. Willett to join them. In his usual fog, Hiram Bowers marched on, looking forward to enjoying a pint with the rest.

When they reached the inn's gate, Montagu and the constable plunged into the crowd, while Longfellow continued on. He soon found the search of Charlotte's outbuildings nearly concluded, and the two women inside idly drinking tea. As long as they were safe, they urged him, might he not do better to see what else was going to happen? After taking a moment to catch his breath and have a swallow of hot tea, Longfellow, too, made for the Bracebridge Inn.

Sadly, he was too late to witness the lengthy initial confrontation between the Reverend Rowe and Edmund Montagu—one an acknowledged pillar of godliness, the other a jealous protector of the Crown's prerogatives. But the latter was only one official protector, in the face of many curious souls. And so, Montagu followed a flustered Jonathan Pratt through a search of the inn's first floor, while the landlord, in turn, trailed a group led by the reverend. Finding nothing, they next prepared to explore the rooms above.

It was now suggested that the inn also housed one other stranger who had been in Bracebridge for several days, and for no good reason—unless one believed the absurd idea that he observed the ways of animals, and was paid to reveal them. This man was also known to have been out of doors at all hours, able to see, and hear, and possibly do evil. This stranger was Adolphus Lee. By the time the reverend and his followers mounted the stairs to the second floor, they were buoyed by the remainder of the crowd that had returned from Charlotte's farm, and those who had completed an unsuccessful search of Jonathan Pratt's outbuildings. Still notably absent were three members of the inn's own family. There was no sign, Montagu realized as he looked around, of the servant girl Mary Frye. Nathan, the smith, was missing as well—so, too, was the landlord's wife.

Jonathan Pratt also wondered why his wife had not come forward at the beginning of the commotion. It was unlike Lydia to let anything take its natural course, if she could hope to direct it and perhaps even hand out blame. Climbing the steps, he heard those ahead corner a bewildered Tim (who had gone up for a better view of what was coming), and demand to know Adolphus Lee's whereabouts. The boy pointed to a door that stood next to the Jamaica Room, behind which the man usually slept for much of the day. A knock produced no result. A path was cleared for the landlord, who by right might open.

But . . . something stood in the way. Apparently, a chest of drawers had been pulled across to slow, perhaps, an unwanted entrance. But enter the stout landlord did, with a push and a shove, until light flooded out to the dark hallway, forcing the visitors to blink—against their will, for none of them wanted to miss a thing.

Inside, as expected, was Adolphus Lee. He sat upon a rumpled bed, wearing only his breeches, his face contorted in a look of fascinated horror. At the same time, through the crack at the door's hinges, frills of a shift could be seen. And although the woman who wore it could not be observed in her entirety, those who noticed suspected they saw a portion of Lydia Pratt within. *Whoever* the woman was, there was no doubt that, as Jonathan Pratt's searching eyes peered around the door, she emitted a squeak.

Meanwhile, caught in a trap with no easy exit, Mr.

Lee looked longingly through the window, as if hoping for some assistance from the natural world.

The hushed crowd shifted its feet uncertainly. Finally, Jonathan Pratt cleared his throat to address his neighbors.

"Seeing that you have not found what it is you are searching for, I hope you will finish with the empty rooms, and then leave my house. It would appear that my guest and I have certain matters to look into." With this, he gently closed the door on the room's occupants.

Even the Reverend Rowe, hearing whispers around him, believed that some things were sacred to marriage— at least, in the first round. He had hardly been prepared for what he'd discovered. Pratt, after all, was one of the largest and most regular contributors to the church, a man who saw to many of its needs; in fact, he'd just sent over that rare and valuable coin the night before. The reverend quickly decided that he had an entire flock to consider first, however much one erring member might have earned his, and the Lord's, wrath. Besides, he had always greatly admired Lydia Pratt himself, feeling that she was something of a kindred spirit. Later, they would talk, and he would show her a better way.

Already envisioning the encounter, Reverend Christian Rowe licked his lips, as he silently led the others in a quick peek at the remaining rooms. Then, they went down the steps and out through the inn's side door.

Watching them go, Jonathan Pratt stood whistling quietly, his cheeks playing with the beginnings of a satisfied smile.

"LIKE SOME BUFFOONERY from a recent novel," was the way Longfellow described the scene later in the afternoon to Charlotte and Hannah Sloan, after he had knocked some of the season's first snow from his coat and planted himself by the fire. Next to him, Lem (who had hurried in the cows earlier) grinned at what he heard, and decided in future to ask Mr. Longfellow for suggested reading material.

"Finding Lee with . . . a lady . . . restored part of the town's good humor, and certainly gave them something to talk about—as well as yet another excuse to adjourn to the Blue Boar."

"Let's hope they stay there for a while," said Hannah, vowing to herself to find more for her own menfolk to do.

Charlotte remained silent as a further revelation came to her. So *that* was what Mary Frye had meant! The maid had probably caught Lydia before, hearing her say she had been one place, when Mary knew the landlady had really been in another. At a small inn, secrets of that sort could only be kept for so long.

"'Diana will be pleased when I tell her," Longfellow added, "though it will make her wish she hadn't slept so late. My sister has wished Lydia gone more than once. And now I suppose she'll have her way. As usual."

"She won't be the only one who's pleased," agreed Hannah.

"They tell me," Longfellow went on, "that Lee's moved over to the Blue Boar until he can finish his work."

"He's staying?" Charlotte asked with surprise.

"Since he's already produced letters from respected men at Cambridge, the village can't very well throw him out for this—at least not without Jonathan's help, which he doesn't seem anxious to give. So, since Jonathan is one of our own selectmen, and I happen to be another, there's not much anyone can do about Adolphus Lee. The situation certainly shows us how times have changed. I doubt if we could have kept poor Lydia out of the stocks several years ago. If anyone had wanted to."

"How is Jonathan?"

"Quite happy, I should say. When the rest left without speaking—general embarrassment was quite plain, and after all, Jonathan hadn't said the first word against her—then I wondered if he might not enjoy having the upper hand, for once. As for Lee, he's a sort of hero now, having deprived the local dragon of her fire!"

At least, thought Charlotte, some steam had escaped from the pie before any further harm had been done.

"But they didn't find . . . anyone else they were looking for?" she asked.

"Who, Lynch's murderer? They didn't find Gabriel Fortier, if that's who you mean. At first, they thought at the inn that Mary had run off with him. But she came back a while later, with her apron full of butternuts she'd been off gathering before the snow started. She says she only saw Fortier in the morning—said Nathan woke him up early, and set him to work mending an ax in the back. Where the Frenchman is now, I couldn't say."

Charlotte again saw the long, bloodless wound in the miller's forehead.

"An ax?" she whispered.

"Many hours *after* the work you're thinking of, from what you've described to me of the body, which, incidentally, I greatly look forward to seeing. I might even try an experiment or two . . . but I believe the miller must have been floating for most of the night—probably since late last evening, I would guess."

"Then—"

"It would seem Gabriel Fortier escaped today from what must have looked to him like a mob coming for his blood. Whether he's guilty of anything or not, he had reason enough to run."

"Then you don't think—"

"I think Mary Frye is far better off today than she

was last night. Beyond that, I have several *other* things to think about, at the moment."

"Richard, I only know a little about anatomy . . . some of medicines, I'll admit, but very little about the rest. It did strike me when I saw Sam Dudley this morning that a physician—"

"—might tell us how, exactly, he died. An excellent idea! Given the circumstances, I thought as much last night, so I sent for a fellow named Warren I met in town a few months ago. I've been meaning to invite him here. I think you'll like Joseph. He speaks his mind, and he listens, too, from time to time. One of the most promising of the recent graduates of Harvard College."

"Oh! I look forward to meeting him."

"You might do a little more, Carlotta, since he's coming all the way from Boston, and he'll be here this morning. As you know, the inn's kitchen is upside down at the moment."

"And yours hasn't held much appeal for anyone lately."

"Well—yes. I'd hoped you'd allow us to share a little something at your generous fireside. Nothing fancy."

"If I'm ever at a loss for funds, I might make ends meet by opening a public house. I imagine you'd steer quite a healthy business my way."

"A privilege I would offer *only* to those who meet your high standards of behavior and taste."

"You're lucky I've heard, too, that Dr. Warren is a handsome man who has a delightful beside manner. Have you heard that as well?"

"Not from any Tories, certainly; he's most noted in town for his republican manner, above anything else."

"Are you trying to frighten me?"

"Would it be possible?"

"Quite! Still, none of us should cast the first stone, I suppose. I've heard we are all by nature political animals;

although I'm not sure the man who said so meant to include females."

"Would that be a quotation from Dr. Franklin?" asked Lem, who had been following only some of the conversation.

"Aristotle," replied Longfellow. "An older gentleman, and not quite as popular. Although he had his day. Look in Mrs. Willett's library, and we'll discuss him later."

A new noise at the front door made Charlotte rise with a hand to her cheek. But it was only Cicero, who brought in Joseph Warren before retiring across the garden.

LONGFELLOW ROSE FROM the table, and immediately went to clasp Warren's hand and shoulder, aware that Charlotte had already begun to examine the visitor for herself.

"I also have it on good authority that most of his teeth are his own," her neighbor offered with a grin.

Warren quickly caught his meaning, and turned to scrutinize his hostess boldly, causing her to look away from his sky-blue eyes.

The physician was, she had already decided, a very pleasing man, exceptionally fair but with a kind of glow. His face could probably hide little. She could imagine that he was as she'd heard—a man who would fly to action whenever the call came, wherever he felt he was in the right. It was said he had an argumentative nature. Still, he would probably prove a rewarding friend.

"I believe our hostess is satisfied," said Longfellow. "But now, we have to go. We'll be back shortly. Bodies, if you'll excuse my mentioning it, may not be preferable to dinner, but they claim precedence—and now we have two."

"Two?" asked Warren, turning. "Your note said only that a young man—"

"Oh, that was last night! This morning, we found another. However, let me show you, before I spoil the surprise. By the way, Mrs. Willett has invited us back here to dine."

"I'll see what can be done," Charlotte answered, looking to Hannah.

"Our thanks, Carlotta. Say, Warren," asked Longfellow, in the highest of spirits, "could we use more company, do you think?"

"From what I hear of these parts lately, we would be wise to seek a crowd."

"You may change your mind about that, when I tell you the rest," rejoined Longfellow, "but one more man wouldn't hurt. *Avanti!*" he cried, stalking out of the kitchen door after Warren. At the same time, he beckoned to a startled Lem, who followed in a rush.

Chapter 21

SOME TIME BEFORE, Mary Frye had been given an order to see to things downstairs—just before Lydia Pratt went up to the second floor, leaving the girl to guess at her quiet business. Then, the others had rushed in from the meetinghouse, bringing the news of the death of Peter Lynch—news that made Mary's heart leap, and race with fear. Hurrying out to Gabriel, she sent him off to a secret place known to them both. After that, she kept back from the crowd, while she strained to hear what it planned to do next.

Now, as the villagers headed homeward and the occupants of the inn watched them go, Mary returned to the empty kitchen and acted quickly. First, she snatched up some bread and meat, which she tied in her apron. Then she ran out the back door, pulling her cloak around her. Under her arm, wrapped in a cloth, she clutched a thin blade with a handle of deer horn—the same knife she'd wanted to bury in the miller on the previous evening.

Soon, Mary began to climb toward tree-covered knolls. As she crossed a tilted pasture, the air chilled her through her woolen garments. She saw that the sky to the north over the river plain had filled with layered clouds the color of pewter, while the heights away in New Hampshire brooded in smoky purples and blues.

In a few minutes she reached the trees, and began to thread her way between the trunks without a backward glance. Once inside the light wood, the girl felt entirely alone; she could hear only her own footsteps treading on the thick bed of leaves, and the distant cawing of a single crow. A sudden volley made her whirl with fear; but it was only icy snow beginning to fall around her. It brushed past high twigs, drummed through upstretched branches as its pellets multiplied, and finally skated across the frost-dried leaves that littered the forest floor.

Climbing on, Mary heard a ground wind rise and cry in the branches. A hiss like rising water came from everywhere, as more pellets began to slide in tiny drifts along ledges of exposed rocks. A deeper sound came suddenly on a downsweep—a roar from the churning sky. As bits of snow were blown against her body like spent shot, she imagined in quick terror the presence of an angry God she'd heard about so often.

Stilling her fears, she chose to challenge this freezing world. Though the inn's warmth was only minutes away, she plunged instead into a realm without duty or privilege, into a primitive land filled with a spirit that spoke loudly, whatever its message . . . and with enough power to cool even her own burning. But she had no intention of letting her passion die easily. Soon, she would see Gabriel. Again Mary felt a familiar thrill, shuffling her feet through the leaves to better smell the sweetness that mingled with the bitter scent of snow.

Looking down at her feet, she missed seeing the Frenchman as he watched her approach from behind a tree; nor did she have time to do anything more than let out a small scream when he leapt out after she'd passed. In an instant, Fortier threw his arms around Mary's slender waist. Before she could do anything at all his mouth covered hers; then hot breath warmed her frozen cheek while tears of pleasure spilled through her eyelashes, and trickled back onto her ears. Suddenly, he pulled away. Twining his cold fingers between her own, he pulled her up and over the granite boulders that guarded his hiding place. When he finally stopped, he took the food she offered, and laid it under a projecting ledge.

"Never leave me," he demanded, rather than asked, and her eyes widened.

"Never," she gasped as he clutched her to him. She could feel the strength of his arms beneath heavy woolen clothing.

"No matter what they tell you?"

Mary watched him lovingly, through a mist of tears.

"What do they say of you," she finally asked, "that couldn't as easily be said of me? We both had reason to hate him. I'll fight too, if I have to! We'll make our plans, and then we'll leave this place behind!"

There was a trace of wildness in her voice, as well as a new strength that Gabriel had not heard before.

"There's more to do first," he reminded her. "For now, I'll wait here. And you will go back to safety."

"But you'll freeze!"

"I'll build a fire when it's too dark for anyone to see the smoke from below."

"Gabriel, I think I know where you can hide inside, where it's warm—somewhere they won't look for you."

"Where?"

"I'll tell you tomorrow. I'll come for you as soon as I'm sure."

"Why do you love me, *chère* Marie?" Gabriel asked, pulling her close again.

"Because you're handsome, which you know is true," she answered, managing a smile. He brushed back her hair, wondering at its new perfume. Again, the space between them closed and words became unnecessary. For a while longer, they huddled together for warmth, then sought something more. The wind continued to howl, and a fresh, clean snow fell like a blanket all around.

"THE KILLER MUST have been an unusually strong man." Joseph Warren settled the quilt over Sam Dudley's throat, softened now that *rigor mortis* had gone from the young body.

Longfellow had watched closely as the doctor made his examination, guessing Warren's conclusions before they were spoken. Now, he looked to Lem, who still stood uncertainly by the door, staring at the neighbor he had long known.

"Impossible," the physician said finally, "to be certain of all the damage done. The crushed area I showed you would have been enough to make the boy lose consciousness; then, his face could have been immersed while he was unable to struggle. If he died from the throttling, there would be no water in the lungs . . . but I don't think there's any reason to look for it. Either way, we know someone was responsible for his death."

"So there's no longer a chance that it was an accident," Richard Longfellow concluded. He watched Lem's face harden. Then, he turned back to observe Warren's expression in the fading light.

"I'd say none at all. No more than with the miller."

"Which is what I thought."

"Although," Warren continued, "how the Devil that leviathan you showed me at the church was overcome in the open is another question I'd like to hear the answer to."

All three were silent for a moment before Warren had an inspiration.

"It could be that whatever struck him was thrown."

"A tomahawk?" Lem asked suddenly.

"I suppose that's unlikely, isn't it? It's probably a special talent."

"Not particularly special, around here," Longfellow allowed.

"I did notice that the blow was a little off center," Warren went on, "if that's any help to you. If it was caused by someone holding on to a shaft, then it was probably held by a person who generally uses his right hand."

"Which would be most of us," said Longfellow, wondering again at the extent of the doctor's dedication to Science.

"And I could be wrong. As you know, this sort of thing isn't usual in Boston, either—for all the wild Indians said to live there."

"If someone did manage to strike at him from an *ambuscade*," mused Longfellow, "say, from somewhere inside his mill where a hatchet was handy—then why, and *how*, did he take the miller outside? He's nearly the size of a side of beef."

"He is that," Warren agreed. "Another difficulty, and again one requiring a powerful individual. As for the *why*, I imagine the killer might have wanted to get the body out of the mill to hide it—although the corpse naturally rose to the surface later, in spite of sinking initially. Most might not realize that it would. But—if he was dragged to the pond after being killed . . . as we believe Sam here was put into the water after he was throttled . . . that could be a further indication, could it not? Showing a similarity of habit."

"Then you feel we are looking for one large, cold-hearted, somewhat tidy double murderer."

"Or, two smaller—who both did the deed, and the dragging?" Warren countered, one eyebrow climbing. "What, Richard, do you say to that?"

For once, Longfellow only scowled, and said nothing at all.

OUTSIDE, THE SKY had stopped dropping snow, at least for a while, and there was a welcome lull in the wind for their walk back. As the three figures started away from the house, a smaller shot around the corner from the back, trying to catch them before they went far. Anne Dudley had been unable to reach the ear of her tall visitor earlier in the day, when he'd been with the constable, and the man from Boston with the lovely buttons. Now, she had another chance.

"Mr. Longfellow, please?" her tiny voice asked.

Longfellow looked down after feeling a tug on his sleeve. He saw again a short blond creature, and noticed familiar tortoiseshell combs inexpertly nestled above her braids.

"Yes, madam?" he asked, bending. "What is it you require?"

"I was told you're very fond of crowns," the child said boldly. Joseph Warren laughed long enough to bring a smile even to the face of the solemn little girl.

"A secret monarchist after all, Richard?" the doctor chided. "This will be quite a story for our club. Sam Adams will be particularly thrilled."

"Friend Adams can . . ." Longfellow hesitated, then addressed the little girl with curiosity. "What kind of crowns?"

"Silver ones—" Anne held her two first fingers apart at the proper distance, to give him a better idea.

"Silver . . . on Spanish dollars, do you mean?" She beamed her approval, and he thrust a hand deep into a pocket to see what he could find, while he asked a further question—though he was certain he knew the answer.

"May I know who told you so?"

"Mrs. Willett. Charlotte's a queen's name, too, my mother says, just like mine. Mine's Anne."

"A very good name." He brought out a coin, examined it for a moment, and then gave it over to a remarkably quick hand, while Lem watched with disapproval.

"Mrs. Willett's quite right. I am fond of them, which is why I occasionally give them to my friends," said Longfellow, straightening. He was rewarded with a low curtsy before the little girl rushed away.

"Not a very honest way to make a profit," Lem threw after her. Dr. Warren seemed interested, and answered the boy's accusation himself.

"So you think talk and flattery are poor things to be paid for?"

Longfellow took the girl's side. "It was well done, and well coached, if you ask me. Young Anne might make a fine actress on the stage some day, if they ever allow a decent one in Boston."

"She has lost something this day, as well as gained," Warren reminded Lem. "Mrs. Willett, I take it, has been here before us," he added to Longfellow.

"A woman of unusual curiosity, Warren, so beware. Though she's an admirable neighbor, and a good example to follow, in most things. You might ask this young man about her; he's apparently begun to formulate opinions on women."

Longfellow leaned over and ruffled Lem's wayward hair, before they began the walk back.

"Do you suppose Mrs. Willett noticed what those

who found him apparently missed?" Warren eventually asked.

"I believe she did. She thought to call a medical man earlier today, before I'd mentioned you were coming."

"One more thing . . . should we report to your village constable before we enjoy our dinner, or after?"

"After. But then, I think we'd do better to go and tell Edmund Montagu instead—"

"Montagu!" Dr. Warren stopped in his tracks. "Is he here?"

"He's staying at the inn."

"Is he?" Warren's pale eyes flashed. "Then there must be even more here than I've seen so far."

"You know him?"

"Of course. As someone who takes a particular interest in what the governor and his quiet men are up to, I would."

"Would you, indeed?" Longfellow asked as he regarded the other, wondering how far his new friend would be willing to explain. Warren, meanwhile, attempted to hide his curiosity from man and boy by scanning the clouds above them, as all three crunched along the snowy road.

Longfellow noticed that Lem, too, usually so dull with company, had seemed quite interested in the doctor's remarks. That, and other things, made him decide it might be time to begin to study this boy more carefully, to see exactly what he was made of—and to guess, from that, what he might become.

IN THE SMALL parlor attached to his bedroom at the Bracebridge Inn, Edmund Montagu sat and stared at a length of steaming wool. He had spread the scarlet cloak over the back of a tall chair, where it continued to drip in front of the fire. Other clothes had been found tied up in the cape, along with a large stone. These were stretched over a nearby table. They, too, matched what had reportedly been worn by Duncan Middleton on the day the merchant disappeared. But why were they here?

Montagu had already looked each article over carefully. The only thing of interest seemed to be that it had all been hidden in the same pond where they'd found the body of Peter Lynch a few hours before. The searchers had hoped to find the missing ax, and find it they did on a later pass with their hooked poles, although the weapon's recovery had been unable to excite the waiting crowd as highly as the first unexpected find. To them, the bundle of clothing was certain proof that someone had wanted to hide what was left of Middleton.

Montagu was still convinced that the merchant was alive. But he couldn't help wondering why the man hadn't simply taken his cloak away . . . or at least the smallclothes that had been pitched into the water. Perhaps the cloak was too bulky, too conspicuous to risk leaving with. But all the rest? Montagu smiled to think of the old rascal itching now in some farmer's Sabbath attire.

At any rate, he hoped there would be no more nonsense from the villagers about a mysterious fire lit by witches. He pulled his hands from his pockets and rubbed them together briskly. His work here was nearly over. But there was something else he needed to reconsider. Someone had very likely helped Middleton in his "disappearance" and his flight. Time had pointed a finger at Peter Lynch, whose mill stood conveniently near the scene of the merchant's fiery show. If the odd pair *had* met before, was Lynch also the agent who was planning to take the tainted rum off Middleton's hands? If so, it was no surprise that Lynch had a gold coin to spare, to give proof to his tale about the Frenchman. Middleton could have arranged for the miller to supply him with a horse and a place to wait until he might leave Bracebridge unnoticed. But now, Peter Lynch was dead. *Why?*

Had Middleton come back later, surprised the miller, and killed him to protect the fiction of his demise? Unlikely, if Lynch was part of his future plans. And it wouldn't have been an easy job for an old man. The captain thought again of the *scenario* Charlotte Willett had followed, when she described Middleton jumping down to hide under his cloak at the side of the road. It had sounded plausible at the time; but now, he wondered.

Another thing—if Middleton had murdered the miller, it meant the merchant had hidden somewhere in the vicinity for at least forty-eight hours. Why had he waited? And where? Someone would certainly have noticed the old devil skulking around, white and crabbed. Who in Bracebridge would not see him and tell others, when everyone was aware of what they thought was the man's spectacular demise? No, Montagu still believed Middleton was long gone, and that there must be a better answer to the question of who had killed Peter Lynch.

The Frenchman, of course, was the most likely candidate. Gabriel Fortier had a very good reason to want the miller dead, and soon. He had youth and agility, even if he wasn't especially large. And further, if Lynch had encountered him in the dark, and Gabriel Fortier already had the hatchet in his hand, surprise or even a quick woodsman's toss could explain how he had avoided the miller's steely arms. Montagu happened to know from experience that a man carrying a candle at night made a superb target. And afterward? For Gabriel to have carried the miller outside by himself was just possible. Montagu also knew, from witnessing events of the battlefield, that a fatal head wound might take minutes or even hours to kill. Often, the most ghastly wounds did not to stop a man from speaking, or babbling at least; an injured man might even get up and run a while before he collapsed and died. The brain was still a mystery to medical men, however much they peered and prodded when they got the chance.

So—the wounded miller could have stumbled out of his mill, dislodged and thrown away the ax in his death throes, fallen, and landed in the water. Or, the hatchet might have been thrown far into the pond by the Frenchman, who would undoubtedly have been following to see a proper end to his work. If things had gone as he had just imagined, thought Montagu, one thing was clear. It would be difficult for Gabriel Fortier to claim self-defense if ever he came to trial.

At any rate, the sodden cape hung before him; it would be something to show to Longfellow and his lovely sister. A fascinating creature, but on the whole, he wasn't sure if he wouldn't be happier spending a quiet evening with Charlotte Willett. There was a woman who came from a different mold. And she was fair in more than the usual ways. Her conclusions concerning the disappearance of old Middleton had been brilliantly simple, and quite possibly correct—although her theory now seemed to him a little skewed. Maybe Mrs. Willett hadn't been *entirely* right, after all. Still, she had certainly led the pack at the start.

It would be interesting to hear her views on the murder of the miller, as well as thoughts she might have on Mary and the Frenchman, and on Fortier's current whereabouts. He even longed to know what she thought about the trials of Pratt the landlord, and the devious wife with her simian lover. One thing was certain. These people he'd met here were hardly the Puritans he had imagined still populated Massachusetts. This place was a good deal like England, after all!

Almost as an afterthought, he added the death of

the boy to this bubbling stew. What had Dr. Warren concluded about young Dudley? Montagu would know before long. But very soon, he would have to let someone
else take over the problem of finding Fortier, and bringing the boy's killer, whoever he was, to justice. His own
problem was still to discover the whereabouts of Duncan
Middleton. And it was barely possible, he had to admit,
that the old man himself was in no way connected to
these two deaths at all.

Still, coincidence could be pushed only so far. And
yet—

Was it also possible that something else was going
on here, something he hadn't even begun to understand?
Reaching for his glass of wine, Edmund Montagu lifted
both feet onto the low table in front of him, settled into
his cushioned chair, and stared intently into the dancing fire.

Chapter 22

AFTER DINNER, WHILE logs crackled in the grate over a bed of squeaking, popping coal, Charlotte offered coffee to Longfellow and Dr. Warren.

Before returning for their promised fare, the doctor had agreed to stay the night in one of Longfellow's extra bedrooms. Now, in no hurry to go, both men took their ease, while outside the window a drier, colder snow fell gently, drifting over garden, lawn, and fields.

It was a shame Diana had chosen to stay at her brother's with Cicero, thought Charlotte, but she had found it necessary—she said—to wash and curl her hair. Possibly, she waited for a visit from a certain captain. And probably, she realized that death must be dinner's main subject—as it had been.

Warren had repeated for his hostess his reasons for believing that Sam Dudley's death had not been accidental. For her part, Charlotte took the story of the

Dutch gold one step further; she told them how, according to the boy's young sister, a piece of gold had been given to Sam. And she explained her notion that the coin had been taken away after his death by whoever killed him. She also offered her earlier thoughts on Peter Lynch's connection to both Middleton and the boy. The next problem was to come up with a way to explain the miller's murder. They had each stopped talking, and spent several moments in thought.

"The miller," Warren began again, "from what I've heard, probably knew several men who might have wished him dead."

"An accurate epitaph," Longfellow interjected with a bleak smile, "if not a very happy one."

"So there probably weren't many he would have welcomed," Warren continued, "on hearing someone in his mill after his usual hour for closing. And untrusting, he would seem to have been a very hard man to undo. An interesting paradox."

"Lynch had at least a few friends, for all his lack of charm. Jack Pennywort, for instance, listened to his boasts and stories, and Wise, the tavern keeper, fed him on a fairly regular basis. There might have been one or two more."

"But not this Frenchman of yours. Surely, though, he couldn't have approached Lynch, at least in a threatening manner, unless it was from behind—which is not the way he was killed. Upon reflection, I don't really believe the ax was thrown after all. I've been thinking, and I believe that if it had been, the gash would have been deeper. I have seen what that kind of an edge can do, when you fellows practice on trees. Yet you tell me that Fortier isn't large. One very big individual, or two smaller—it comes to that again. Now, if one of a *pair* had provided a distraction, then the other might have come up close behind. At the last moment, Lynch might have turned, and—"

Warren brought the side of a surprisingly delicate hand up like an ax against his forehead. Longfellow's lips twisted, while he looked to their hostess, hoping to see her shudder. He only saw that Charlotte seemed far away. Following her eyes, he, too, watched the snow fall into the shivering maples beyond the curtains.

"Or it might still be one person," she murmured, "if the helper happened to be some kind of unseen agent."

"Agent?" asked Warren alertly.

"If you mean whiskey," ventured Longfellow, "don't forget that Lynch was a man who could hold his liquor. He'd had a good deal of practice."

"What if he'd been lulled half asleep," Charlotte said, still apparently trying the idea on herself, "befuddled, or even frightened by something else he didn't know was affecting him? What if he'd been given some sort of concoction—a medicine, or even a poison? I know several things to quiet an illness that are easy enough to come by; so do most women who nurse their families. If I wanted to attack the miller myself, I'd first try to make him as helpless as possible."

"A good idea," Longfellow responded uneasily. He was alarmed by the avenue of thought this opened up to him, but the doctor seemed encouraged.

"Would you, Dr. Warren," Charlotte asked hesitantly, "think to look for signs of anything of the kind, while you were examining a corpse?"

"With an obvious injury to blame, no. I probably wouldn't."

"I remember that the miller had a slight rash."

"Yes—a recent brush with nettles, I'd thought. But you're right! Such a rash could have been caused by a reaction to some kind of plant, or even a poison. Unfortunately, my knowledge of botany isn't great," he added.

"I can help you there," Longfellow threw in. "Lynch might have been affected by a great many things. I know of several plants that plague our farms by causing harm to animals . . . although I've not seen detailed descriptions of how they affect man. At any rate, there's Jamestownweed, for one—what Linnaeus calls *Datura stramonium*. Bad for sheep and cattle, though it's sometimes smoked to relieve constriction of the chest. Then there are the banes. The Mediterranean henbane has unfortunately been introduced, and now grows wild here, dropping seeds that sometimes kill chickens; hence, the name." He paused, and Charlotte took a breath to speak.

"But—"

"Wolfbane, or monkshood—aconite," he continued, "is particularly deadly, though it's sometimes used in small amounts as a sedative. Its blue flower is attractive, so it is frequently found in pleasure gardens. There's also the wild arum, or wakerobin; cowbane, or water hemlock, very deadly; garden foxglove—to name but a few."

"I'm aware of problems with yew," Warren added thoughtfully. "Especially when its red berries interest our children."

"In short, we have a plethora of plants that might be used to sicken or kill a man, woman or child, growing right outside our doors."

"But," Charlotte tried again, to no avail.

"And yet some, as you say, Richard, are used for medicines as well. Poison or medicine might be only a matter of degree. What holds off the gout in one man may kill a patient unused to it outright."

"You speak from experience?"

"Well, I've only begun to practice, so I've not yet been in a position to kill off *many* on my own," Warren retorted dryly.

"You'll get to it, if you're like the rest. I'll tell you,

though, that if you're looking for a killer, certain poisonous metals seem to be the preferred thing today."

"You're referring, of course, to the therapeutic use of mercury, arsenic, antimony—"

"But what," asked Charlotte quite loudly, "about the *miller*? Could you discover now, Dr. Warren, if anything had been introduced into his system before he died, that might alter his abilities, or his perceptions?"

"Tests of that kind are difficult enough when the victim is alive," Warren admitted. "I need to observe symptoms while a patient is able to tell me how he feels, to be reasonably sure of the cause. I believe it's circumstance that catches most poisoners—where they obtained the poison, who saw them applying it, that sort of thing. That, and their natural desire to talk about what they've done. It's something we read about in the newspapers, time and again."

Longfellow nodded. "Just the other week, there was a story in the *Mercury* about a man in Newport—"

"Yes, I saw that!"

"Many times, too, it's a woman who does the deed, remember."

"Yes, well, I'll grant you poison is known as a woman's weapon. Certainly, a man might be wary of a sex that would use deadly nightshade drops, simply for beauty's sake. He might wonder—would they shrink from experimenting on him, especially if their minds had already been affected by the action of the plant?"

"It does make one think."

"Not that females neglect the metals, either. You'll remember Captain Codman, no doubt—fed arsenic by two slaves for weeks, until he finally died of it. Although he probably deserved his fate." Dr. Warren went on to mull over the details, as well as the ghastly fate of a co-conspirator, whose mummified body still hung in chains on Charlestown Common, across the river from Boston.

Charlotte had given up trying to speak, and scarcely listened. Instead, she rose quietly and went out to look through the library shelves in the blue room. After that, she laid out a sheet of paper, opened some ink, took up a quill, and paused to consider. If she belonged to the circulating library in Boston . . . but at £1.8 per year! If only she were allowed to use the one at Harvard College, like her brother Jeremy. But that was unthinkable. No woman would ever be welcome in that place. Poisoning, Warren had said, was generally a woman's work. Slightly peeved, Charlotte took small pleasure in their apparent concern at how easy it might be. But in several more minutes, when she returned to the table, she discovered that her guests had moved on to another topic altogether.

"I must apologize for beginning to talk shop, Mrs. Willett, but I've just remembered meeting your merchant once, at the house of a surgeon who gave me instruction in dentistry. I've begun to tell Richard about the man's work," Warren explained, well aware of a social duty to win back his hostess's approval. She nodded for him to go on, for teeth were a subject of painful interest to most people, sooner or later, even if they cleaned and cared for them as well as—

What was it in the passing thought that made her jump in her chair? She had nearly remembered something important. She was sure of it . . . something that was trying to join itself to a statement the animated doctor had made but a moment before.

"They can be wired directly onto your own, and fill in a gap or two quite well. There are, of course, now whole plates made of gold, and set in front with ivory teeth from all kinds of tusks; these make quite a good show if your own are completely gone. Not that they would be of any actual use in eating, but they do improve the appearance."

"Did you say," Charlotte interrupted abruptly, "that Duncan Middleton had his teeth cared for by this man?"

"Not his teeth, exactly. Prescott usually works in construction now. Although he still looks at live teeth, too. Which is fortunate, for you'd be surprised how many do nothing but pull and staunch the blood, when with a little planning, some could be saved. But since Middleton had none—"

"Are you saying Duncan Middleton has *false* teeth?"

"Oh, yes. He came to see if Prescott could adjust them. Middleton is as toothless as a turtle. Mrs. Willett, are you feeling well?"

Quite well, thought Charlotte, if amazingly dull-witted. She remembered how Duncan Middleton had looked at her, with the eyes of a man who had something familiar on his mind. She recalled his pale complexion . . . almost as pale as Diana's had been the next afternoon. She thought of the valise she had examined in Middleton's room at the Inn, with its absence of toothbrush or cleansing powder, both of which a Boston man of wealth, certainly one who took the trouble to carry a shoehorn, would more than likely carry with him. Unless, of course, he had no use for them at all!

Again, in her mind's eye, she clearly saw the old man take a large bite of the new apple she'd given him. And she remembered how she had heard it crunch between what were obviously several sound teeth.

"The simplest things," she replied to both Longfellow and Warren, who were watching her face with some alarm, "are sometimes the least obvious. But I think—I really think that the 'old man' I saw on the road on Tuesday afternoon wasn't old at all. And he most certainly *wasn't Duncan Middleton!*"

Chapter 23

THE MAN I saw," Charlotte Willett hurried on, "wore the merchant's scarlet cloak. And rode his horse. But he had to be an imposter." She went on to explain about the teeth, causing Longfellow, who was speechless for a time, to slap his thigh.

"Montagu was so sure!" he exploded.

"Sure that the merchant is missing from his home, and that we have his horse and clothes and traveling bag here. Beyond that, the captain had only our vague descriptions to go on, and I'm afraid they might have been misleading. Now that I stop to think, the figure I described was nearly covered by a hat and wig, a full cloak, probably face powder and possibly even some other kind of theatrical disguise, as well. The high voice that I heard speak very briefly, and that Mr. Lee also remembers, proves nothing, since we'd never heard it before—and remember that he took care to *say* almost nothing, except to Lydia. For all we know, the man might even have been an actor hired to play a part."

Longfellow threw down his napkin and leapt up, to begin pacing the floor. "It would explain why Middleton's business and assets are intact. The real man only wanted to throw Montagu off his scent for a time! Drawing him here, the merchant would have had a few days clear. I wonder what else he has up his sleeve?"

"And the horse!" Charlotte exclaimed.

"Of course! Something did bother me when I heard Nathan's description, so I had a look myself. Then, I managed to forget all about it."

"How do you mean?" asked Warren.

"It's too absurd. No—let me tell you. The horse had been habitually and *recently* flogged, a thing I always find irritating, and a damning indication of a rider's poor sense and temper. Yet Nathan mentioned that its sides had already begun to heal when it got here. It was as though it had carried an altogether different rider on the day it came. And so it had."

On an impulse, Charlotte rose and closed the curtains. Then she moved away from the windows, closer to the fire. She remembered the tired animal that she, too, had seen. At least, she considered, the impostor who rode him into town was kinder to horses than the real Duncan Middleton had been. But what if . . . ?

"There is," she said quietly, "another possibility."

"Which is?" Longfellow inquired, watching her sink back into imagination.

"It could be someone knows that Middleton has died, and wants to hide the real cause and place—by making us think he came to Bracebridge. Don't forget that Captain Montagu said Middleton left home on Monday. The man we saw didn't arrive here until Tuesday, almost at evening."

"In that case," said Longfellow, "our imposter might also be . . ."

"A murderer."

"And where to you suppose that man is now?" Warren's quiet words continued in a placid way that made the others remember he was a trained physician, after all. "If I were you, Mrs. Willett, I would take great care. You've just told us something that might also have occurred to the imposter as well. You, alone, saw this man in an unguarded moment, in an attitude outside his pose. He may feel that you, of all people, are able to identify him—by this, or even by some other little slip he could have made. Or might make."

"There's still a good chance he left the area after performing his fireworks," Longfellow ventured cautiously.

"And you believe the two other deaths that occurred here were unrelated? In that case, I'll be glad to get back to the safety of the city! Everyday village life appears to be very bad for one's health."

"Warren, I think it's time for us to visit Edmund Montagu. And time for you, neighbor, to bolt your doors and windows again." Longfellow took Charlotte's hands and rubbed some warmth back into them. "Inside," he added with a grimace, turning for his hat and cloak, "it's *possible* that you might manage to stay out of further trouble, Carlotta."

The physician, too, rose. "Walk me over to your study, Longfellow, and I'll write out a quick report of my examinations of the miller and the boy. It might come in handy. Thank you again, Mrs. Willett, for your generosity. You will take care of yourself? And if there's ever anything I am able to do for you—"

Charlotte pressed a folded piece of paper into Warren's hand. "I did wonder earlier if you would look something up for me, and send me word of what you find. I know you're welcome to use our best scientific library."

"At Harvard College, you mean? Certainly. In fact, the place is on my way."

"It's a list of complaints—or what you'd call symptoms. They've been the talk of Bracebridge lately. Witchcraft has been whispered as their cause. But I believe something natural might produce many of them. I suspect it's an herb. I visited John Bartram's botanical garden in Philadelphia a few years ago, and we spoke at length about the healing properties of some of his specimens, but I'm afraid this is something quite different. While you and Richard were talking, I leafed through my father's copy of Josselyn's herbal, but it only contains New England species, and I don't think it's a native plant we're looking for. I know Richard has a great deal of knowledge about these things, but I'd hoped that as a physician you might also be interested."

Concentrating, Warren studied the list, and then returned her earnest look.

"There really should be some universal reference for poisons, or plants that might induce illness rather than health, but I don't believe one exists. I'll see what I can do. Though I *have* heard of a treatise on wounds and the appearance of various causes of death, written by a man in Leipzig. What an interesting new science to pursue— medicine, as it affects criminal behavior. A fascinating thought. Well, if you can spare your young man, he could ride in with me to Cambridge; I'll send him back with whatever I find. Since I know the librarian, I don't think I'll have much trouble in borrowing a few volumes for a week or so. And Lem might like to see the sights of Harvard for himself."

"He could be needed here, especially now—" Longfellow began to object, but Charlotte stopped him.

"I think he'd like that," she said, giving the doctor her hand. She also promised to have Lem ready to ride, when Warren called early in the morning.

• • •

CHARLOTTE'S FRONT DOOR had barely been opened to the cold when Diana Longfellow mysteriously appeared, nearly hidden under a forest cape whose shoulders were dusted with snow.

"I've come to keep you company, Mrs. Willett. I'm afraid there's very little hope of society at the house where *I'm* staying. But I see that you have some of your own! Good evening, Dr. Warren," she finished with a brisk curtsy, after moving inside so that the door could be shut again.

A few moments more and the men were off, leaving only their regrets behind. For consolation, the ladies sat to drink a pot of tea by the replenished fire.

"Now there's a curious man. Still, he's not unattractive, and he's unattached." Diana gave her neighbor a meaningful glance. "By the way, did you see what I did with the small bottle of perfume I showed you at the inn yesterday afternoon?" she queried, slipping off a pair of her brother's jockey boots that had previously hidden under her skirts.

"The dragon bottle? No, I don't think so."

"How maddening! It's irreplaceable," Diana said with a sigh, settling herself into a chair in her stockinged feet, "and I hadn't even grown tired of it yet. Oh, well— perhaps it will turn up somewhere. I'm forever misplacing things, especially when I come here. At home I have much more to lose, but Patty always keeps an eye out. I've just come from the inn, where I had my own small dinner party with Captain Montagu, who still thinks he's the most exciting man in town—which, unfortunately, he is. I wonder, though, how other women deal with his smugness. Deep inside, you know, I'm convinced he's a passionate man. That doesn't surprise you? You know how I love to find what's underneath others' pretenses, when there's anything worth finding. In his case," she added, poising a fingernail delicately in the air and dimpling at the thought, "I think there is. If I can get under his skin just a little further . . ."

Charlotte had seen Diana's pursuits before, and didn't doubt that it would be an interesting time for both parties, whenever Miss Longfellow and Montagu might meet again.

"You'd better watch your step," she warned her coquettish friend. "The captain seems to be a clever man who usually gets what he wants. And I'm not sure he would approve of some of your friends."

"Well, neither do I, when it comes to that. Especially the ones who *will* dwell on business and politics. Hurrah for Captain Montagu, if he can keep them quiet on those subjects when he's around! Incidentally," Diana continued in a different tone, "you might like to know they've found the red cloak and other things in the millpond. Oh, and I should tell you before I go on—Mary stopped me as I was leaving, and asked me to thank you for all you've done. Now—have I told you about the patterns from Paris that Lucy Devens brought back last month? She swears it's the new fashion to dress like a shepherdess and picnic in the woods! Can you imagine?"

As dusk turned to dark, the ladies talked of many things, each cleverly managing to keep the other (or so she thought) from worry.

EDMUND MONTAGU REACHED out and accepted Dr. Warren's report from Longfellow's hand. Before examining it in front of the fire, he provided his guests with claret.

While he read, the others examined the cloak and smallclothes, which still hung from the furniture.

"This has more to do with your problems than mine," said the captain when he had finished, handing the paper back. He recrossed his silk-clad legs and cleared his throat before continuing. "I had planned to help with your investigations only as far as they advanced mine. Now, I find I have to leave them to you. Only a moment ago, I received word from friends in Boston who tell me that a body, naked and as yet officially unclaimed, was washed up along the coast near Providence. On Tuesday."

"Duncan Middleton," Longfellow returned quickly.

"A guess, of course."

"Hardly that. A scientific deduction, based on fact."

"How?" asked Montagu. And how were they always a jump ahead of where he imagined them to be? He watched Longfellow set the tips of his fingers together carefully, and draw them apart again.

"Actually, I had it from Mrs. Willett. The man she saw here, she now tells me, was an impostor. As to the how, she notices little things. And little things with her often lead to larger ones. For instance, there was the time when one of her hens disappeared, and she eventually discovered— but I digress, Captain, when you have more serious things to consider. I take it you still plan to return to Boston, in order to watch what happens to Middleton's estate?"

"Indeed," Montagu replied, further annoyed. He would have to guess about the hen, and would miss learning more about Mrs. Willett's methods. Whatever they were, they succeeded. For an instant, he imagined he saw the shorebird of the same name. Rather unspectacular, until she decided to fly; then, the willet displayed an arresting wing pattern, white and black bands that could hardly fail to catch the eye and raise the spirit. Another instant decided him.

"But please," he insisted, reaching for the decanter of claret. "Go on. I would like to hear Mrs. Willett's reasoning."

"It has to do with teeth," Longfellow went on, as his

glass was refilled. He related all that Charlotte had concluded after dinner. At the end, Montagu had to admit that the affair was far from finished.

"Do you have," he queried, "further plans of your own?"

"I had meant to ride to Worcester tomorrow, to see Mary Frye's father. Now, that seems unnecessary, strictly speaking. But I believe I'll still go and talk to him, and ask a few others if anyone has seen a man of means who might have arrived there on Wednesday, possibly carrying Dutch gold. I may have some luck. And I'll inquire about the miller's stay earlier in the week—if in fact Lynch went that way. He might have dropped hints about this imposter he was in league with."

"You will save me the trouble. And I'm sure someone of your experiences can speak with a frontier person better than I. Send me word if you discover anything of interest."

The three men rose, but Montagu had not quite finished.

"Please give Mrs. Willett my regards, and my regrets at not having more time to spend with her. You might also take my respects to your most unusual sister. I suppose our paths will cross again, in town. Dr. Warren, I look forward to seeing you as well."

"The question is, will I be seeing you, Captain?" Warren asked knowingly.

Montagu nodded slightly, acknowledging the hit. "That's a question I wouldn't wager on, either way," he finally smiled, putting down his glass and walking them to the door.

THE NIGHT HAD begun to clear by the time Charlotte retired to her feather bed. She curled her toes around a squat stoppered jug full of kettle water, while she watched the stars that crept westward behind racing clouds, winking like distant eyes. Drifting toward sleep, she began to imagine others in their beds throughout the village.

Diana, of course, would be in her scented boudoir, draped in satin, kept warm by who knew what secrets and desires. Always a late riser, she was probably still at a book, or writing in her diary.

Then there were those at the inn. Charlotte wished she had managed to speak with Edmund Montagu again—Diana had told her he planned to leave in the morning. Together, they might have discovered why certain things, like the coins, connected the three confirmed murders. (She had been only partly relieved to hear from Richard, when he returned for his sister, that the merchant's body had, in fact, been found far away.) Willing herself to forget about serious matters, she pictured Captain Montagu readying himself for bed, his wig beside him on a chair looking like a small, sleeping dog; she smiled to think what he might look like without it.

Resting near Edmund Montagu would be Mary, and Jonathan, and Lydia. Where would Lydia be sleeping now, she wondered? In a room usually kept for guests? It would be a cruel wound to Lydia's pride, though a source of amusement (and a warning) for most of the village. She wondered what Nathan would have to say on the subject in days to come.

Mr. Lee would probably be in an upstairs room at the Blue Boar, if he was in bed yet; more than likely, he was still in the noisy room downstairs. He would certainly be the victim of many jokes in poor taste. But he would probably be the receiver of more than one free pint as well. Would he be telling further stories for his supper? Surely, he would be urged by the rest of the men to "spill the beans." She wondered if she might find a way to talk with him again, without setting tongues wagging. As a naturalist with a knowledge of plants, he might be able to instruct her. Beyond that, Lee could have learned more from Lydia when they were, well, together ... about what exactly Lydia had discussed with Middleton or, more accurately, with the imposter, on the day he disappeared.

As sleep began to overtake her, a darker image of Gabriel Fortier loomed in her thoughts. Somewhere out there, in the wind, she seemed to see—no, not Fortier, but a short, dark figure with its back to her, coming closer—a back bent over and unaccountably moving along like a crab, sideways, but growing larger, and larger, until it flapped its dripping red cape, and turned to show a face that had been eaten away—a sight which woke her abruptly, and left glistening sweat on her lips and forehead.

In a move as familiar as childhood, she patted the side of her blankets and whispered softly. Orpheus, thus invited, rose stiffly to his feet and climbed up beside his mistress, where he settled with a happy groan.

For a long time after, comforted by the soft breathing beside her, Charlotte continued to look up at the flickering stars.

Chapter 24

_⌒ Saturday

FRIDAY'S SNOWFALL WAS followed by a day of clear sun and brisk wind, with the sky a deep blue. As usual on Saturday, people hurried about, trying to complete the week's chores before sundown when the Sabbath began. In homes along the road, birch brooms swept at the open doors, beans simmered in pots, and linen fluttered on lines and trees.

Two horses clopped and snorted through the early morning air, over a landscape covered with shining, melting snow. As they left Bracebridge behind, Warren amused Lem with stories of life in Boston, sensing unborn ambition in the boy. In fact, he might well benefit from encouragement, Warren thought, and become a force for change, or at least resistance to all that was threatening the future of Boston. Most people who were given purpose, the doctor believed, could do amazing things. He himself had left Harvard in '59 to enter not only into medical studies, during his indenture to Dr. Lloyd, but into political life as well. A member of what was softly called the Long Room Club, he met others at unannounced meetings above the office of the printers Edes and Gill, who put out the *Boston Gazette*. Here, men worked to develop friendships, public spirit . . . and treason, according to some.

Warren believed young men should be helped to knowledge that might allow them to lead their countrymen, especially when they showed a talent for leading. He had recognized something he liked in Lem Wainwright on the previous afternoon. If someone—say, Longfellow—were to sponsor the boy at Harvard, anything might happen—as long as the lad held onto his native reserve and pride, and kept a natural suspicion of both the British and easy money.

Eventually, through the fields, they saw the spires and rooftops of Cambridge ahead. The town of about fifteen hundred souls was no larger than Worcester, but its atmosphere was vastly different. Here, the bells of Boston could often be heard coming across the water, and that city was a nourishing presence which provided a good deal of money, as well as a constant flow of new thought and information.

They soon passed a large Congregational church, whose yard held many of the Commonwealth's founders, Warren observed. Then, on the left, they saw an open quadrangle of buildings neatly fenced off from the ordinary world.

There was Massachusetts Hall, four stories with a large clock that faced the road, Harvard Hall with its bell towers and unbelievable library of 3,500 volumes, and Stroughton Hall—all three constructed of redbrick around a large, bare courtyard, where students crossing and recrossing between meetings continually wore out the grass.

Warren had already told his youthful companion about Professor Edward Wigglesworth, the scholarly old man who still prepared most of the future theologians of Massachusetts, while he also taught the students Greek and Latin, rhetoric, logic, and ethics. Now, the doctor told several amusing stories about the far less ancient John Winthrop, who was responsible for teaching mathematics and natural philosophy, as well as calculus, astronomy, and geography. It was Winthrop who had created and still presided over the experimental laboratory on the second floor of Harvard Hall. There, a twenty-foot telescope had enabled him to learn more of the nature of sunspots, and comets. Winthrop also had an orrery in his apparatus chamber; this showed, by means of hanging brass bells moved by a wheelwork, the paths of the principal bodies in the solar system.

But when they entered Harvard Hall and looked in at the laboratory on their way to the library, it was a hanging skeleton that stopped Lem and held him dumb. Warren took the opportunity to show his new friend just how Sam Dudley had been approached and strangled, to the considerable interest of several students occupying the room.

Somewhat later, Lem sat under the eye of a watchful librarian, looking through a book he'd found on a huge oak table before him. As his eyes flitted over the pages he let the smell, the sight, and the sounds of the place work on his agitated mind. Poring over a single volume by the fire had once been a thrill. But now, that prospect gave him only a brief glow. Here, an entire world of books surrounded him, all of them waiting to be tasted, acting on the boy like a bonfire—even if, as Dr. Warren had warned him, three-quarters dealt with divinity.

Lem's own questions had more to do with the stars and their names, details of inventions, places mentioned in the newspapers, and the curious habits of weather and atmospherics described in the Almanac. *How*, and *why*, figured largely in Lem's unspoken thoughts, along with an occasional and sometimes even heretical *why not?*

One question that didn't trouble his mind at the moment (although he was later to wonder why about that, too) was this: What was going on at home, in the house of Charlotte Willett, which he had left unprotected? And why, he might have wondered (had he been looking down from his favorite hillside perch at that moment)—why was a crouched figure creeping up to Mrs. Willett's kitchen window, looking around to make sure Hannah Sloan continued on her way down the hill on a quick errand, then stealing like a shadow to the unbolted door?

EDMUND MONTAGU, TOO, had passed Harvard College as he came through Cambridge very early, on his way back to Boston. But Montagu had no thought of stopping. Continuing on, he reached Roxbury and crossed over the Neck.

Nothing much, he decided with satisfaction, looked to have changed. Boston claimed a population these days of well above fifteen thousand, and its business kept on growing, in spite of the latest conflagration in 1760 which he'd often heard mentioned, and a currently rumored depression. He could see the masts of ships that had hurried to cross the Atlantic before the worst of the winter storms, clamorously unloading now on the wharves at the ends of east-running streets. As he rode on, he passed farm carts from the western mainland towns rumbling along the Common, bringing produce to markets and warehouses, as well as the cargo holds of the tall ships.

Commerce would always take care of itself, he

thought—unlike one particular participant of the Boston trade, whose business was finished. Soon, Montagu would mount granite steps he'd only watched before. A constable had already made inquiries there, when word of Middleton's disappearance first arrived from Bracebridge. Later, he'd received word that Constable Burns had what nearly amounted to a wrestling match with the merchant's housekeeper, a Mrs. Elizabeth Bledsoe. It appeared to have been a draw.

This time, the captain would try himself. All through his journey, a homily had rarely left his head: Where there's a will, there's a way. And a will was just what Montagu wanted to find, now that Duncan Middleton was known to be really and truly dead.

Leaving his horse at a nearby stable, he stopped briefly at his rented quarters in a house in Pond Street. After that, he strode the half mile down to the big house off Water Street, near Long Wharf. Eventually, he lifted the heavy knocker on the large carved door.

After he had knocked several times more, the door was opened by a kitchen maid with greasy hands and a crooked cap, and coal dust around her nose. Montagu was about to ask to speak to someone else, when a bleating sound behind him announced the timely return of the housekeeper.

"Good afternoon, sir." She slid by him, shooing away the unpresentable maid. Mrs. Betty Bledsoe was, as reported, a very ruddy and cheerful woman. She was also very round, and despite the cool weather, her face was covered with perspiration from her morning's marketing. There was no doubt that she could use a good washing. The image of Mrs. Bledsoe in a bathtub helped considerably as the captain struggled to maintain a pleasant smile, while both caught their breath, for quite different reasons.

"Good day, madam," he finally responded, and bowed.

Mrs. Bledsoe had already admired the fashionable young gentleman from behind; now, she enjoyed admiring him face to face, while trying to decide if his visit promised fair weather or foul.

"I'm afraid the master's not in at the moment. Might I be of some service?"

"Certainly, for it's you that I came to see, Mrs. Bledsoe."

"Oh! Then you'd better come into the parlor. Unless—you might like to follow me into my kitchen? Nice and warm there, sir, and I could offer you a pot of tea, and some fresh buns, too."

Having won a small victory, Mrs. Bledsoe led the way, taking just a moment to send the maid upstairs to polish a distant pair of andirons.

When the kettle was on the fire, the housekeeper lowered herself into a chair. Montagu watched her feet rise into the air, before hearing them meet the floor again with a plop. Curls like yellow sausages hung beside her flaming cheeks, and bobbed vigorously as she began uttering pleasantries, which soon moved toward the colony's many faults. Montagu had quickly discerned that she was an Englishwoman. As it turned out, Mrs. Bledsoe had been born in Portsmouth, and proudly considered herself more loyal to the king than most of those around her. Had she, he asked, suspected that some of Middleton's dealings had been less than aboveboard, when it came to their monarch's interests?

Oh, they all stretched the laws a bit, didn't they, businessmen? Especially these colonials. And didn't the government generally overlook these things, for its own good reasons? Not that she could ever condone what sometimes went on. . . .

"Anyways," she concluded, "wherever was I to find an honest man to work for? My own Mr. Bledsoe always believed America to be the land of opportunity, but when he left . . . when he *died*," she stressed, "I had very little. I really had no choice but to take a post here in Boston. Unfortunately, my upbringing was not *quite* fine enough to get me a position in the house of a real English gentleman."

"Of course," said Montagu, bringing the conversation grandly back to his own design, "one doesn't always have a choice. But I give you one now, as a personal representative of His Majesty." He almost expected the woman to raise a hand in salute, considering her new expression. "I can only tell you so much, you understand . . . but I can say that you might assist your king and country greatly—and perhaps yourself—by answering a few questions."

He now dropped a Dutch gulden on the table, causing Mrs. Bledsoe's pale eyes to widen. "Certainly," she replied, moistening her lips, "I'd like to accommodate a gentleman like yourself, especially if, as you say . . ."

"Mrs. Bledsoe. Betty . . . have you seen many of these before?"

"Didn't they come in with the *Jenny Dean*! One of our ships, that was, back from Curaçao just this August. I remember quite well, as I saw Mr. Middleton counting them out before he hid them away in his strongbox."

"And where is this strongbox, Mrs. Bledsoe?"

"Oh, sir—" A sudden coldness in his expression decided her. "Well . . . it's in the master's study."

Montagu again smiled affably. "Show me," he said firmly, sweeping the gold to one side of the table, without taking his gaze from her.

Mrs. Bledsoe licked her lips again and swallowed. Then, seeing that the coin was not about to disappear by itself, she led the way down a hall. Rising to follow, Montagu quickly pulled a small flask of rum from his coat pocket, and poured a dollop into her teacup.

She stood waiting at the door of a dark, shuttered room with a fireplace full of ashes, and a dusty feel about the rest of it. After walking to a pine highboy with soiled knobs, she opened a low drawer. She removed a painted tin box with an iron device over its clasp.

"It's locked, I'm afraid, sir."

"Please don't trouble yourself any further, Mrs. Bledsoe."

"Would you be needing anything else, just at this moment?" she inquired with an air of innocence that would have been out of place, he thought, in a child of four.

"Perhaps you need to attend to something in the kitchen? I'll do quite well alone," he assured her. "You go and have another sip of tea." And he set to work with a pocket knife and a small metal pick, as soon as the door had shut behind her whispering skirts.

The contents of the flat box were, at first, a disappointment. On top were some signed papers promising payment of money borrowed against eventual delivery of goods, at an exorbitant rate of interest; a few hopeful letters from other firms, and one or two that less politely requested payment; lists of cargo; lists of captains and crew members.

Under these, he found two pieces of newspaper, both from the *Boston Gazette*.

The first was a brief homage to Veracity Middleton, who left no one, and was probably missed by few. A second yellowing page was an account of the wreck of a cargo ship, the *Gloria Jones*. Out of Providence, she had gone down with all hands on the harbor rocks of a small port in the Canary Islands. It had happened during a hurricane that had savaged the area, and must have meant something to the old man. Then Montagu remembered that under similar circumstances the last remaining brother, Lionel, had perished as a sailor three years before. According to Montagu's informants, who had taken a look at the city's tax lists, Lionel's name had, in fact, been removed.

And then he found the packet containing a series of old wills, most of them made when Duncan Middleton's brothers and sister were still alive.

Presumably, the first slim document had been made at the urgings of his elder brother Chester, to whom it left most of a very little nest egg; small bequests went to a sister and two former servants. Next came a will leaving out the elder brother, presumably dead by now, and recognizing a younger one named Lionel, who had come of age. He was set to share a somewhat larger fortune with Veracity. A third will specifically excluded a disfavored Lionel, and left the sister all. The fourth and final document, made shortly after Veracity's death in 1761, named only one person as the recipient of a smallish sum, to be given after the man carried out Duncan Middleton's last wish. It seemed that the bulk of the now weighty estate, with all other claimants gone, went to—and here Montagu heard himself laugh out loud—a home for drunken sailors, to be established in Marblehead on Duncan Middleton's death. As the merchant made very clear in a stinging paragraph, sailors were welcome to their vices, which he believed were far less wicked than those of most of his Boston acquaintances.

When Montagu returned to the kitchen, Betty Bledsoe again sat at her table. The gold coin had disappeared, as had several sugary buns from the previously offered plate. Standing, and giving a sly look toward his coat pockets, the housekeeper offered to pour another cup of tea.

"When your master left on Monday last, where did he tell you he would be going, my dear?"

"He didn't tell me. But not to where he ended up, I'm sure . . . this place called Brainbridge—or Bracebridge. If that is where he ended up."

"You doubt it?" he asked with a look that led the woman on.

"I really don't know. It sounds like one of his tricks

to me! I'm not a superstitious person myself, so I don't see him burning up, like they say. And I can't see him going off and leaving all this behind. As it is, no one's told me *what's* to become of his fortune—although I can tell you he promised me my living, for the great many things I've done for him over the years. At any rate, no one has told me to leave or to stay, so I'm sure I don't know what's to become of Betty Bledsoe!"

Neither did Montagu, but he suspected that fate would soon arrange a new life of small pleasures, and considerable future pain, for some unwary son of England.

LATER, CAPTAIN MONTAGU paid a visit to his benefactors at Town-house, who gave him little reason to go further in any particular direction. They did, however, alert him to the curious fact that the wagonload of tainted rum was still nowhere to be found.

Duncan Middleton's final will had told him very little. On the other hand, what it didn't tell him brought new questions to Montagu's active mind.

First, he decided, he would have a well-earned dinner. Then he would view Middleton's body, and talk with the man who had brought it home. After that, he planned to change his clothing and spend some time prowling the lower parts of town, where he hoped to find a few among the living who could tell him what he now wanted to know.

They said all roads in these parts led to Boston. Let's hope so, the captain said to himself as he walked to the door of a welcoming tavern. With any luck at all, he might be able to avoid a long ride to Providence.

Chapter 25

SEVERAL HOURS EARLIER, Richard Longfellow had mounted the dappled gray in his stable yard and had spoken severely from his high seat to the small collection of humanity that stood below.

"Stay close to home, the two of you! Tell Cicero if there's anything you need. He's seen you through difficulties before," Longfellow reminded his sister especially, "and I expect you to rely on him."

At this, Cicero watched the weather vane on the roof of the barn, neither acknowledging the compliment, nor admitting to Longfellow that, in his opinion, the battle to restrict these two ladies' behavior had been lost long ago.

More than ready to ride, Longfellow leaned down to take up a small package from his neighbor.

"It's a meat pie, and a flask of perry," Charlotte informed him.

"I'll probably be back for a late supper." The horse jerked his head up into the bright morning air and snapped it down and up again, wheeling while his rider paused to hold on.

"Do try to stay calm," urged Diana, knowing her brother's distrust of what he considered to be irrational animals. "They can sense it when you're not. You really should take the chaise, you know."

"Too slow. Besides, the ride will do both of us good."

"Godspeed, then," his sister sighed. "But I can't stand this cold any longer!" With that, she turned and went back inside.

"Will you be stopping at the Three Crows?" Charlotte called.

"I will. The horse will need rest, and I have in mind a few questions I might ask Thankful Marlowe."

"Be sure you measure out the oats yourself. They have a new stable boy every week. You'll give the lady my regards?" she added, allowing a small smile to have its way.

"If I see her," he replied vaguely. Longfellow chucked and nudged his horse with his heels, while he loosened the reins. And before any further leave taking could begin, he was flying off to Worcester.

Left all alone in the snowy yard, Charlotte knew Diana would expect her to hurry back inside for another bite of breakfast, at least. She could easily have done so, and revealed her own plan for the rest of the morning, before taking her leave.

But that, thought Charlotte, might be unwise.

Instead, she turned and went her own way. She prayed the weather of the night before would have kept Adolphus Lee inside like everyone else, so that he would now be rested, rather than asleep. But would he be willing to speak to an unlikely (and an inquisitive) visitor? Probably, he would. She even suspected he might be ea-

ger to listen to her questions and to answer them, if only
for the pleasure of her company. It was a thought that
made her less than happy, but it was based on good evidence and sound reasoning.

After a brisk walk of fifteen minutes, Charlotte arrived at her destination. She entered the Blue Boar by
the front door, where she was relieved to discover few
guests inside. In fact, there were only two travelers resting at a table near the ale barrels, engaged in their own
business. While her eyes adjusted—and her nose became
a little used to the strong smell—she saw Phineas Wise
approach, his hands busy at his apron.

"Mrs. Willett! A surprise this morning! How might I
help?"

"I would like to have a word with one of your
guests."

Wise scratched his stubble, speculating before he
replied.

"You mean my only guest, at present. Seeing you, I
half supposed we'd made a date to barter again, as I'm reminded of the lovely cheeses."

"You drove a hard bargain for the cider, I thought,
but a fair one," she replied, knowing it was the sort of
thing Phineas would enjoy hearing. "I can bring you another, tomorrow, but . . . would you think it out of place
for me to see Mr. Lee alone this morning? Only for a moment or two," she added, seeing the other's eyes dim. (As
a man reliant on the selectmen for the renewal of his
tavern's license, she knew he would be unlikely to allow
anything that might influence the town against him. Of
course, what its wives, in particular, didn't know . . .)

"I would of course be pleased to see you any morning, Mrs. Willett, whenever you might care to drop by.
And I believe Mr. Lee *is* upstairs. I gave him the large
room, the one with the windows. But let me call him
down," he offered, still hoping to have his own way.

"I think that I'd rather ask him my question upstairs, instead of down . . . so the others wouldn't be bothered . . . if you see what I mean."

"Well, better upstairs than outside, since you are no doubt cold from your walk here. It would be unwise to stand too long out of doors—or anywhere else without a fire. A few minutes, of course, might do you no harm. But *questions*, you say? Is it something to do with Lee's recent behavior? You haven't been sent—"

"No! It's only curiosity, on my part. About the old man on the road. Duncan Middleton."

"Him, again!" Phineas growled. "First, he's dead, and now they say he's alive after all. Which is it to be?"

Charlotte said nothing, but her eyes were grave. Waiting to hear no more, Phineas Wise threw up his hands and led the way up a flight of winding stairs.

"Stomp your foot when you're ready to leave, if you want me to help you down again. But the kitchen door at the back will be open. They say, you know, that curiosity killed the cat. That is what they say," he repeated, reaching the middle of three doors and knocking.

A series of small noises came to their ears before footsteps approached, and Charlotte felt her heart race faster. But the sight she saw when the door opened did much to dispel her uneasiness, while it encouraged her lively imagination.

Inside was a cramped room quite unlike the large and tidy one Adolphus Lee had undoubtedly enjoyed at the Bracebridge Inn. Here, instead, were jammed together boxes and bottles, books, and what appeared to be several small wooden presses, all residing on or under a long plank table that stood between the door and a narrow, rumpled bed. In addition, several cases suitable for carting stood around the walls. It had become more of a work room than a bedroom, and might even be heading in the direction of becoming a sort of museum, she thought after a brief look around.

Mr. Lee, Charlotte was glad to observe, was fully dressed and quite alert, as she has suspected he would be. After a moment of amazement he flung himself backward while he opened the door more widely, sweeping a hand inward at the same time with a gallant bow.

"Mr. Wise and Mrs. Willett! What a surprise . . . and a pleasure, to be sure. Have you come on an errand of mercy? For I've surely been wondering what to do with myself this morning. I would be most happy if you would both come in, although . . ." (he added with a grimace) "I would not be surprised if you thought it . . . unwise."

Taking a breath and lowering her head, Charlotte did plunge inside. Even as she heard the grumbling proprietor shut the door, she saw an expression of real pleasure play across the malleable face before her.

"I'm quite delighted! And I promise, you have no cause to fear anything at all while you're here, at least from me. I believe I've learned a lesson, of sorts."

Hardly knowing what to reply, Charlotte walked to the long table. It was stained and burned with use, and probably came as a temporary loan from the barn outside. Her eye was next caught by a particular box with a glass front, partially covered by a cloth. She thought for a moment to lift it, but decided to send a question with her eyes, instead.

"Ah—now I remember that you are interested in Science. Could this be your reason . . . ? Well, no matter. If there is anything you would like explained, I'll be happy to try. What you are wondering about at the moment is an example of one of your local fliers, which, of course, are beginning their winter's sleep, so I had little difficulty in capturing it. I would guess many of your sex would be put off by this sort of thing. But if you'd like to see it more closely . . ."

Watching her eyes widen, Lee gently lifted the cloth, causing the bat beneath, hanging upside down from a stick, to twitch slightly. However, it kept its eyes tightly closed. Its skin, thought Charlotte, was beautiful—much like a dull satin, worn perhaps for mourning. The thought reminded her of the purpose of her visit, and she resolved to get on with it.

"Have you other . . . live things?" she asked after a second thought, with an eye to her own safety.

"One or two," Lee replied. "But perhaps it would be best not to wake them."

"Actually, I'm more interested today in plant life."

"Somehow more fitting, I think, for a lady. Or, possibly, a healer?" he asked shrewdly.

"Most of us do live some distance from more educated hands."

"I see. Well, I've pressed several things here, which I'm preserving until I can take them back to a water colorist in Connecticut. You probably know most of them yourself. We're attempting to catalog some of the marsh plants, which I suspect have more uses than we realize. It may do some good."

"I'm sure you're right," Charlotte agreed quickly, glad to speak with a man who gave a thought to the future in something other than terms of his crops and his land, or his business. While Lee probably had little in the way of wealth, he must have enough for his simple needs. He certainly seemed far removed from the worries of most farmers she knew (who generally found it difficult to support the land they'd been left, even while they scraped and saved to acquire more).

"I'm interested, just now," she said finally, "in plants that might do harm, rather than good."

"Oh? And what," Lee asked, absently picking up several pages of notes revised with smaller scribbles in their margins, ". . . what exactly is it you look for?"

"Something that might produce visions, and could make someone subject to unusual fears. Something that might also impair the workings of the limbs, as well as the mind."

"Many things might fall into the category you sketch," Lee said thoughtfully. "Can you tell me anything else?"

"A rash—something to cause a small, red rash about the face. And, something that might be found growing locally."

"I'm afraid I can think of no one thing, at least not immediately." Lee took a few steps, and turned. "Combinations of two or more might also be worth thinking about. But I'm scarcely a physician. I, myself, am more interested in the rare specimen no one else has yet seen. Or very few," he added, smiling. "You see, I have no wife, no children. But if I were to make a discovery or two, and if they were to be called after me, it would keep the name of my line alive just as well, to my mind. And, perhaps, some day, some might even thank me for my trouble. It would not be much, but to another scientist, surely, it would seem worthwhile."

"I know one or two who would agree with you," Charlotte returned kindly.

"Mrs. Willett. I must ask you one thing. You are not planning . . . that is, you wouldn't think of using this plant on someone else? No—I'm sorry to even think such a thing. Certainly, you must have quite another reason for your concern."

"As for that," Charlotte said, "I do." Deciding that the man might be trusted with what she'd found, she went on to explain that the supposed Duncan Middleton seen by Bracebridge, and heard by Adolphus Lee himself, was not the actual Boston merchant at all. "What I wonder," she added as she finished, "is if you have seen anyone here, Mr. Lee, whose voice you might recognize as the one you heard speaking to Lydia—or Mrs. Pratt . . . but of course, you know . . ." Her voice trailed off awkwardly.

After thinking for a few moments with his eyes closed, Lee responded. "I did see several gentlemen come and go while I stayed at the inn, and I spoke to most of them downstairs, over a glass of one thing or another. There was the man from Boston who came to visit a niece, he said, who lives somewhere nearby—but his voice was so hoarse you might have taken him for a bullfrog, and I doubt if he could have disguised it, even if he'd wanted to. Then there was Purdy, from Gloucester. But he left the day before Middleton, or whoever it was, arrived. Wait—what about . . . no . . . no. Mr. Mayhew, from the Vineyard, of course, could not be the man, for he stayed until the day *after* the merchant disappeared. There were several others, but they all were far too old to be the gentleman with the good set of teeth you've just described to me. Is there anything else about him you can recall? Anything in the least?"

"I'm afraid not," said Charlotte, turning to go. It had been a wasted trip, after all, for she knew no more than when she'd come in. Now, if she could only manage to leave without being found out . . .

"You know, Mrs. Willett," said Lee, moving as well, "the few afternoons I spent with Lydia Pratt were not only for my own pleasure. Please—do listen. I sensed something in the lady immediately, when I first saw her last year . . . something I recognized, that spoke to me of a loneliness . . . and a need. I don't know why I tell you this, and I hope it will not offend you. But as a woman, and a friend of Science, you must agree that some things are only natural. Not that I believe I was right—far from it! But there are certain habits, learned in youth, I'm afraid, which are very hard to break. That, too, for a man at least, and a traveler, is only natural. And I am a naturalist myself." He grinned, leaping around her to the door, an eager and almost childlike fellow, she finally had to admit.

Lee held the door open, then looked at Charlotte for a moment in all seriousness. "It is important for me to know the world will not despise me for my past sins, which I deeply regret. Is it possible that you, as a representative of this fine village I've grown to admire, can forgive me? I would, I assure you, never in the world hurt one of the female sex. On my honor."

Just what that might be worth, Charlotte was not quite sure as she heard the door close behind her. And yet, somehow, she did believe Adolphus Lee. She had favored him with a slight nod, and a small smile. But again, she thought as she crept down the stairs, she had learned nothing new or especially useful from this unusual man. Except, perhaps, that it might be only fair to think somewhat differently of Lydia Pratt. Lonely? She supposed it was possible. And certainly, she herself knew well enough what loneliness could mean. Should she try to comfort the woman, when few others were in a mood to do so? So far, she had avoided seeing Lydia and posing the few questions she would have liked to ask. The landlady might indeed be able to add something to the description of Middleton, having spoken to him at some length, as Lee had just mentioned again. Of course, there was another possibility concerning Lydia—one that had already been suggested, which she might also explore. . . .

Avoiding Phineas Wise, Charlotte walked out into the cold air and shivered suddenly. Somehow, in answer to her last question, she didn't think it a very good idea. And besides, Saturday chores were still to be done, before anything else could be accomplished. Tomorrow, possibly, she would ask herself once more.

VERY MUCH LATER, toward the end of the afternoon, Mrs. Willett walked in a corner of her kitchen garden, still considering loneliness. Only this time, after thinking deeply of Lydia Pratt's situation, she thought of her own. Longfellow had gone off to Worcester, Lem and Warren were in Cambridge, even Edmund Montagu had by this time arrived in Boston. At the moment, Mrs. Willett wished she could rise and sail like winged Pegasus, to see beyond the horizon.

She stooped to pluck the last blossoms of some meadow saffron, gathering them into a bunch. As she sniffed her nosegay, she even began to feel a little like the unfortunate girl in Monsieur Perrault's fairy tale. *She* had been cruelly kept from a ball, while her sisters put on all their finery and went to enjoy the social world.

But—was a horseback ride to Boston, or Worcester, worth the saddle aches, and possibly even frostbite for her trouble? Not really, Charlotte decided. There was a great deal to be said for taking journeys beside one's fire, with an improving book . . . or even one that wasn't very improving. She would have to ask Richard to pick out something amusing for her from the bookstore on King Street, when he went to take Diana home.

Curiously, Diana had earlier mentioned something about cooking. That in itself was amazing; given the circumstances, it also seemed highly unlikely. But Charlotte hadn't been summoned to join Diana this afternoon, which left both of them free to get on with their own business.

Maybe she was still hoping a crystal slipper would come into her life again, she thought with some regret. Her eyes settled on the clump of horehound holding onto its pale, woolly leaves, growing in the shelter of an old rock wall. Perhaps this year she could bring herself to boil down the hard candy again. She stiffened, and walked on. It was almost as if her mind, now refreshed and cleansed by the astringency of bittersweet thought, could finally turn to the problem she had come outside to ponder.

Just like the characters in the fairy tale, she knew that real people often spent time dreaming of change, and especially of gain. Maybe it was wealth, or maybe it was position that they hoped for. Maybe it was love. But who, exactly, she wondered, stood to gain *in some material way* from the deaths of the last several days? In her own experience, death had added to her stock in life more than once. It wasn't something one liked to think about, but it was something one *did* think about, after—and sometimes even before—someone died. It was, after all, only human.

What about Peter Lynch, then? Had the miller left an heir? Had he possessed the foresight to contemplate the certainty of his own death? Surprisingly, many people didn't. But he certainly had enough property to consider making out a will. He had no family in Bracebridge. She had no idea if he had relations away from the village, or if he was alone in the world. Peter Lynch hadn't been a man many would have cared to ask about his personal history. She only knew he hadn't always lived there. Then again, he might not have cared to leave his goods to a family he had forgotten long ago. He might have preferred to leave them to a family he'd planned to have in the future. Could he have promised money to Elias Frye, or even to Mary directly? Her rejection of him had seemed total, but that hadn't made a difference to Peter Lynch! If he planned to use his wealth as a bargaining point, Mary might at least have heard where he planned it to go at his death.

No one had yet come forward, and so it was something the selectmen would probably need to look into. She would ask Richard Longfellow, as soon as he came home.

The cries of a pair of hawks circling above echoed strangely through the newly empty trees. She drew her shawl tighter, chilled in spite of the thin yellow sunshine that fell at a slant onto her shoulders.

As for the other two deaths: she had no idea who might benefit from Middleton's removal, nor did she particularly care. Anyway, Edmund Montagu would no doubt see to that end of things. And it was, of course, sadly unnecessary to ask the question of young Sam, who had owned next to nothing—only a well-worn musket, and one gold coin. In fact, at the end, not even that.

The walk hadn't given her much insight after all. But an earlier suspicion, while it hadn't blossomed, had gained another inch of fresh growth in her mind. It involved someone she had hoped wouldn't suffer from the week's evil events. Suspicion was not proof, she reminded herself. Nor was it a reason for withdrawing one's support from a fellow creature—especially one in need.

She snapped off some last stems of purple asters for the table, adding them to the crocus blooms. Then, Mrs. Willett wound her way to the kitchen door, intending to set some wool-dying herbs to boil. But first, she would make herself a strong, welcome, comforting pot of tea.

Chapter 26

THE DAPPLED HORSE traveled over snow patches, puddles, and mud, through a wooded countryside spotted with ponds and open meadow. At first, Richard Longfellow enjoyed watching the sunlit silver trunks moving by, while he listened to the voices of migrating waterfowl. Tiring of that, he began to listen to himself.

While much of Bracebridge looked to the East for news and ideas, Longfellow knew that most of Worcester—when it looked beyond its limits—looked to the West. New land was still to be had past the mountains, if one could take it. Dynasties continued to be carved out of the distant forests and marshes; Indian trails and war roads led the way. Worcester saw itself as part of the future, allied with Springfield and Albany, and all the other towns just starting to expand on the web of great and lesser inland waterways.

Had it really been nine years since representatives

from all the colonies made their way up the Hudson to Albany, to consider Dr. Franklin's plan against the French and Indian threat? That these men were not able to agree to its sensible provisions for joining together struck Longfellow as a perfect illustration of the divisive and selfish ways of mankind in general, and those of the men who sat in the various colonial legislatures in particular. But it was all water over the dam now, with European peace upon them again.

Eventually, he was sorry that his ride was almost over, when he trotted past Lake Quinsigamond and reached the town of Worcester. He saw the courthouse and the Congregational church, the bowing elms of the Common, the large, painted clapboard houses of the wealthy, and the shops and businesses that had grown up around the county seat. But he didn't stop until he'd reached a comfortable inn on the other side of town.

There, he pulled his horse up and dismounted at the thick plank steps of the Three Crows, where, sure enough, an unfamiliar boy ran out to take the reins and lead the gray to the stable for its dinner. At the door, Longfellow was greeted warmly by the proprietor, who sent him in to her sitting room fire while she went for some refreshment.

"It's a brisk day," Thankful Marlowe commented moments later as she swept in to see Longfellow's cold-reddened fingers come from under his gloves. Her look told him she approved of his unusually high color. She herself was anything but pale, in either appearance or personality. Everyone knew that Mistress Marlowe had already enjoyed a pair of husbands (both of whom she'd outlived). And it was presumed that, at the age of twenty-seven, she might consider one or two more. The sole owner of a well-known inn and tavern, the widow could afford to pick and choose, which was something Longfellow had been aware of for a little over a year—

since, in fact, Asa Marlowe took his leave. For this reason, he now never failed to consider his possible peril when he stopped during trips to and from the western villages. (That Thankful might doubt he would do for *her* was something Longfellow hadn't considered, and so he worried while he relished her robust presence. In this, it might be said, he had considerable company.)

"What are the chances," he asked, sipping the toddy she'd brought, "that this impostor of ours came through here on Wednesday, possibly carrying some Dutch guldens?" He had already gone over the news, detailing the latest observations and conclusions of those in Bracebridge.

"To the Three Crows? I'm sure he didn't. Most of my stopping customers I know, or I soon get to know . . . although not quite as well as Lydia Pratt, apparently," Thankful couldn't help adding with a wicked laugh. "I'll ask Angus if he's noticed anyone spending guldens in the taproom, but I think he would have mentioned it to me. We're all well aware of what the man was said to look like. I tell you, we've been watching our shadows since this whole business started!"

She stood by the mantel, and soon leaned down to prod the logs with a brass poker until she was satisfied.

"It's certain he looks nothing like what he did, without his disguise," Longfellow cautioned. "We really have nothing to go on there, other than the fact that he's not overlarge . . . or oversmall."

"What about this fiery display of his?" Thankful asked with curiosity.

"That? Just a parlor trick. I could do it myself. In fact, I think I might attempt it for the effect it would have on the town. They need someone to teach them a thing or two about believing in black magic."

"You had better pray they don't go after you next! Of course," she continued, sitting and picking up a bowl of nuts, "lately there's been the usual talk of spirits here, too. We generally hear it more during the autumn. I suppose it's mostly done for amusement. But it's not only between the young and the simple, you know. For every girl who casts a ball of yarn through the window to see her future husband pick it up—oh yes, they still do it—there's a sensible man wondering who might have made his pig sick, or a calf die."

She twisted a wooden screw into a walnut shell, and gave her guest the results with a handsome smile.

"So you were already looking out for something unusual," Longfellow commented, looking along his outstretched legs to the riding boots he wore today over woolen knee breeches. In the heat of the room, both had become somewhat uncomfortable.

"Oh, yes. But we've always got new people coming through, and many of them are noticeably odd, especially those going to the West. A good half of Worcester moves that direction every year, as well. Lately, though, some of them have come back with stories that are *truly* frightening."

"Pontiac?" He sat up, and set his glass on a table to look at her more carefully.

"It seems the war's not over yet, after all. Not his war, at least, and not for the Ottawas. It's farther away this time, but it's led to even more fear and hatred than there was before. No one here knows them any more— the Indians, I mean. So they don't look on them as warriors worthy of respect—and that's no way to go to war, if you want to keep your scalp! But our young men see only the few who stayed around here—most nothing like they once were. In fact, it's tragic to see what they've become."

"What about the French Neutrals in the area?"

"That's another charming story. I'd say they're worried, and with good cause."

"About the frontier?"

She shook her head, frowning. "They don't have much to gain there any more. No, mostly they fear some of the good people of Worcester, and what they're likely to do to them, now that Gabriel Fortier is gone missing. They say he's being hunted for your unpleasant miller's death. Is it true?"

"Mmm, although I think it's unlikely they'll find Fortier now, unless he's a very simple fellow. Which I doubt."

"I've had him here—this summer. He helped clear stones from some of the old fields around the place, the ones Asa couldn't be bothered with. Gabriel should have stayed a farmer; it's apparently what he wanted. But his family had him learn a trade. They bound him to a cooper. He served his time, and then was let go. It seems he wasn't the most pleasant soul to have around, even in a barrel shop—being very sensitive to things that were said of him. You know how men are always going on, especially about politics and the war. Now, I suppose Gabriel is at loose ends, with no tools and no custom of his own."

"You know about the girl?"

"Frye's daughter? Yes, I've heard. Poor thing."

"That's why I've come. I plan to see him, if you'll give me directions."

"Oh-ho! Would you like to take along one or two of the dogs? He's been known to hide from certain visitors, and to turn on others with a cudgel."

"I think he'll talk to me. In fact, I think he'll be expecting a visit."

Thankful Marlowe gave her guest directions to the Frye farm, and walked him to the front door.

"Good luck, then. Will you be back tonight? No? Come by again when you can stay longer. There's always a bed for you here, no matter how full up we are. And be sure to give my regards to the very patient Mrs. Willett."

"Of course," Longfellow replied uncertainly. Only after he had ridden away did Mistress Marlowe let out a peal of laughter—which rang so loudly that one of her lodgers stuck his head out of his window, wondering what he'd missed.

ELIAS FRYE SAT on the porch of his house in the woods, sipping at intervals from a cup he replenished from a stone jar by his knee. As Longfellow rode into the cabin clearing, the gray's nostrils flared at a dozen different smells and sights that confronted them. Ahead, a wolf's pelt was nailed to the logs of the house to cure; to one side, the thick red fur of a fox hung beside several lesser skins from the limb of a dead tree. Assorted gnawed bones lay strewn about the snow-spotted yard, between the ribs of broken casks and old wheels, and a few rusting beaver traps. It was a scene Richard Longfellow was prepared for. But it was still enough to disgust him.

Drawing himself up, he squinted at the unpleasant old person under the mossy roof, who gave him back a false smile. Longfellow dismounted, kicking away a pack of curious dogs who turned out to be more sniff than bite, and tied the horse's reins to a branch of a tree.

It soon became evident that Elias Frye had no qualms about discussing his old acquaintance.

"I did hear tell of Peter being dead—killed by that boy, I imagine," said Frye, taking another sip and watching Longfellow prod a clump of wood fungus on a stump with his boot.

"No one knows," he finally replied, "though as a selectman, I can tell you we're not making any accusations just yet. But we have a few questions for you, concerning the miller."

Elias Frye lowered his eyes; he seemed to be trying hard to recall something.

"Peter Lynch was here on business," he finally began, looking up again. "On Monday, it was, he stopped to see me, like the good friend that he is. Or was," he said with a frown. "Asked me how my family were, and he give me a few jugs of cider, too, as a present. He's spoken for my oldest girl, you know."

Frye fastidiously picked a bit of food from the sleeve of his filthy jacket, and flicked it off onto the ground.

"Did you *actually* want to marry your daughter to Lynch?" asked Longfellow, pinning the man with his eyes.

"Course I did! Why not? Hadn't he money, and property? That's a fine mill to run, too. And didn't he ask me proper, paying me for the honor?"

"Oh, I'm certain he did that. Just as Jonathan Pratt paid you to have your daughter work for him for three years, rather than see her go from childhood into the miller's arms. You relied on Pratt's sympathy, didn't you? It was worth money in your pocket. And there was always later for the miller, although he would have preferred sooner. At any rate, you'd have been glad to do another favor for Lynch if he asked you—isn't that right?"

"What kind of favor?"

"Oh, you might say that he was somewhere, when he wasn't."

"I told you he was right here, on Monday."

"Yes, even before I'd asked you."

"Well, I knew *somebody* ought to come and ask me about him, because he's dead, ain't he! And we both know who did it," Elias Frye whined.

"Yes, he's dead. That's why you can tell me the truth now, and not just what Lynch told you to say. I believe he was nowhere near here on Monday. I think—I *know*—he had another errand to do. Perhaps on the coast?"

At this, Elias Frye paled; even his dogs seemed to sense the fear that had shaken through his narrow body. They slunk quietly in a row around the corner of the house, with hardly a backward glance.

"What do you want from me?" Frye eventually managed, his throat tight and bobbing.

"The truth. And a promise that you'll leave Mary alone, so she might make up her own mind about what to do next."

"Well, the Frenchman can have her, and welcome— if he keeps his neck free of a noose! I've got more. I doubt anyone *else* would have her, now. I only tried to get her something better for herself, and for us all! Though there's some say I ain't done as well as a father might for his motherless children, I done what I could, all alone, with what I got," he wheezed, pulling a horrible handkerchief from his pocket and dabbing at an eye, then mopping his forehead.

Longfellow looked slowly around, sensing that there were others hiding nearby. One young girl in particular was in his thoughts . . . Mary's likely successor in Frye's plans.

"Let me warn you about something," Longfellow began again. "If you don't tell the truth, you could very well anger whoever it was that murdered the miller. In any event, I'll see that the courts and the lawyers tear apart this story of yours. And they may do far worse! This thing is far from over. Very possibly, it's about much more than Lynch's murder. So there *will* be more questions, until we learn the truth."

Frye said nothing. But a girl of twelve or thirteen, wearing a ragged homespun dress, now walked out of the door behind him and stood facing Longfellow defiantly. At first, he thought she meant to join her father, but such was not the case.

"The miller never came here on Monday, sir. He

never came at all last month. Old Man barely knows what truth is, so you'd be foolish to trust him!"

"Your father had no contact with the miller at all?" Longfellow asked with some surprise.

"He went to see Peter Lynch last week in Bracebridge, and stayed the night," the girl replied. "We don't know what they did, but if it was wrong, it's not the first time he's shamed us. Might be the last, though." She gave a sour little smile to the back of her father's head. "One day soon we'll leave, and then *he* can drink himself to death . . . if he can find the money."

"Has Mary been here recently?" Longfellow pressed her. He watched the young girl's expression change abruptly.

"Mary hasn't been able to come since winter, but she writes us, and I can make most of it out," her sister replied anxiously. "Did she send you?"

"No, but I've seen her, and she's well. My name is Longfellow. I live next to the inn where Mary stays. If you have information about your father and Peter Lynch, you might be asked to testify in court. Then again, you might not. You could prefer to keep what you know in reserve . . . in case someone should try to make you do something you don't care to—as Mary was nearly forced into doing. If anything like that should happen, go to the Three Crows, and ask Mistress Marlowe to send for me."

The young girl nodded sharply, though he thought he saw a question in her gaze. At the same time, the old man seemed to deflate. He again applied his handkerchief in a gesture that asked for pity. A sudden wail from a child sent the girl flying back inside. Longfellow's eyes followed her in silent admiration.

What the girl had said probably proved some kind of collusion, he thought when she'd gone. As he had supposed. Satisfied for the moment, he started for his horse.

"She'll do what she likes, that one will," Elias Frye

rambled on to himself, after taking another long pull from the jug. "She's smart, she is, there's no doubt of it. Go away and leave her old father alone. Ah, let her go! Let her try to find a man herself. She's no beauty— not like my Mary. My very own, very nice Mary," he snickered drunkenly to himself, apparently thinking of happier days.

Was *that* the real reason the father had kept Peter Lynch on a string—fear of his anger at learning, on his wedding night, the vilest of family secrets? By sending his daughter to work at the inn, had Frye hoped to put the blame for a sin of his own on someone else, if and when time revealed it? Suddenly, the stench of the place became unbearable.

It was enough, thought Longfellow as he rode away, to sicken a man. Surely it was enough to make a child do whatever it could to be free of the abuse, the squalor, and the ugly lies that life at home had always held. A young woman would naturally dread the continuation of such a life, in the arms of another man equally cruel, or quite possibly worse. That kind of fear, Longfellow realized, might have driven a person like himself to go beyond the law, beyond the rules of sense and decency. Might it even, he thought morosely, in a like situation, have driven him to murder?

Chapter 27

I F THERE'S ONE thing I know, it's human nature," Diana Longfellow confided. Seated in a chair to one side of the kitchen hearth, she smoothed her skirts, while Cicero shook his head at the old Dutch oven whose three feet straddled a mound of glowing coals.

"How *could* he have done what they say?" she went on airily. "There's certainly no real proof against the Frenchman, and I don't intend to help your village ruffians tear him to pieces, before they find the real culprit. He's far too handsome for that! Which is why I'm allowing him to hide in Richard's greenhouse."

Cicero's gasp did nothing to alter her serene smile; it rarely bothered Diana when she shocked others.

"He's already out there?" the old servant finally asked unhappily, knowing trouble when he saw it. And right now he saw it sitting next to the kitchen fire.

"Well, you didn't think I'd be making this pot of

stew and the kettle cake all for us? I'm sure the poor man hasn't eaten decently for days. That's why we're going to feed him. After it's dark, when he can come inside. Mary told me he almost froze, out alone in the woods last night."

Women who are forever petted and praised, thought her temporary guardian, often display as much sense as the little dogs they keep on their laps. At least this time Diana hadn't brought along Bon-Bon; not a good traveler, the ratlike thing preferred to stay at home where Diana's maid Patty stuffed it with sweetmeats. Cicero longed for a chance to try his own hand at stuffing the animal; he had seen a well-mounted skunk in a shop window once, in Boston.

He poured the yellow batter he'd mixed into the greased pot, covered it, and turned to attempt to reason with his charge.

"What," he asked somewhat severely, "will we do if someone looks in and sees him? Have you thought of that?"

"Well then, of course, we ... well, we say we have no idea how he got here. But most of the town will be inside by sunset, because it's the Sabbath. Besides, it's quite cold out, and I doubt if anyone *really* wants to interfere with this house; there's talk Richard is clever enough to raise the very Devil whenever he wants to. Besides, as we all know, one must occasionally make sacrifices for others."

Cicero looked at her sharply. It was not the kind of thing he was accustomed to hearing from the rosy lips of this particular young lady. His own lips moved slightly.

"Pardon?" she challenged.

"I only wonder if there's a new young minister in Boston," he muttered, leaning forward to look into the stew pot that hung over the fire.

"I grant you that good works are not my usual occupation, for I generally have enough trouble trying to make sure *I'm* happy. But today, everyone *else* has something to do, and here I sit, twiddling my thumbs!"

"Go home, then," the old man suggested, seeing a glimmer of hope.

"To Boston? Back to more of the same? Balls, and dances, and whist parties, and dinners where everyone chatters on and on, like a flock of parrots? I suppose I shall have to, soon enough. But I propose to have some excitement first."

"This wouldn't be something you want to do to bedevil your brother, would it? And what if the town finds out, with him in a position of responsibility?"

"Richard can take care of himself," Diana countered saucily. "He always has; he always will. It's a trait of the Longfellows."

"And if Captain Montagu discovers what you've been up to?"

At that, her eyes twinkled along with her rings in the firelight. "It *would* be amusing to find out what he would do with me," she answered with a graceful smile. "You, of course, he'd probably hang. But he's not here, is he? We'll tell him all about it some other time—after the whole thing's over. Now, we will cut up five or six large potatoes, as soon as we bring them up from the cellar, and then we'll add them to the pot. Don't be long," she called after him, wiggling with anticipation on her cushioned chair, while a sighing Cicero took himself down the creaking wooden stairs.

ACROSS TWO GARDENS, Charlotte entered her own kitchen. A rushed Hannah Sloan had just hurried in with some items for the pantry. Anxious to return home before sunset, she was soon through the back door and gone.

Alone again, Charlotte warmed the teapot and filled

it. Several ideas crowded into her mind, one on top of another. First came thoughts of supper. With Lem gone, fried hasty pudding with maple sugar would do, with dried blueberries soaked in cream for after. She was in no hurry. The kitchen was warm, and the fire right for making up a batch of dye.

She let Orpheus out when he whined softly at the door. She was surprised that the garden walk hadn't been enough for him. She supposed that the dog, too, felt restless, probably sensing her own state of mind. Putting dried goldenrod from a corner rafter into a pot of water with a bit of indigo, Charlotte stirred and hoped for a green as good as the one she'd made the year before. She had enough alum for fixing several pounds of wool and a smaller amount of flax for napkins. There would soon be plenty of time to put it to the loom, when the snow drifts began to grow up the sides of the house and barn. Time, and time to spare.

On Monday, bayberries could be set to boil. Hannah's youngest had already collected gallons for her from the marshes and rocky wastes—enough to melt off a film to skim and add to beeswax for a few dozen special candles. And she would have books from the Harvard library to explore, if Dr. Warren kept his word. It would be another full week.

Slowly sipping the tea that seemed bitter as dregs today—it was, in fact, the last of the August-bought tin, and full of powder—Charlotte began to imagine the road to Boston once more, a road as full of memories as any she knew.

Outside the kitchen windows, the sun hit the limbs of a beech behind the barn, and played among the final leaves of the darker oak branches nearby. As day turned to evening, the world seemed to crackle with electricity. While the frost prepared to fall again like a lace coverlet, the eastern sky turned the color of lapis lazuli, complete with faint gold stars. And the setting sun lit up the barn's windows, until they appeared to be turned into Indian rubies! She had seen it all many times before, but tonight it was particularly vivid and clear. So were the huge flocks of geese flying through the upper light in long, trailing forks—hundreds, thousands of spots of darkness covering up the sky . . .

Charlotte suddenly realized she had been staring blindly into the night through the dark window, seeing nothing, only imagining. Her eyes were wide. Her breath came in swift shudders. And her mouth was dry. Mechanically, she finished the cup of tea, wondering what was wrong with her surroundings. An unlit candle stood beside her. Without thinking, she got up and went to the fire. Fumbling with a splinter, she produced a flame on one end—touched flame to wick—then blew the source away. The resulting smoke coiled up into the air in a thick rope like a monstrous, twisting cobra, hissing and dancing hypnotically. She stared in amazement, then looked away with growing fear.

And yet the hearth fire still sparked and crackled softly. The pot had begun to steam, the tea was still before her.

The tea! It was something to do with the tea. Bitter, and musty; she could still taste it on her dry tongue. And the books, what was it about the books she'd been thinking of? Her head echoed with sounds she knew came from her own imagination. With great effort, she concentrated on the few things that still seemed real.

Of course—this must be what it was like to feel first-hand something that had afflicted others around the village during the week. Curious signs that marked their victims as being . . . what was the word? Oh, yes, *possessed*. She had been possessed once; as a wife, she thought dizzily, possessed and cherished. Till death do us part. No, that was over. This was her own kitchen, though a new world. Yet not unlike the old . . .

Scratching her fingers against the back of her hand, she looked down to see a red rash. She had seen the same rosy dots before, when she looked down into the miller's horrible face—

She saw that dead face again, growing out of the table in front of her. It was a thing too terrifying to look at for long. But at the same time, the words of someone, she couldn't quite tell who, sounded in her ears. It was a man of Science. Something he had told her. Emotion. No place for emotion in science. She heard herself laughing merrily, and wondered why.

Clinging onto the back of her chair, Charlotte twisted and rose to her feet, then took the candle to a small mirror by the door. On her face were more blotches, and she could hardly believe that the eyes she gazed at were her own. All black, their pupils completely covered the blue. These were the eyes of paintings, eyes of the beauties of Italy, and Spain. Black eyes, like round chips of shiny, hard coal—eyes as big as saucers, *belladonna* eyes. Wasn't that a serious problem? Didn't people sometimes die of it? The thought was frightening—or might have been, except for other thoughts that overrode her fears.

"In the midst of life, we are in death." She knew that to be true, always. Though Death was hardly a friend, he was not entirely a stranger. She decided to sit and watch for him to come, if he would, while she strove to calm the pounding of her heart.

Had the fire grown brighter? The room was hot, stifling. It was smaller, too, and the china winked with eyes, like cats sitting on the cupboard shelves, waiting to leap down and begin to fiddle in the firelight. There was altogether too much going on in the little room, she told herself, beginning to admire her own control. Perhaps a solution to all of her problems lay outside the bolted door.

It was difficult at first to raise the latch. But once opened, the door swung inward on its hinges, and Charlotte stumbled out. Suddenly, she felt much cooler, though she soon ceased to notice. The night sky, filled with stars, seemed boundless. As she turned, she saw the constellations twirling, some of them caught in the ensnaring arms of trees, some pulling free. And then, at both sides of the sky, they began to disappear.

Near panic, she forced herself to be still, and to look down to earth again. What little she saw around her feet was vague and blurred. Something pulled at her; she felt her feet responding. When she next looked up, nearby shapes grew menacing, and her heart leaped to her throat as they seemed to lunge forward, only to subside again into surrounding calm. For a moment, the acrid smell of wood smoke clawed at her throat and made her sneeze. When she again opened her eyes, the ground churned and rolled under her, and seemed to groan. Suddenly, her empty stomach rebelled; with a rush, she felt herself turning inside out.

Finally, the spasms ceased.

She realized that it must have been her own voice she had heard groaning, and noticed that she had fallen to her knees. Once more, her breathing quickened as she sensed an unknown presence drawing closer, and closer still.

Abruptly, her arms were filled with fur. Orpheus had found her on his return from the fields. He whimpered as he searched her face and hair with his nose, wondering what was wrong.

Her own wild giggles brought momentary comfort, and a partial return of reason. But that was soon lost in a further blur of motion and sound. Again, the wet nose bent over her, and a large tongue licked her forehead.

Once more, Charlotte lifted her head and stretched out her arms to encircle the dog's neck—and then slid back and out of the world entirely.

Seeing his mistress lying silent, Orpheus lifted his head to the cold stars, and howled.

WHEN SHE AWOKE, Mrs. Willett was puzzled by the change in the air around her. Now delightfully moist and warm, it was filled with a strong, flowery scent. She opened her eyes, half expecting to find the Heavenly City around her. But instead of ethereal light, there was almost total darkness, and a snaking dragon coiling itself in front of her face. Was this place Hell, then?

The dragon moved away and, she saw light come through the slits in a small copper lantern, on a stone beside her. It was a hard slate floor she lay on, but hardly Hades. Rolling her head to look up, she saw the long fingers of a palm frond against the starry sky, and suddenly knew exactly where it was that her body had somehow landed. How it had arrived there, she couldn't recall. And why her head, when she tilted it to one side, caused her such agony was another mystery; she'd felt no pain before.

Focusing her eyes, she saw the dragon approach once more. But this time, she recognized its painted face. It was the same creature she had seen on the little bottle that Diana had shown her at the inn. It seemed like weeks before; was it only two days ago? But now, the bottle was in the hands of Mary Frye.

Gabriel Fortier also knelt to one side, his face full of concern. The Frenchman bent forward to help when Charlotte struggled to raise her head, and she noticed that Mary's little bottle went swiftly back into the pocket beneath her skirt. Fortier helped her to slide back against the warm brick wall, and then smiled ruefully.

"I am unlucky for you," he began, but Mary wouldn't let him go on with the thought.

"It would have been far worse if Mrs. Willett had frozen to death in her own garden, with no one there to find her! It's a good thing that you heard the dog, and went to look."

Mary stood to remove a canvas drapery from its pegs, which she then drew around Charlotte's shoulders. "But she can't stay here, and neither can we. We'll take you in to Miss Longfellow. You haven't even worn a shawl," she chided, shaking her head with disapproval, as if at a child. "And then to faint in a lonely spot like that!"

It was too much to explain, Charlotte realized; and so she didn't try.

Mary and Gabriel had begun to help her to her feet, when the outer glass house door made a sound, and moved. All three turned as one, expecting the worst. Instead, they saw Cicero, whose soft cry at seeing Charlotte on the ground was answered by sighs of relief.

Mrs. Willett, the old man saw immediately, had somehow managed to get herself into the middle of more trouble. He stooped to look deeply into her eyes.

Soon, they were on the path to the house, with Orpheus leading the way.

"What on earth. . . !" Diana boggled, when the kitchen door opened and she saw the procession enter. In an instant, she had gone for a heavy quilt to wrap around her friend.

When everyone was settled, with a fresh pot of tea brewing and smells of a simple dinner rising from the table, the story was slowly pieced together.

"Then someone must have gone into your house," Diana concluded when Charlotte had finished, "and left something in the tea while you were in your garden. It was certainly a coward; who else would choose such a way to silence a woman?"

"Would you have preferred a duel?" her neighbor asked with a laugh that was still not quite her own.

"I would have preferred for you to stay indoors, as Richard suggested. Oh! I'm starting to sound like my brother. But never mind; it wouldn't have helped much if you'd done that, anyway. The poisoner might simply have found a faster, surer way." She hesitated, shocked by the picture this brought to her mind, before she continued. "I suppose it's uncertain whether he wanted to actually kill you or not. But with you wandering outside, out of your senses, the cold certainly could have done the job. As it is, it's a good thing I'm here to watch you. I doubt if you'll be able to think clearly for quite some time."

"Otherwise, she would have been wondering by now why you're hiding a fugitive in your brother's greenhouse," Cicero said pointedly.

"Yes, I *was* going to ask you that, Diana. Especially since Richard said—"

"What he always says? Oh, well. He's not here to think for us, so I suppose it's up to me to say they *can't* stay here now. Whoever was after you might have been watching all of us tonight, and seen all of *you* come inside. I suppose it was the impostor—the one Richard tells me everyone thought was Duncan Middleton?"

"He was not?" asked the Frenchman, unacquainted with the newest developments. Charlotte related the story of the old man's teeth, or lack of them, and her own slight connection with the red-cloaked stranger—as well as the warning given to her by Dr. Warren.

"If he is still alive then, at least no one has reason to blame me for being a sorcerer," Gabriel proclaimed with relief. But they soon realized that the news did little to change his position as someone who might well have sought the death of Peter Lynch. To the village, at least, he was still outside the law. And it was likely that Mary's part in helping him would soon be discovered.

"Go back to the inn," he begged, his fingers gently touching Mary's hair. "For now, there is no future with me. Soon, I can be far away, in a place where I will work for money. When I have earned enough, then I will send for you."

"Unless . . ." Charlotte ventured, raising a hand to her aching head, and thinking as clearly, and as quickly, as she could.

"Unless I go with you now," Mary finished, holding her own head proudly, staring in the face of trouble that was likely to come.

". . . unless you stay until tomorrow, or the next day at the latest," Charlotte suggested quietly. "I know it's a risk, but when I can put two and two together again, and we have a few more facts, I think we will be able to clear Gabriel's name for good. Although there's a chance that would bring other dangers," she finished, looking squarely at Mary, her blue eyes grave.

"I think," Mary responded, bravely, "that I know one more place where no one will find you. And if the worst should happen, I swear by God that you won't die alone!"

It was an extremely foolish oath, Charlotte knew immediately. Foolish, and deadly serious—and very likely to be carried out, if things should go against Gabriel Fortier.

Charlotte reached to stroke Orpheus's silky fur, and thought for a moment about the selflessness of love. She knew it was something that might hold two people together even in the face of death—sometimes, even after death itself. Looking at the lovers before her, she hoped that the strength of their passion might not also prove to be their undoing.

Chapter 28

꜀ Sunday

'HE DISCOVERETH DEEP things out of darkness, and bringeth out to light the shadow of death,'" boomed the Reverend Christian Rowe, reading from the Book of Job, while his congregation fittingly huddled in the unheated meetinghouse. Some probably shivered, too, while taking the sobering words to heart.

Did it mean, wondered Charlotte Willett, that it was only the Lord's business to make known these deep things—the depths of human iniquity and frailty? Or was it for man (or woman) to help matters along? Am I my brother's keeper? If so, am I to be his executioner as well? She wished she knew.

Charlotte was herself a great deal fonder of earlier words in the same chapter, those exhorting man to listen to the beasts, and the fowls of the air, and to learn from the earth as well as the fishes of the sea. Certainly there was much to be learned by using one's senses and examining Nature, in the manner of Mr. Lee, among others. On the other hand, Reverend Rowe clearly relished the somber passages that came later; his eyes flashed with pleasure as he went on.

" 'Man that is born of a woman is of few days, and full of trouble. He cometh forth like a flower, and is cut down; he fleeth also as a shadow, and continueth not. And dost thou open thine eyes upon such an one, and bringest me into judgment with thee?' "

God, we're told, Charlotte continued on her own, helps those who help themselves—and He requires that we help each other. But what she now considered telling meant something more than help for the living, or even a quiet rest for the dead. It might also bring dreadful harm. Was it her business to interfere, by pointing a finger? She was certain now that at least a single murderer was still in their midst. But just how did one decide what to reveal about one's fellows, and what to leave to others, or to God?

Three men had died . . . although one of them had really been only a boy. Peter Lynch had been a menacing, grasping man; but the taking of his life, too, was surely of some importance, if even a sparrow counted. Every death had meaning; each meant loss. " 'And therefore never send to know for whom the bell tolls,' " she remembered Aaron saying. " 'It tolls for thee.' " Once more, Donne's lines provoked many thoughts within her. But soon they whirled with all the rest of the morning's words in a glittering mass inside Charlotte's head, which still ached from the previous evening's adventure.

And what about preserving one's own life, if it were threatened? It was true she could have died in her garden—might well have died of the cold, at least, if it had not been for a combination of lucky circumstances, or perhaps divine help. That, too, was a thought. Before leaving home this morning, she had taken several cups of strong coffee to fight off a fatigue that sleep hadn't cured. Now, its effects caused her body to tremble. The rash had gone, but an irritating itch remained.

Still, she'd taken a little time this morning to study the books Lem had brought back for her from Boston. But on the face of it, she'd decided it might be impossible to prove anything, even if she *had* found a likely herb. After all, knowledge of what had been used still didn't say who had left it, even though she felt she knew.

Looking for distraction, she studied Richard Longfellow and Diana in their front pew. It was a position her neighbor had paid well for, as was expected, although she knew he would have preferred a less conspicuous place.

At the same moment, Diana, too, was feeling constrained by her highly visible position, but at least she didn't feel the cold, wrapped in a thick, fur-lined cloak, with her feet on a warmer full of coals. What a bore the preacher was, she thought, and had been for two hours and fifty minutes, according to a small gold watch she glanced at from time to time. She was used to sermons dealing with urban life, with politics and personalities chastised or supported from the pulpit. Sundays *could* be very exciting, especially if one knew the individuals referred to, and could turn to look at them. And sermons in Boston were generally shorter. She wondered if Edmund Montagu went to meeting today in the city, or if he had found some official excuse.

Once again, Diana reached into a large satchel that held several comforts, to get a scented handkerchief and perhaps a lemon drop. It was then she saw a gleam from within, indicating something which, on further fishing, turned out to be the lost enameled dragon vial with its delightful perfume. She had been wrong; she'd never lost it at all.

Only now, she remembered dropping the bottle into

a small pocket in the larger bag, for safekeeping. Well, that was fortunate. She would have to tell Charlotte not to keep looking for it, when the sermon ended. The thought of Mrs. Willett made Diana sigh again, as it recalled her mind to more serious matters.

Seated beside his sister, an attentive Richard Longfellow continued to frown at Christian Rowe, trying to decide if the minister's hairline receded as quickly as his own. Longfellow had already gone over his conversation with Elias Frye several times in his head, until he had run out of new conclusions. It was now very likely that the miller had not been in Worcester when he said he was; wherever Lynch *had* been, it was also very likely that he'd been up to no good. It might have been Providence . . . but there was no proof. Still, he couldn't have been the one to attempt to poison Charlotte. Tea from the same canister had been drunk since Lynch's death with no ill effects, by both Charlotte and Hannah. And there had been no other guests in the Willett house since then. So, someone *must* have crept into Charlotte's kitchen when no one else was there on Saturday afternoon, and left a nasty calling card. As a selectman, Longfellow felt especially unhappy about the way the thing had been carried out. Had it really come to this—had people to lock all of their doors when leaving now, if only for half an hour? It was undoubtedly a sign of the growing lawlessness of the times.

On Longfellow's left, Cicero sat gazing at the preacher with what appeared to be admirable piety. But his thoughts, too, were wandering. It had been another interesting night, and a neat trick to get Gabriel and Mary out the back door, while Longfellow came in through the front. Later, he would enjoy hearing Diana's explanation of the brief use she'd made of Longfellow's glass house. Last night there had been enough to say about the attempt on their neighbor's life. All three had resolved to do everything they could to keep such a thing from happening again. They had also agreed that no one else should be told. It was enough that Charlotte had been singled out twice in one week—first, by Peter Lynch, then by the preacher, in front of his mob. Cicero knew it would do little good for even Longfellow to challenge a man like Reverend Rowe, if he should get it into his head to stir up more trouble. But, there were other ways to persuade the fellow, should the need arise.

" 'For thy mouth uttereth thine iniquity, and thou choosest the tongue of the crafty. Thine own mouth condemneth thee, and not I: yea, thine own lips testify against thee,' " intoned the reverend.

That's why certain pious people really should be more careful, thought Cicero, of what they wish for, even to themselves, after a few toddies on a cold night at the taproom of a village inn. Especially when they're standing near a corner nook that hides an old man with excellent ears. Cicero's smile grew until it nearly connected those two prominent features, and he raised his kindly face as if exalting in the Word. If some of the ladies present only knew!

Two pews away, but in another world, young Lem sat among his large family, remembering the novel things he'd seen and done at Harvard College. If he worked hard, Dr. Warren had told him, he might become a student, although an extremely low ranking one to start. Still, with sponsorship—and if he learned his Greek and Latin—Warren had also said he might earn a degree with the best. Odder things had happened. In fact, it seemed to Lem that odd things lately made up the bulk of his limited experience.

Nathan Browne, the inn's smith, sat in the middle of the room, thinking how curious it was that both Jonathan and Lydia Pratt sat next to him in church today, as though nothing had happened. Well, no one *could* say, for sure . . . and given another chance, Lydia might change her spots, he supposed, but it was not a thing he'd be willing to wager on. Still, in the last two days she had spoken surprisingly kind words to them all. At the same time, Mary was in such a nervous state that those around her had begun to fear for her health. One moment the girl would be flushed; another she was as pale as a snow bank. Something else had happened to make Nathan hide whatever feelings he'd once had for her. So far he'd told no one, and wondered if Mary knew herself. The way things were, it might be dangerous to say too much . . . but he'd made new plans. . . .

Toward the back of the meetinghouse, others filled less polished pews. Phineas Wise sat with glazed eyes, next to Jack and Esther Pennywort, who actually appeared to be listening. Across the aisle, the four remaining Dudleys, their eyes cast down, privately mourned one of their own, speaking through their hearts to their Creator. On a corner bench, Hannah Sloan, her husband, sons, and daughters had begun to imagine their afternoon meal together, while in front of them Constable Bowers and his large fidgeting family held onto their prayer books and each other, and prayed that Mr. Bowers would not be the next one murdered for his official part in the ongoing investigations.

And then, abruptly, Christian Rowe ended his reading on the woeful ways of man, to the relief of the entire congregation. No doubt he'd worked up a thirst. He may also have sensed that after three hours he'd lost most of his listeners. At any rate, the preacher released his flock for their dinner, prior to a second service in an hour and a half. Some noisily bustled out on their way home. More made their way to common pastures to wait—heading for the Bracebridge Inn, and the tavern at the crossroads.

•   •   •

"I KNOW IT'S cruel to keep him out," declared Esther Pennywort, who sat in her faded cloak, sipping a cup of warm cider by the Blue Boar's fire. "Though what's a woman to do but treat a husband like a child, when he acts that way? Not that I'd keep a child of mine out in the cold," she corrected herself, "if it had no place else to go. But Jack always has his ways, and he can shift for himself if need be."

Charlotte raised a glass of sherry that Phineas had brought her against the new season's chill, quite glad to be out of the drafts of the meetinghouse. Earlier, she had excused herself from Longfellow and Diana, saying she needed to have a brief word with a friend. Now, at her suggestion, she and Esther Pennywort cast their minds back to the evening of the old man's burning.

"Do you know just where he weathered the night?" Charlotte asked with a certain amount of hope. She watched as the small, fussy woman's eyes narrowed in thought, while worn hands rubbed one another.

"Well, when Jack's had enough, he usually goes to sleep in a barn or a shed, next to wherever he's found whatever it is he's been drinking. If he's been here at the Blue Boar, I'm told he goes across to the mill to sleep under some flour sacks. I know drunkenness is common enough in country and town alike, but I won't put up with it in my house! So when he came home carrying that strange tale, and with the fumes of a whiskey barrel about him, it made my blood boil! We have little for what we need, with the children growing. And for him to spend it on drink is too much!"

"It is hard," Charlotte sympathized. "But did he tell you where he went on that *particular* night?"

Again, Esther paused to think, her upper lip puckered into soft, vertical waves.

"Now, that's funny. He didn't say, but I thought he might not have gone to bed at all—he was so tired when he came in next morning. He slept for most of the next day and night, and after that he was up and gone again early."

"The morning Sam Dudley died."

"Yes," Esther replied hesitantly, "that would be the day. My Jack isn't a bad man, when he's sober," she insisted, worried more than a little at what Mrs. Willett might be thinking. "Although most believe him to be dim-witted. Oh, I know they do. Still, he's good enough for me."

"Times haven't gotten any easier for you lately, have they? No extra money has come in to make a difference?"

"Extra money! No, I'm afraid not. But as you mention it, lately he *has* taken to carrying on just like he's 'somebody'—even carrying snuff about. Imagine! A habit for his betters, if indeed it's for anyone at all! Quite nasty, I call it, sniffing tobacco up your nose, even if a lord cares to do it—even if it's soaked with something sweet."

"Where do you suppose he came by it? Perhaps someone gave it to him?"

Mrs. Pennywort looked around her, then lowered her voice. "I doubt that. I'm afraid to say it, but Jack has been known, occasionally, to be a bit—well, light-fingered. It's not all his fault, and I'm not sure but it's fair play, really. You see, his *friends*, as he calls them—these friends of his think he's simple, and encourage him to drink for the joy of watching his antics. It's never been all because of drink, either. It's his medicine, you know. For his teeth."

"Ah," said Charlotte, letting her breath escape in a sigh of enlightenment.

"They're none too good, nor are most of ours at this age, I suppose. But his are something dreadful, what's left of them in back especially. And he's too afraid to have them pulled! But he went to Boston one day, and in a tavern by the docks, he met a fellow—"

"Who gave him something for the pain?"

"That's right!" smiled Mrs. Pennywort. "They use it in eastern lands, he told Jack. Little seeds he was to chew on. Something like clove—he used to put a clove on a tooth for the pain, like most of us do. Well, these did him far more good, but they do make him quite queer. Sometimes, he can't tell what's what after he chews them. Still, they help him over the worst. He got a dreadful rash at first, but he's over that now. They call it henbane—funny name, isn't it? Anyway, that's why so many think of him as childlike. So do I, sometimes, I'll admit. But it isn't good for grown men to be teased and laughed at, or treated like children, is it? Nor for women, either, although men treat us the same as Jack often enough, and for less reason. It's a shame, really."

Charlotte sat very still, while Esther Pennywort sighed at the world's folly, took another sip of cider, and sat back with a small frown. Then she began to examine the company around them, unaware of the great secret she'd just betrayed.

So Jack Pennywort had left her henbane, thought Charlotte with a tiny smile . . . probably for fear of what she might suspect about his dealings with the miller. She'd already guessed that Jack knew more than he'd told. Had he feared, after their interview, that she might soon guess more?

She had given him tea on Thursday; that might have planted the idea in his mind. And perhaps he had only tried to discredit her, by causing her to act as he often did himself. After that, in the same way that others had always laughed at him, they would laugh at her, whatever she told them. Surely, her death hadn't been part of his plan. After all, he chewed the seeds himself. And she believed for Jack Pennywort that one murder would have been enough. As for Peter Lynch—how easy it would have been for Jack to offer his powerful "friend" one pinch of tainted snuff . . . then, another. And in a while, if the miller had begun to worry, or if he had rushed toward the smaller man, threatening—

She thought it likely Jack had only resorted to murder after he'd witnessed the miller commit one of his own. Poor young Sam must have seen the miller getting rid of the evidence of "Duncan Middleton" in his pond on Tuesday night; the boy had probably agreed to meet Lynch at a later time, when things had calmed down. If Jack had already gone to rest in the dark mill on Tuesday night, and overheard Sam talking with Lynch—and if he had followed later, to see the miller choke the life out of the boy—he might well have thought his own life was in danger. As it probably had been.

It all fit. So did the many reports of "the Devil's work" heard during the week. No doubt Jack had enjoyed offering others some of his own medicine in an innocent pinch of snuff. After all, he had been chosen to tell a shocking story to an admiring world, only to discover that it had all been a hoax. The whole thing, his whole life, had been a peculiar sort of amusement for others. Perhaps, thought Charlotte, there were more than a few people in Bracebridge to blame for Jack's recent sins.

She drew her mind back to the buzzing room full of farmers. The smells of ripe stew, lunch baskets, tobacco and wood smoke, wet linen and wool, and the pungency of several infants all swirled together over the subtler fumes from mugs and glasses.

Right now, Jack would be out behind the tavern with a few other men, enjoying tall stories and the cheap comfort of jug liquor, out of view of their women and children who preferred the crowded warmth inside. If he should enter now, what would be his reaction at seeing her sitting beside his wife?

And what about the man who had started the whole thing by coming to Bracebridge with the red cloak and the gold coins belonging to a dead man—an impostor whose own location no one, as yet, seemed to know? Had the stranger truly been responsible for the real Duncan Middleton's murder, with perhaps some help from Peter Lynch? Whoever he was, he was probably far away. Or then again, it was possible that he could be about to walk in through the tavern door at any moment.

Thinking it all over, Charlotte came to one final conclusion. She had very little idea of what would happen next.

Chapter 29

ODDLY ENOUGH, THE next person to actually sweep through the front door of the tavern turned out to be Diana Longfellow, who had never been known to visit the Blue Boar, but who seemed to find it worth a brief look now.

"You'll wonder," she said to Charlotte Willett with feigned ennui, "what draws me here, and all alone. It's a question with two answers, really. First, Richard and Cicero are quite busy on the bridge, debating whether the flow of water would be increased if the millpond were reduced, and whether that would alter the pleasures of some kind of fish. For my part, I wanted to tell you I've found my dragon vial. It was just where I'd left it, I'm afraid. But why don't we all go for our dinner now, if you're through with your business?"

"Then it wasn't Mary—" Charlotte began. Immediately, she thought better of denying what she'd been forced to suspect earlier ... that the young woman might be a thief, and worse. It *had* seemed odd that Mary would be interested in taking such a thing, while her lover's life was at stake. Diana's news, then, meant that there must be *two* identical bottles in Bracebridge. But why had Mary been so quick to hide one of them the night before?

"Didn't you tell me that bottle was one of only half a dozen just arrived?" she asked Diana instead.

"Yes, brought in by Will Harper. If I'd been in Providence to ask him directly, I'm certain I could have gotten it at a much better price. For a song, really," Diana concluded, her eyes taking on a dreamy expression. "Did I tell you that I met the captain once before, while I was in London?"

"But then, Mary's bottle must have been brought from Providence, as well," Charlotte labored to explain. "So that means Peter Lynch was in *Providence*, not Worcester, on Monday ... and that's where he intercepted Duncan Middleton! As he may have been *told* to do—by someone far smaller, who would be able to impersonate the merchant here. Then, both came back to Bracebridge on Tuesday, with the clothes, the horse, and the money. The impostor took the money, put on the clothes, and rode the horse to the inn. I saw him; so did Jonathan, and Lydia ... although she tried to hide the fact—unsuccessfully, for the two of them were overheard by Mr. Lee. And then later at the Blue Boar, Gabriel went out first, and Jack followed them both onto the road, just as they knew he would—"

And at that instant the end of the story came to her, along with the knowledge of where her reasoning had gone wrong before. Stunned by her conclusion, she barely heard the faint clatter of horses' hooves outside. Then, realizing that delay might be dangerous, Charlotte turned and started to explain to Diana exactly who it was they should be extremely careful to avoid, and why. She had time to utter a name which put a look of astonishment on Diana's features. But before Mrs. Willett could go further, a commotion rose above the room's babble. One by one, heads turned to see five horsemen dismounting under the bare trees in front of the tavern.

Those outside quickly gathered around the newcomers, obscuring the view through the windows. But Charlotte and Diana had seen the vivid finery of Edmund Montagu, surrounded by the lesser uniforms of four others. Two, in loose blue and white, were sailors, while two more in scarlet coats and white breeches were clearly members of the king's regiments. It was an unusual spectacle this far inland, in time of peace, and more than a little grumbling punctuated the immediate excitement of the men outside.

Curiously, the sailors followed Montagu into the tavern while the redcoats kept watch over the horses, in the face of an increasingly agitated and demanding crowd.

Montagu at once spoke in low tones to Phineas Wise, who had seen his arrival and hurried forward. As he spoke, the captain's eyes caught those of a worried Charlotte Willett. He stared at her with concern of his own, before he was captured by a look from Diana Longfellow. The conference with the tavern's owner lasted only a moment more. Then, while Wise continued to shake his head, Montagu approached the two ladies whom he'd so often thought about lately, for different reasons.

"Captain Montagu!" Charlotte exclaimed softly. "I think we have proof our miller killed your merchant in Rhode Island."

"Yes, but how the devil—"

Rapidly, Charlotte began to explain.

"There was a perfume bottle, given to Mary Frye by Peter Lynch, while he pressed her to marry him. She took the bottle because she was forced to, but was ashamed to show it to anyone. Diana has its twin, one of a very few lately arrived on a ship now at anchor near Providence—" Montagu held up a hand in supplication, and she let her sentence trail off.

"Peter Lynch was seen along the waterfront, boasting and spending Dutch gold, as you say, Mrs. Willett. But of far more importance now is the man I've come for, the imposter in the red cloak you saw on Tuesday afternoon—"

Now, Edmund Montagu was forced to halt, when a group of boys burst into the Blue Boar. They soon set the place whirling like a hurricane.

"We've found the Frenchman! The murderer's in the mill!" They chanted it eagerly, over and over, forcing all other conversation to stop short. "We've *found* him, and he's gone into the room above!" their leader screeched. Behind him, someone climbed onto a table to shout, "Let's get the beggar, and finish it!" A rasp of voices sounded an angry chorus.

"Throw him in the millpond, and see what he says!"

"Don't wait to send him to Cambridge, or Worcester, where his friends be! Let's do it now, and have it done—"

"Come on!"

A flurry erupted all around the room, as some tried to get to the door so as not to miss the excitement, while others attempted to pull themselves and their children out of harm's way, out of view of what promised to be a grisly scene. Charlotte watched Esther Pennywort jump up and join the rest, no doubt going to find Jack—just as Richard Longfellow pushed into the room against the tide.

"Edmund," he began as he reached the captain, "what's to be gained by bringing—"

"Do your duty," Montagu quietly ordered his two sailors, who turned and disappeared into the crowd. "You two stay here," he added to Charlotte and Diana, while he grasped Longfellow's shoulder. But they weren't able to leave quite yet.

"Save him!" Diana implored, pulling on Montagu's hand with strength enough to turn him back to her. It was a tense look he gave her—one that she would long remember with a thrill, and a certain pride.

Then the captain and her brother were gone, following the crowd that headed for the mill.

THE PLACE HAD already been thoroughly searched. A few concerned with trespass had lately avoided it, as did many more who believed rumors that the mill now had its own ghost. All of these ideas made it a likely spot for Gabriel Fortier to hide.

Somewhat earlier, Mary had imagined herself unobserved as she crept around behind the millpond on the small path. But several boys playing a game of settlers and Indians had seen her going by. They, in turn, had eagerly and carefully crept after, and proved her undoing.

Like King Philip a century before, leading the Nipmucks, the Narragansetts, and his Wampanoag brothers against the settlers, the boys had been careful to keep out of sight until the moment called for action. They imagined that they, too, wielded guns and tomahawks, and that these tomahawks were much like the hatchet the Frenchman had recently used to destroy the miller, as most of their fathers maintained. And so it was with a mixture of terror and delight that they came to see a young woman in the arms of that very same murderer.

When they screamed, hoping to make him let go of her, they expected the woman to run behind them to safety. Instead, both had stood with looks of disbelief frozen on their faces. And then she had turned and run *up* the stairs to the mill's second floor, where the large post of the grinding stone was held in place; next, the boys had seen the Frenchman go running after her, calling out her name.

Now, their shouts had created an extremely satisfactory chaos outside the mill, where fifty men debated what to do. Some wanted to smoke the Frenchman out; others urged someone should wait with a rifle, until he showed his face. Most simply wanted to storm the building.

All of their plans were short-lived. Edmund Montagu, back on his horse now and followed on foot by Richard Longfellow, cleared a way for the two redcoats who carried muskets set with bayonets. At the water's edge the captain turned to address the enflamed crowd.

"There is *no reason*," he shouted over a barrage of threats and suggestions, "to go in after Gabriel Fortier, *or* to endanger the life of the young woman with him. But there is *every reason* for all of you to listen to me! The man who was said to catch fire last Tuesday evening was *not*, as you must know, the merchant, Duncan Middleton. But he *was* someone who arranged for that man to be killed! Middleton's body was found washed ashore on Tuesday morning, near Providence. Yet on Tuesday afternoon, *after* the discovery of that body, someone else walked through Bracebridge wearing Middleton's clothes, carrying a supply of Dutch coins obtained by the merchant in a recent exchange. *That* man then caused himself to disappear, to cover up the real murder of Middleton, which he himself could not have committed—but which he had *caused to happen* by promising payment to your own Peter Lynch!"

Now a different sort of cry rose from the crowd—one of outrage mingled with disbelief.

"Who was it killed the miller, then?" one man shouted. Others quickly turned to ask each other the same. In the new commotion, Montagu's horse tripped and turned with a discomfort that matched its rider's, while those next to it warily moved back.

"That is of only secondary importance at the moment," Montagu argued with consternation.

"What about my boy?" came a sharp cry from Rachel Dudley, who had followed the crowd hoping to learn more of her son's death. She finished with a sob that did much to still the violence in those around her, at least for the moment.

"They're saying it was no accident that killed Sam," the bereaved woman continued. "Well, no one cared about this man Middleton—no one knew *him*! All they really cared about was his gold. No one even minds what happened to Peter Lynch, who surely deserved what he got. But Sam was only an innocent boy! So you tell me, who would want to murder *my son*?"

"It's nearly certain that he, too, was killed by the miller, for something he saw," Montagu called down to her, "and for that, I'm truly sorry. I believe your boy frightened Lynch, though he might not have known it. But there's one here who's responsible for *all* of this! A man who arranged to have his own brother killed—a man assumed dead by all those who insist on believing *what they read in the newspapers*—a man thought to be drowned in a shipwreck three years ago! I have brought two of his former shipmates from Boston; they can rely on their own eyes to tell them the truth, and will say if *Lionel* Middleton is still here, maintaining his masquerade!"

Montagu pointed, and the crowd turned to see the two sailors in an upper window of the Blue Boar, waving their arms, then shaking their heads violently—while from another window Diana, and Charlotte behind her, leaned out and pointed back. Taking the hint, many turned around again, to see a stream of smoke rising from the base of the mill; it was immediately followed by a sheet of flames that began to climb the outer walls of the old wooden building with a roar, racing into its upper story.

Suddenly, the crowd was electrified by the knowledge that two innocent young people were trapped inside, and would soon burn before their eyes. Immediately, water pails and a ladder were rushed from the tavern; others ran to nearby homes to bring more buckets. Few noticed a lone figure leading a horse from the stable behind the Blue Boar; few heard the approaching clatter of iron shoes on the road.

There was a scream from the crowd as Mary and Gabriel appeared in an upper window. Together, they stood on the brink, in the midst of a flow of black smoke that was already filled with bright sparks. Both were choking, trying desperately to fill their lungs with air. Then, still together, hand in hand, the pair leaped out into the air, and fell down into the millpond.

In a few moments, Mary Frye was pulled out of the pool by several men, to be bundled into a blanket and rushed off by a group of solicitous women. Gabriel still clutched at water weeds and struggled to get his footing on the millpond's muddy bottom, until the strong arm of Nathan Browne reached out to him, hesitated briefly, then slowly pulled him to the bank and safety.

By this time, two lines passed to and from the fire; these were manned by most of the able-bodied, while the two old quails, Tinder and Flint, stood back and shouted lustily at the flames, as if together they might somehow blow them out.

"But where," cried an elderly farm wife, who had been trying to think of something to do, "is this *other* man the captain accused? The one who's responsible for all that's happened? Is he going to get away?"

As it happened, her question was answered almost immediately. Six redcoats and a third sailor now rode down toward the town bridge from the direction of Boston. Between them, his hands bound and his head low, rode the finally defeated naturalist, Adolphus Lee.

Chapter 30

WITHIN THE HOUR, the Blue Boar and the Brace-bridge Inn were filled with sooty, happy patrons who gave thanks for an end to the fire, and to their fears of the past week. Warmed by their own efforts, they raised their glasses to the saved mill and to each other, and there were some who said a prayer for their reprieve from any further preaching that day.

Meanwhile, in Charlotte Willett's kitchen, Long-fellow and Diana, Charlotte and Edmund Montagu feasted on toasted bread dipped into heated cheese, a few bottles of French wine, and a heaping plate of apples. Much had been discussed, but more remained unclear.

"So Lionel Middleton," Diana tried again, "arranged for the miller to kill his brother, which each of them did for money . . . and then the miller, already a murderer, killed the boy when he thought Sam had seen too much . . . and when Jack saw Lynch kill the boy, he decided to kill the miller?"

"Actually," Montagu corrected her, "when I spoke with Pennywort half an hour ago, he assured me he only meant to find out if Lynch had any further plans for *him*. Then, when he suspected he had, Jack thought he might make the fellow less dangerous with some of his doctored snuff. He hoped it would give him his chance to get clear, and planned to alert the rest of the town so that Lynch would be taken into custody. But when the miller threatened to kill him then and there, Pennywort swears he only did what he had to, as soon as he got the chance. Luckily, the ax was handy. After that, he watched the miller reel into his pond, wrench the thing from his head, and drown."

"And now Jack will look something of a hero," Longfellow added, smiling at the irony of the situation.

"Maybe it won't be such a bad thing," Charlotte told him gently, remembering again what Esther Pennywort had told her.

"Even though he tried to kill you, too, Carlotta?"

"But I don't think he did, Richard. Remember, he'd already put ground seeds into the snuff he carried. If that same mixture was what he put into my tea canister, he meant no real harm. My illness might have been as much from drinking an infusion of the *tobacco*, as the other. I doubt if he would have realized that."

"But how on earth did you know enough this morning to warn me about Adolphus Lee?" Diana asked her, a slice of red apple in her hand. "I can understand why Captain Montagu suspected Lionel Middleton was here. But even he didn't know for sure who Lionel *was*, until his former shipmates identified him. You concluded it was Lee from the other way around." She shook her head. "I don't see how."

"Mr. Lee gave himself away twice, really. I finally realized that he must have lied, when he said he'd heard Lydia Pratt talking to Middleton in the room next to his—remember? Because Lydia, with her love of meddling, never mentioned it to Captain Montagu when he questioned her. She couldn't have, since it never happened. She went along with Lee's story because she thought he'd invented it for *her*, to make it seem they hadn't been together on Tuesday afternoon. The truth, of course, was that they'd been very much together. And Lee had no real *reason* to make up that lie; he certainly hadn't been challenged. The discovery of their . . . activities together only came on Friday. But he knew Lydia wouldn't refute the story, and must have decided that it added a little sauce to his claim that he and Middleton had been inside the inn at the same time. When she knows the rest, Lydia Pratt will be more than a little ashamed of not having told the truth before . . . especially when she sees that Lee—or rather Lionel—only used her. I don't suppose Lydia has had many offers of that kind before . . . certainly not from a man so attentively energetic, which made Lee, or Lionel, all the more difficult to resist."

"But still, you only *suspected*—"

"But when I did, and I saw his eyes again, I remembered the way the old man had looked at me on the road. It's possible to disguise quite a few of one's features and intentions, but the eyes generally give the game away. Don't you think?" Charlotte queried, looking from Diana to Edmund Montagu.

For the moment, Diana said nothing. Then Montagu took the lead.

"Lee, or I should say Middleton, will go back to Boston tonight under close guard. I have little doubt that his trial will be a brief one. By the way, what was left of the gold that he paid to Lynch has been found in the mill. It seems it had been under floorboards that were warped by the fire."

"What will happen to Jack now, do you think?" Charlotte asked Montagu, feeling a pang for the man's family.

"I imagine he'll be tried for attempting to poison you. If you'll accuse him."

"Do *you* think I should accuse a local hero, Captain Montagu? I would guess it might do me more harm than good."

"It's possible you're right, Mrs. Willett, and I've no desire to meddle in village affairs. At any rate, Pennywort is now in the inn's cellar. Perhaps it *would* be best for his wife to have him back, after his day in court for the way he stopped Lynch."

"You had some opportunity to speak with Lionel Middleton as well, I suppose." Longfellow had just burned a finger on good English cheddar, and examined the digit as he spoke. "What, exactly, is *his* story?"

"Apparently," Montagu continued, dipping a piece of apple more cautiously into the pot, "when Lionel survived the wreck of his ship, and found he was listed as dead in the Canaries, it was a simple matter to adopt a slight disguise, sign onto another ship, and return to Providence, where he'd sailed from originally. His brother had disinherited him long before, after a family quarrel. But Lionel realized that if his brother made *another* will, and left him out of it entirely, then Lionel might still claim his share as an overlooked legal heir, after Duncan's death. Keeping his ears open, he learned that there *was* talk of a new will, made after his sister Veracity's passing. He knew that with clever counsel, he might stand to gain a fortune."

"And yet," mused Charlotte, "he made himself a good life during the time he waited. Richard said he'd become at least a convincing scientist more than a year ago, and he seems to have pursued his work happily since then."

"He had a knack for it," Montagu agreed, "and his years of travel gave him a great deal of experience. But he was also a man with an obsession—a burning desire, if you'd like. Strangely, if the Crown's trial against his brother had proceeded, there's little chance there would have been much left to inherit, after the government took its share. If Lionel had learned of the possibility, he might have reconsidered. Then again, it might only have made him hurry, I suppose."

"But how did Duncan Middleton happen to make the acquaintance of Peter Lynch?" asked Longfellow.

"It was hardly chance. After following his brother for several weeks, Lionel suspected what Duncan was up to with his adulterated rum. Duncan had already made some profit trying the scheme on his ships going to South America. Now, Lionel thought his brother would jump at an inland contact who could help him transport some of his poisonous drink to the frontier. And it happened that on earlier collecting trips, Lionel had met Peter Lynch. Thinking him a likely candidate for a murderer, as well as a smuggler, Lionel approached the miller. Lynch agreed to help him. Lionel told Lynch that Duncan was about to make one of his trips to Providence, and would stay at a particular inn he was known to frequent. Lynch went there and gained Duncan's trust; after that, it was only a matter of choosing a time and place for the old man's removal. A letter was written, and Duncan Middleton rode to Providence with a sackful of gold on Monday night—gold meant to pay for stores and transportation, which ended up instead financing his own murder. And I suspect we never will find a wagonload of poisonous spirits, because the miller never actually intended to deliver or transport anything at all!"

"Yet getting entirely rid of Middleton turned out to be more difficult than it seemed," Longfellow commented, cutting himself another cube of bread.

"Neither Lionel nor Lynch thought anyone would connect a body that eventually turned up on a beach in Rhode Island—if in fact it ever did—with a man's disappearance by most mysterious circumstances in a place like Bracebridge. Nor would there be much chance of identifying someone who had been floating in the water for a while, especially one so far from home. And they were nearly right. But Lynch knew little of tides or currents, being neither a sailor nor a coastal man; when he threw Middleton into the water, he didn't realize he would come back so quickly, and in such good shape. Of course, neither of them knew of *my* continuing interest in the merchant's whereabouts, or my man watching in Providence."

Charlotte had gazed long into the fire. Now, she spoke again.

"So they were all entangled in nets of their own making. Soon, the last of them will pay the price. It seems a sad defeat for a man who might so easily have continued to prosper on his own."

"A defeat for vengeance, a victory for love—and for a certain handsome Frenchman and his bride," Diana reminded her, lifting a glass of claret from Bordeaux. "And who would have thought that Paris scent would ever undo a man in such an *unusual* way? I must say I adore it now even more than before. To all things French!"

"Are you ready to switch your allegiance, then," asked Montagu in a particularly offhand manner, "to France, from England?"

"Oh, my *dear* Captain Montagu—you know we Americans are of independent mind. Most especially the ladies! I think you'll find it extremely difficult to pin us, like butterflies, to any flag—or alliance."

"My employers," Montagu hurried on, addressing her brother, "will have more for me to do as soon as I return. I'll be leaving very early tomorrow morning—"

"In that case," Diana interrupted, "perhaps you'd let me come along? I happen to have a riding dress with me, and if you don't mind going a little slowly . . . You know, these roads aren't entirely safe for a lady without an escort. Really, if I were to go back alone, my honor might even be at stake."

Charlotte reddened to a shade resembling one of her apples, as she tried to hide her amusement.

At the same time, a snatch of poetry floated unbidden through the captain's thoughts.

Full many a flower's born to blush unseen,
And waste its sweetness on the desert air.

Looking at the two women in front of him, Montagu was quite positive that Gray's verse hadn't been brought to mind by Diana. But perhaps it didn't really describe Charlotte Willett, or this place, either. He found himself wondering just how often Mrs. Willett might make the trip to Boston. And he thought that he would like to have a look at the next husband she chose for herself— just to see what kind of man he would be.

BY MONDAY MORNING, most of Saturday's snow had melted in air that was again almost warm. After Lem returned from leading out the cows, Charlotte Willett walked alone through the same clover, and climbed the orchard hill until she reached the low fence on top.

Perhaps, she thought, she was drawn to the family graves in sympathy with those who had suffered in recent days. It was also the end of another harvest season; time to give thanks for all that had been gathered in, as well as for things held only in memory, but held dear nonetheless.

When she arrived, Charlotte placed a sprig of rosemary on Aaron's stone. Reflecting, she looked off down the hill, where she saw her cows ... and Richard Longfellow. As she continued to watch, her neighbor turned from his own track through his field and began to climb the other side of the hill, long before he could have known that she was there among the low ring of hawthorns, now bereft of nearly all of their bright leaves.

When he did see her, he raised his felt hat, and his expression turned from pensiveness to one of pleasure.

"I was just thinking about love," he confessed. "My sister maintains that love often turns men into little more than beasts. But I have been concluding that so does the need of it, the *lack* of it, sometimes—as does a lack of simple respect from one's fellows."

"As I recall, love or the lack of it is rumored to have caused a great deal of trouble in the past," Charlotte agreed.

" 'Look to the future' is my motto. Speaking of that, have you heard what young Fortier and Mary have decided?"

"Let me imagine. They're to go ahead and marry now, with Jonathan's blessing?"

"The real news is that they'll soon be going to Nova Scotia, and that they plan to take the children from Worcester with them, leaving the father on his own—which will be smaller punishment than the wretch deserves! I hear a great many of the Neutrals are returning, probably hoping that no one will ever call them by that pitiful name again. I suspect they'd much rather be known for who they are, than what they were. Fortier says he is thoroughly tired of running about, and of living in the woods. I suppose they'll be quite happy plowing their own fields."

"We all need to tend our own gardens," replied Charlotte, gazing across her farm. "Do you know what's going to happen to Peter Lynch's property?"

"It's quite likely to wind up in the colony's treasury, like Middleton's, although we will be able to keep the mill for the village, since it's on common land. We haven't learned of any other relatives, and he did die a suspected felon. All this should do wonders for the governor's morale. Although I suspect at least *some* of the gold Lynch got his hands on won't find its way to Boston, after all," Longfellow added, with a look that went off toward New Hampshire, or possibly as far as Acadia.

"I've heard some news myself," Charlotte said with spirit, "about another impending marriage. It seems Nathan has been courting a woman in Concord, and he's planning to bring her here to live. Knowing Nathan, I imagine she'll be well worth having as a neighbor."

"I hope she's a match for Lydia Pratt . . . although our Lydia seems to be a changed woman. She actually manages to speak with respect and affection to her husband, which is certainly a very good thing . . . though it's one most of us never thought we'd live to see."

"Some help themselves by helping others," Charlotte replied, glad to have her long-standing opinion of Jonathan's good sense confirmed once again. Had he chosen, he could have seen to it that Lydia paid a steep price for her dalliance—but it would have cost him a valuable asset. "And have *you* any plans for the future, Richard?" she queried, quite interested in his answer.

"As a matter of fact, I'm thinking of putting on a little show tonight, around dusk, not far from the Blue Boar. Perhaps you'd like to attend. It seems there are still a few who persist in believing that witches were responsible for an unholy fire on Tuesday night. So I thought I'd treat them to a scientific demonstration. However, I have it in mind to change the formula a bit. For the turpentine, this time, I'll try substituting rum. And I plan to make a few other adjustments, as well."

"That," said Charlotte, with a smile, "should be most instructive. But if you don't mind, this time I'll stay at home."

THAT EVENING, CICERO sat under the portrait of Eleanor Howard in Longfellow's warm, quiet study. Things were nearly back to normal, and he was glad of it. Diana had gone back to Boston with Captain Montagu—God help the man to keep his wits about him, with no one to intervene for him the next time. And Longfellow had gone out to have a little fun with his chemicals, in a bright mood. Now, Cicero looked forward to enjoying a little peace, at least until the next crisis came.

He took a bite of cake and a sip of tea from a tray on his lap, and looked deeply and contentedly into the fire. Excitement was well enough for some. But after a certain age, he had decided, philosophy was better. He lifted a small volume from the table beside him, and again began to savor its classic phrases as he ran them softly over his tongue.

The dark face he suddenly glimpsed out of the corner of his eye, as someone tall strode past the window, startled him into dropping his book. There had been something very familiar about the figure, and its apparel.

It was when the man entered the study itself, and Cicero smelled the acrid scents of burning wool, and hair, and pitch, that the story came to him in a flash. His face dissolved into a beatific smile. Things *were* back to normal.

AND FINALLY, ACROSS the gardens, Charlotte, Lem, and Orpheus sat in front of their own fire; this time, it was one that burned in the hearth of the blue room. Lem waded through elements of Latin grammar from a book once used by Jeremy Howard and his sisters. As the old dog watched him sounding out new words, its eyebrows rose and fell to match the reader's own.

Meanwhile, Charlotte concentrated on a letter she knew should have been written days before. She would send it to her brother in Europe, and duplicate its information in one to the Willetts in Philadelphia. Even in the City of Brotherly Love, she had found a taste for shocking events, no matter if they sometimes came at the expense of one's neighbors. That was the way the world went, she reminded herself, dipping her quill into the inkpot again. Life went on.

Then she heard a rhythmic bumping, as a long tail began to thump against the bare wood floor. She looked down, and followed Orpheus's gaze to a spot in the middle of the room. Nothing seemed to be happening there at all. It was at that moment that she smelled the familiar scent of horehound, although she also noticed that it was fainter than usual. In another moment, she saw Lem raise his head and curiously test the air. After that, Charlotte watched him yawn and return to his work, and kept on watching with quiet pleasure, while the old dog before her settled with a sigh.

About the Author

MARGARET MILES currently lives in Washington, D.C., with her husband Richard Blakeslee, and a black cat named Rocket. After writing and coproducing short films and videos for nearly twenty years, she now enjoys spending most days in the eighteenth century.

If you enjoyed the first mystery in the Bracebridge series, A WICKED WAY TO BURN, you won't want to miss Margaret Miles' second mystery, TOO SOON FOR FLOWERS.

Look for TOO SOON FOR FLOWERS in hardcover at your favorite bookstore in January 1999.

TOO SOON FOR FLOWERS

A *Bracebridge Mystery by*

MARGARET MILES

Coming in January 1999 in hardcover from Bantam Books

1764 OPENED WITH A GRIM PORTENT when fire destroyed much of Harvard College during a blizzard one January eve—an event like none other since the creation of that great institution, well over a century before.

No one was quite sure how the blaze started; some put the blame on logs burning high into a chimney, others on a stealthy burrowing beneath a hearth. Fortunately, few scholars were endangered, for most had gone home for a month of rest. But the college housed temporary lodgers, including Governor Sir Francis Bernard, members of the Massachusetts General Court, and notable alumnus John Hancock—all of whom bravely joined together to fight the conflagration. (As Fate would have it, at least one would be well repaid for his losses that snowy night. Before the year was out, the sudden death of his merchant uncle would make young Hancock the second wealthiest soul in all the colonies.)

But a far greater threat already stalked the old Commonwealth, which was the reason these men of Boston had been driven across the Charles River to meet in Cambridge. For an ancient plague had once again begun to rage. A dozen victims of small-pox had been discovered in this town before Christmas; of these, all but two had died. Then more sickness, and still more was dutifully reported, until the Boston Neck was awiggle with a tide of people hurrying away, leaving behind flagged and guarded houses, feverish souls, and worried families.

At first, afraid that inoculation might encourage the pestilence, the authorities refused to condone the procedure, though it was widely called for. Finally, faced with an epidemic, they bowed to public and clerical pressure.

Many weeks later, warm May breezes carried rising hopes that an end to the outbreak was in sight, while it was often claimed that Science had triumphed. There was no doubt that among the thousands inoculated, only a few score had died. Death was far more likely in those who took the disease the usual way, and their symptoms were generally more severe—even after one allowed for a gradual weakening of the strain. Yet, in spite of inoculation's obvious benefits, some continued to reject the relatively safe and simple procedure, as Richard Longfellow complained to Edmund Montagu one spring morning, while both trotted along the Boston-Worcester road.

"Arguing with Diana is more difficult than trying to convince a cat," Diana's brother went on philosophically as the two men traveled abreast on stallions, while behind them a black and white mare pulled a chaise and two ladies. "Reason doesn't have much effect, so one is eventually forced to offer rewards. In Diana's case, she agreed to submit when I promised to take her on a voyage, *and* to leave a great sum with her dressmaker. But in the end, I won my point. She will be protected, in spite of her fear of scarring. I think you can see a useful lesson there," Longfellow added.

"I suppose so," the Englishman beside him mused. He kept to himself his own suspicion of exactly what lesson Diana Longfellow might have taken to heart, and just how long ago. He glanced over the gilded epaulet on his right shoulder, catching her eye. Odd, how Longfellow refused to admit that his much younger half-sister had grown into something beyond a silly, spoiled child. Today, Miss Longfellow was clad in pale yellow brocade, patterned with raised red roses, while her auburn hair was arranged in a style less elaborate than she usually favored in town. Diana was even more lovely than usual, Captain Montagu decided with a sigh. His eye followed the ringlets that fell among the ribbons of her lace cap, barely hiding a delightfully white neck which she encouraged him to brush with his hand, from time to time.

During the recent upheaval, these moments had been few. Certainly, nothing had occurred recently to inflame Edmund Montagu quite like last October's meeting in Bracebridge, when he had first found himself alone with the young temptress, in Longfellow's kitchen. Yet he wondered—how many others had Diana encouraged before? Or since?

Captain Montagu touched his hat. and received

a flirtatious answer that involved both bright green eyes and loquacious lashes, before Diana turned her head away.

"I suppose he'll always believe it was his doing," she went on to Charlotte Willett, who sat beside her, holding the pair of reins and keeping her own eyes on the road. "Which is all the better for me! Richard has increased my allowance to pay for my clothing, without argument, through September at least. Beyond that, I've extracted his promise to take me to see the Dutchmen in New York. Actually, some weeks ago—I did tell you, Charlotte, that I'd visited in Newport? Well, I had a letter while I was there from Dr. Warren, answering one I had sent to *him*, asking for his advice. After I considered his reasons I decided to take the inoculation—not wanting, of course, to be the last one in town. They say nearly five thousand have submitted and very few have succumbed. Better still, the given disease is lighter than the natural, and the chance of pocking lessened. Which I will admit still fills me with dread. . . ."

As Diana's anxious voice trailed away, her plainly dressed companion gently turned the conversation in another direction.

"Is Dr. Warren still on Castle Island?"

"Yes, inoculating the poor, at the town's expense. But some very rich men are also there, paying quite well, I imagine. And they'll be a boon to his practice later. He's been quarantined in the harbor for some time now, and it's said that after this, he'll know *everyone* in town—which will be quite a waste of his time, in my opinion. Though I believe Dr. Warren finds it amusing, heaven knows why. The best news, however, is this: Warren's to be married when it is all over. Oh yes! He'll get a large fortune with Elizabeth Hooton, and that is always pleasant. She has a pretty face, too. Still, she's only eighteen, and it seems to me that a wise woman would wait a little . . . to see what might develop, you know. But she's already vowed to everyone that she's in love with him, so I suppose she might as well. It's a practical move for the doctor, certainly. It will also discourage many ladies in town—and perhaps certain ones a little distance out of it?"

Diana bent for a glimpse of her friend's face, hidden beneath the brim of a straw hat. But Charlotte Willett merely stared ahead, though her eyes danced with amusement. She could easily recall what it was to be twenty, as Diana was, however different her own life had been just five years before. Now, while the two-wheeled carriage, with its calesh top collapsed to let in the breezes, took her closer to home, Charlotte (like Captain Montagu) thought back to the previous autumn.

Last October, Dr. Joseph Warren had made his first visit to the village of Bracebridge, mid-way between Boston and the frontier town of Worceser. While Captain Montagu had come on the governor's business, seeking a rich merchant, the physician had been invited by Richard Longfellow—who, as a village selectman, had asked Warren to examine the corpse of a man rumored to have been murdered. Charlotte had quickly decided that the young doctor would make a pleasant and useful acquaintance, and perhaps even a superior husband—for someone. But not for her. Her sense of Aaron Willett was still strong, and though her husband had been dead three years, his presence continued to make itself felt, in ways that were difficult to ignore. It was too soon for her heart to consider marriage again. Not yet. She, too, had married young, when not quite eighteen. And she, too, had married for love.

Feeling a familiar pain in her breast, Mrs. Willett silently wished Dr. Warren long life and happiness with his new bride, while Diana continued playing with her parasol, and relaying additional news of Boston society—such as it was these days, with most of it camping out somewhere else. Meanwhile, the wind caressed, the bright clouds flew, the birds called to one another arranging their own affairs, and the three horses clopped along.

Charlotte was glad to notice that Longfellow seemed enthusiastic in his discussion with Captain Montagu, who had often been in attendance during the three days passed at the home of Diana and her mother—once Longfellow's home, as well. Though one day it would be his again, the place was now occupied solely by women, a fact that seemed to feed his tendency toward melancholy. Fortunately, exchanging barbs with Montagu had brought sparks to his eyes, and held his darker moods at bay.

Edmund, too, seemed to be enjoying their conversation. Today, thought Charlotte, the British captain was far more affable than when they had all come together for the first time, on this same road, little more than six months before. The natural reserve of his breeding was lately less obvious, and his cold, aristocratic way of speaking (as if, some said, he was officiating at a hanging) had softened somewhat. If Diana seemed less inclined to pursue him as if he were a mouse and she a cat, Charlotte suspected the young lady might increasingly be thinking of retaining the captain as a live prize. As for his own ideas, well, no one could ever be sure what

Edmund Montagu really thought. His handling of the death of the old merchant the previous autumn had revealed deep waters. Beyond that, an officer and an agent for the Crown had duties and obligations that were not known to everyone.

It was probably just as well, thought Charlotte, that Edmund would soon leave them at the junction with the post road, having arranged to spend some weeks in New Hampshire as one of a summer party, at an estate along the Merrimack. After tomorrow's inoculation with the smallpox, Diana would be unlikely to enjoy visitors for a week or two, at least.

"What are those little things?" Diana demanded, pointing to the edge of the road.

"Which?" asked Mrs. Willett, squinting to see more clearly.

"The little yellow ones, in amongst the grass. They're pretty, don't you think? I believe I'll soon have a bouquet. I wonder if they have a scent?"

In answer, Montagu coaxed his horse ahead, then dismounted. He removed his triangular cocked hat with a flourish, and deposited it safely beneath one arm, leaving his powdered and pomaded wig to glow in the sun. While the others watched, he bent to pinch several blooms from a clump of fragrant primroses at the highway's edge; soon, he straightened with a handful. In another moment, the captain approached the chaise Mrs. Willett had brought to a halt.

"May I suggest a brief walk, to say farewell?" Montagu, offering the bright bouquet to Diana. He was rewarded with the young lady's hand as she climbed down. He kept it while he guided her away from the road, toward another wave of flowers. By the time they reached it, he had captured an entire arm under his own.

"I wanted you to know," he began haltingly, "that I . . . have asked your brother the favor that I be called, in the event that—if the unexpected should occur," he finished stiffly, quite unsatisfied with his choice of words. Would he ever be able to speak plainly and simply to this woman, or would their every meeting end by making him feel a loaded pistol were pointed at his head?

"Be called at my demise, do you mean? Or before?"

Carefully, he disengaged his arm.

"In the event that you might want to see me. One last time," he added, pleased at the feeling the cruel words gave him.

"Well, I *could* wish to see you in that event, I suppose," Diana replied steadily. She leaned forward with some difficulty (for her busk and stays cruelly contained her slender waist) to pick a bloom for herself, and added it to those he'd already given her. Though the exertion gave her some discomfort, its effect was very graceful.

"But what," she asked abruptly, "if I do not die, but instead become disfigured? Should that occur, Edmund, what do you suppose your feelings would be?

Both stood silent in the field, recalling painful scenes. Women who had been badly ravaged by the smallpox often chose to remain immured at home forever—while others ventured out only with gloves, and thick veils. A few, among the poor and aged, did expose twisted hands and scarred faces, that frightened children and even their elders. Now there would be more such creatures. Most in Massachusetts were born after the last great epidemic. In—, one in six residents of Boston had died in a few months' time. But everyone was well aware that there was still no cure.

Montagu was the first to shake off the disturbing vision of disfigurement. He patted puffs of dust from the arms of his new blue coat, whose military lapels were held back with many brass buttons, set off by gold piping.

"If you were to be seriously afflicted," he answered Diana, "I would come to compliment your bravery—and to see if seclusion had made you any better at the whist table where, as yet, you lack a great deal as a partner."

"You complain because I failed to help you win a fortune this winter, poor man. And so you must survive on your pitiful pay. Like so many of the nearly-titled."

"Very true," he answered with a wry smile. This lady could be cruel, as well, when she chose to be. It was common knowledge that Miss Longfellow's dowry would be large. She could certainly expect to marry a man of means.

"It's possible, you know," Diana continued airily, "that I was determined to spare my neighbors, to keep their money from flowing back to London. After all, I seem to remember that you are one of those who urge the colonies to hold on to all the coin they can get."

"You've been keeping those pretty ears open around your betters, Miss Longfellow," he said to tease her. Seeing that he'd achieved some success, he went on in a practical vein, appealing to the lady's intellect. It was a tactic that had been known to flatter (even sometimes to astonish) a female, especially an attractive one who was most often allowed only insipid conversation.

"Though I would still encourage you to hold on to your reserves of both gold and silver, especially with the upheaval in trade these colonies have lately suffered," he added seriously. "But what do you plan to give your dressmaker for your imported satins and damasks? Potatoes? When I see the ladies here wearing home-spun woolens and linens, I'll know you've learned your place, and become true converts to sound economic policy—and, incidentally, that you have at last learned common sense. Though the Lord knows Boston's politicians have been talking enough lately of self-sufficiency, with a keen eye to obstructing British interests. . . . But," he concluded, "I have no wish to argue with you today, my dear."

"Well, go and argue with someone who will listen in New Hampshire, then," Diana replied, holding her head high as she affected a sulk. "Though I'm sure the ladies there will be no more likely than we to dress themselves in sackcloth."

"We'll see," Montagu answered thoughtfully. "But none could appear more charming than one Boston lady I know, either in brocade or burlap."

Diana tossed the curls away from her lovely face, dimpling with pleasure.

As he knew she expected, the captain was quite affected by her show of spirit, as well as her ability to laugh at the future. It was something she did far better than he, and far more often. Listening now to her musical laugh, he noticed with something of a shock that the flowers in her hand had already begun to wilt and fade.

He looked up, and took careful note of Diana's

peerless complexion. Then Edmund Montagu took her soft hand in his own once more, while he listened to a trill of foreboding (which he knew well) play upon his racing heart.